To Dearest Max

lots of love

from all your

Parsons Cousins

xxxx

The Complete Adventures of
BLINKY BILL

Blinky Bill, the mischievous little koala, is one of the best-known and best-loved characters in Australian juvenile fiction. In this omnibus his complete adventures have been collected; it contains the three books, *Blinky Bill, Blinky Bill Grows Up*, and *Blinky Bill and Nutsy*, each of which has been an established favourite with young readers; and together they form a continuous and absorbing story.

The remarkable and ever-growing popularity of the Blinky Bill books is not due to any freak of fashion, but to Dorothy Wall's understanding of just what children want from a story. Her skilful blending of imagination, action, and humour, combined with simple yet vivid characterization of familiar bush creatures and accompanied by a wealth of delightful illustrations, makes *The Complete Adventures of Blinky Bill* a book that cannot fail to have an immediate and lasting appeal for every child who reads it.

THE COMPLETE ADVENTURES OF
BLINKY BILL

CONTAINING :-

BLINKY BILL
BLINKY BILL GROWS UP
BLINKY BILL AND NUTSY

TOLD & ILLUSTRATED BY
DOROTHY WALL

ANGUS & ROBERTSON PUBLISHERS

ANGUS & ROBERTSON PUBLISHERS
London • Sydney • Melbourne

This book is copyright. Apart from any fair dealing for the
purposes of private study, research, criticism or review, as
permitted under the Copyright Act, no part may be reproduced
by any process without written permission. Inquiries should be
addressed to the publishers.

First published by Angus & Robertson Publishers, Australia, 1939
495 reprinted 1992

Copyright Angus & Robertson Publishers, 1939

National Library of Australia
Cataloguing-in-publication data.
Wall, Dorothy.
The complete adventures of Blinky Bill.
First published as one, Angus & Robertson 1939.
For children.
ISBN 0 207 14541 3.
1. Title.
A823.2
Printed in Hong Kong

ANGUS & ROBERTSON PUBLISHERS
London • Sydney • Melbourne

This book is copyright. Apart from any fair dealing for the
purposes of private study, research, criticism or review, as
permitted under the Copyright Act, no part may be reproduced
by any process without written permission. Inquiries should
be addressed to the publishers.

First published by Angus & Robertson Publishers, Australia, 1939
34th impression 1985

Copyright Angus & Robertson Publishers 1939

National Library of Australia
Cataloguing-in-publication data.

Wall, Dorothy
    The complete adventures of Blinky Bill.

    First published, Sydney: Angus & Robertson, 1939.
    For children.
    ISBN 0 207 94700 7

    I. Title.

823'.2

Printed in Hong Kong by Everbest Printing Co., Ltd

DEDICATED TO

MY SON
PETER
AND ALL OTHER
PETERS
AND
JOHNS
AND
BOBS
AND
TOMS
AND
MARYS
AND
BETTYS
AND
JOANS
AND
PATS
AND
ALL KIND CHILDREN

CONTENTS

This is Me

CHAPTER ONE
The New Arrival

THE bush was alive with excitement. Mrs Koala had a brand new baby, and the news spread like wildfire. The kookaburras in the highest gum-trees heard of it, and laughed and chuckled at the idea. In and out of their burrows the rabbits came scuttling, their big brown eyes opening wide with wonder as they heard the news. Over the grass the message went where Mrs Kangaroo was quietly hopping towards her home. She fairly leapt in the air with joy. "I must tell Mr Kangaroo!" she cried and bounded away in great hops and leaps. Even Mrs Snake, who was having a nap, awoke, gave a wriggle, and blinked her wicked little eyes. The whole bushland was twittering with the news, for a baby bear was a great event. Mrs Koala had a baby every two

1

years, and as Mrs Rabbit had very, very many during that time, you can just imagine how surprised everyone was.

In the fork of a gum-tree, far above the ground, Mrs Koala nursed her baby, peeping every now and then at the tiny creature in her pouch. This little baby was the funniest wee creature. He was only about an inch long and covered with soft baby fur, had two big ears, compared to the size of the rest of him, a tiny black nose, and two beady eyes. His mother and father always had a surprised look on their faces, but they looked more surprised than ever now as they gazed at their baby.

He peeped at them and blinked, as much as to say, "Aren't you glad I'm here?"

Mr Koala puffed out his cheeks with pride, and his wife hugged her baby tighter than ever.

There had been quite a lot of quarrelling and jealousy among the bush folk as to who should be the baby's nurse.

Mrs Kookaburra was the first to offer her services, and she came flying over to the tree where the Koalas lived. Knocking on the tree with her strong beak she asked if she might come in.

"Certainly," said Mrs Bear, "if you don't laugh and wake the baby up."

"Do you want a nurse for him?" Mrs Kookaburra anxiously inquired.

"Yes, I do," Mrs Bear replied.

"Will I do?" Mrs Kookaburra asked.

"Oh, no!" said Mrs Bear. "Your laugh is so loud and you chuckle so long that you'd wake the baby up."

Poor Mrs Kookaburra was very disappointed and flew off to tell Mrs Magpie about it.

"I'll go over and see if I can be the nurse," said Mrs Magpie. "Mrs Bear is very particular and I'm sure I will suit." She gave her feathers a fluff and sharpened her beak, then straight to the Koalas' home she flew.

2

"Go away Mrs. Snake!"

"Come in," called Mrs Bear on hearing the peck at the tree.

"Good morning, Mrs Koala. I hear you are wanting a nurse for the baby. I'm sure I could keep the young scamp in order as I've had a few dozen myself."

"Thank you, Mrs Magpie," said Mrs Bear very politely, "but I don't like the look of your beak. You could give a very nasty peck with it."

"They all want a peck sometimes." said Mrs. Magpie.

"They all want a peck sometimes," said Mrs Magpie in a very cross tone. At this the baby bear popped his head right out of his mother's pouch and blinked very hard.

"If you are so particular, I'll send along a friend of mine who will suit you very well." And saying this Mrs Magpie gave the tree a savage peck and flew off. Imagine Mrs Koala's surprise when she peeped down the tree later on and saw Mrs Snake slowly wriggling her way upwards. Oh, she was frightened!

"Go away, Mrs Snake!" she called in a loud voice.

"I've come to nurse the baby; Mrs Magpie sent me." And Mrs Snake wriggled higher up the tree. Right on to the branch where Mrs Koala sat she came, and coiled herself round the fork.

"I don't want a nurse." And poor frightened Mrs Bear tried to push the baby's head back in the pouch. But he *would* peep out.

"He's a nice little fellow, and like his daddy," said Mrs Snake

The New Arrival

slyly. "I can take him along on my back for such lovely rides up and down trees and in and out big black holes."

Hearing this Mrs Bear nearly fell off the tree with fright, and began to cry.

Now Mr Koala had been listening to Mrs Snake as he sat on a branch just round the corner. Slowly he climbed over to Mrs Snake and caught her in his claws. Before anyone had time to see what was happening he pushed her off the branch and she went tumbling to the ground below. Two very frightened bears peeped down from the tree, and there they saw Mrs Snake slowly crawling away in the grass.

They were just beginning to recover from this fright when a thump, thump, thump, was heard on the ground at the foot of the tree.

"Who's there?" called Mrs Bear in a very frightened voice.

"It's just me!" came the reply.

"Who's me?" growled Mr Bear.

"Angelina Wallaby," called a very soft voice.

"Come up, come up," Mrs Bear replied.

"I can't climb; my tail is all wrong," said Angelina.

"Well, I'll come down, if Mrs Snake is nowhere about," said Mrs Bear. And she slowly started to scramble down the tree. Very carefully she went, always grasping the tree with her strong claws, her back showing all the time, while she cleverly looked over her shoulder now and then to see that all was safe below. It took her quite a time to reach the ground and she felt very nervous.

Angelina Wallaby hopped over to her and gazed in wonderment at the baby.

"What a dear little fellow!" she said, her great brown eyes rounding with excitement. At the same time she put out her paws to touch him

"Oh, don't!" cried Mrs Bear. "He is so small and your nails might hurt him."

"I've been all the morning blunting them on a stone so that I could pat him," said Angelina in a disappointed voice.

"Oh, I'm sorry," said Mrs Bear. "I did not mean to be rude, but Mrs Snake gave me such a fright."

"I'll be ever so gentle," said Angelina, "if you let me pat him just this once."

"Very well," smiled Mrs Bear as she opened her pouch.

Angelina Wallaby patted him twice, then sniffed him all over with her soft muzzly nose. Now her eyelashes caught in his little toes: but Angelina did not mind, as she had had babies herself and knew just what to do.

"I wish I could mind him for you sometimes, Mrs Bear. I'd be so gentle with him."

"I'm sure you would be the very kindest nurse," replied Mrs Bear. "But what could you do for him?"

"I would come along in the evenings, and take him out for a walk. I've got a pouch just like yours, and I'd tuck him in it and hop along very gently, so he wouldn't feel the bumps."

"I think that is a good idea," said Mrs Bear.

So it was arranged that Mrs Bear should climb down the tree every evening and meet Angelina Wallaby who would take the baby for a walk in the bush.

The New Arrival

Imagine how proud Angelina felt! She hopped home very quickly that evening to tell her friends the news.

Next day, just as the sun was setting, she came to the foot of the gum-tree and thumped three times on the ground with her tail. Mrs Bear peeped around the corner of her home and, seeing Angelina at the foot of the tree, called out:

"I'm coming down with the baby, so watch for Mrs Snake." Then she carefully and slowly climbed to the bottom of the tree.

"Is the coast clear?" she anxiously asked.

"Yes, Mrs Bear. I passed Mrs Snake on the road a mile away."

"Well, do be careful, Angelina; and bring him back before the day breaks. Is your pouch warm?" And Mrs Bear inspected Angelina's pouch.

"Yes, Mrs Bear. It may be a trifle large, so I padded it well with grass; but it's very warm and not a bit draughty."

So the baby was carefully taken from his mother's pouch and gently placed in Angelina's.

Waving a paw to Mrs Bear she took a hop and then peeped down at the baby to see what he thought of it. Taking several more hops she soon started away for the bush track and in no time came to Mrs Rabbit's home. Thumping her tail on the ground, she waited a moment. Mrs Rabbit popped her head out of the burrow.

"Good evening, Mrs Rab. I've brought the baby to show you."

"Good gracious, how lovely!" said Mrs Rabbit as Angelina gently drew the baby bear from her pouch. Several more bunnies came round to inspect the new arrival.

"Just look at his ears!" cried Mrs Rabbit. "I'm sure I'd never hear with those furry things. And, oh dear, no tail!— Well, well! Take care he does not catch cold. I really think he should have a tail to keep him warm. I have a spare one hanging on the wall of the burrow. Poor Mr Rabbit was shot, and I found

"Here's just the thing!"
Mrs. Rabbit cried.

The New Arrival

his skin near by; but I managed to bite off the tail and bring it home." Here poor Mrs Rabbit burst into tears.

"Never mind, my dear," said Angelina soothingly. "If it will please you, we will tie it on the baby."

Mrs Rabbit dried her eyes with her paw and went sniffling down into the burrow.

"I won't be a moment," she called from somewhere down under the ground.

Up she came in a very short time carrying the tail in her two front paws.

"What can we sew it on with?" inquired Angelina.

"We'll tie it on with a piece of grass." And Mrs Rabbit hopped round until she found a nice long piece.

"Here's just the thing!" she cried, and came hopping back with it in her teeth.

Angelina excitedly pulled the baby out of her pouch, and together they fastened the tail on. It did look funny, as it was almost as long as the baby; but it certainly would keep him warm.

Bidding her friend good night she hopped on her way. The moon was now shining brightly and all the bush was hushed, except for the sound of those little animals who are always busy at night-time. Angelina sniffed the night air with delight and felt very happy as she thought of the baby in her pouch. Hopping along between the great grey gum-trees she was suddenly startled to see Mrs Snake lying right across her pathway.

"Ha, ha, Mrs Wallaby," called the wicked Mrs Snake, "so you're the baby's nurse. Well, I want to have a look at him."

"Oh, you can't!" cried Angelina. "He'll catch cold if I take him out of my pouch."

"No, he won't, the night is warm," said Mrs Snake. "Show him to me at once."

9

Angelina thought very quickly, and darting her paws into her pouch she untied the rabbit's tail and pulled it out.

"There you are, Mrs Snake," she cried. "Isn't he beautiful?"

Mrs Snake did not stop to look. She sprang at the tail and bit it savagely.

"Ha, ha, ha," she laughed, "there will be no baby to take home now."

Poor Angelina got such a fright she did not waste a moment, but hopped away as fast as her legs could carry her. On and on she went, breathless with fear, not daring to look behind. She reached the foot of the gum-tree and thumped wildly with her tail. Mrs Bear came scurrying down the tree and listened to the story. Then grabbing her baby she quickly climbed to safety. Angelina waited at the foot of the tree until she saw Mrs Bear safely home, then hopped away to the bushland.

She sprang at the tail and bit it savagely.

After that, Mrs Koala decided to keep her baby at home. Every day he grew bigger and stronger, until he was six months old. Then his mother thought it quite time he learnt to ride on her back, as the pouch was getting too small to hold such a big baby. So with Mr Bear's help they taught the baby to cling to the long fur of her back and only during the cold nights was he allowed to climb into her pouch. He was now growing very big. When eight months old he could no longer crawl into the snug pouch at all. So his baby days were over. He became very cunning too. When his mother was feeding, he learnt to stretch out his arms and pull the tenderest leaves into his mouth. He soon reached the age of one year, and measured ten inches, while his weight was about three pounds. Strange as it may seem, Mrs Koala had not thought of a name for her baby. Now, she thought it quite time he was christened; so one day she talked the matter over with his father. "Shall we call him 'Walter' or 'Bluegum'?" she inquired.

"No," grunted Mr Koala. "Let's call him 'Blinky Bill'." So Blinky Bill he became from that moment.

"Well, my dear, I'll arrange about the christening," said Mrs Koala. "My cousin the Reverend Fluffy Ears will perform the ceremony. And, of course, we must choose his godfather and godmother."

"Jacko Kookaburra will be his godfather," said Mr Bear. "We will send him a message over the wireless, as he is so well known; and Angelina Wallaby would be sure to jump with joy if we asked her to be godmother."

So that night when all was quiet Mr Koala tapped out a message on the gum-leaves calling the Gippsland bush folk.

"Will Mr Jacko Kookaburra speak, please—Koala senior is calling."

Rat-a-tat-tat—came the reply on the leaves.

"Jacko here. What can I do for you?"

"Will you be Blinky Bill's godfather?" Mr Koala tapped back.

"Only too pleased," came the quick reply.

"I'll be along next week. Sorry I'm broadcasting every night this week."

Angelina, who seldom uttered a sound, purred with pleasure when she was asked to be godmother, and hurried home to make a present for the christening.

The great day arrived. In a quiet corner of the bush, down by a little stream surrounded with bells and flannel flowers, everyone came from far and near to see young Bill christened.

The Reverend Fluffy Ears looked very important with a white collar made from the bark of the paper-tree. He also held in his paws a book of gum-leaves, from which he read.

Mr and Mrs Koala smiled at everyone, and everyone smiled at Blinky Bill. Jacko looked spick and span, and of course, being a widely travelled gentleman, he took things very quietly. At the same time, he gave a dig in the ground with his beak every now and then and swallowed a fat worm. Angelina looked sweet in her nut-brown coat, and her large eyes watched Blinky Bill all the time. She had made a ball of fur for him to play with, and he cuddled and hugged it closely all the time.

Mrs Rabbit rang the bells and everyone sat down or perched.

The Reverend Fluffy Ears spoke as he took Blinky Bill in his arms.

"What shall I name this young bear?" he asked.

"Blinky Bill," said Mr Koala.

At once the bush was filled with laughter. Wild kookaburras who were no relation to Jacko had

"Silence!" roared the Reverend Fluffy Ears.

The New Arrival

flown into a nearby tree, and they made a terrible din, chuckling and laughing at the top of their voices. Nobody could speak for the noise.

"Silence!" roared the Reverend Fluffy Ears. But it was useless. They took no notice.

"I'll speak to the young larrikins," said Jacko, and he gave the call for all to listen.

Immediately the laughter ceased.

"I'm Jacko," he said, "and if you birds up in that tree don't keep quiet I'll tell everyone over the radio what rude kookaburras you are and that you are no relation to me."

Hearing this, the wild kookaburras became very quiet, as they wanted everyone to think they were related to Jacko. He was such a wonderful bird that if they were asked in turn who was their cousin or uncle all would reply—"Jacko". So you see, they had good reason to keep quiet. Blinky Bill had water from the stream sprinkled on his head, much to his surprise, and the ceremony ended without any more interruptions. He was carried home again on his mother's back, feeling very important after all the fuss and petting. That night up in the fork of the white gum-tree Mrs Koala told him that he was now a youth and that if he were a human being he would be put in knickerbockers.

CHAPTER TWO
A Tragedy

THE Koala family lived so happily; never thinking of harm, or that anything could happen to disturb their little home, as all they asked for were plenty of fresh gum-leaves and the warm sun. They had no idea such things as guns were in the world or that a human being had a heart so cruel that he would take a pleasure in seeing a poor little body riddled with bullets hanging helplessly from the tree-top. And they had no idea this same being would walk away, after shooting a bear, content to see him dead, no matter if he fell to the ground or not. That same being might just as well take his gun and shoot

A Tragedy

baby kookaburras, so helpless were they all and so trusting.

Poor Mr Koala one day was curled up asleep in his favourite corner, when the terrible thing happened. Bang! He opened his eyes in wonder. What was that? Did the limb of the tree snap where that young cub of his was skylarking? He moved very slowly to take a look and, bang! again. This time he felt a stinging pain in his leg. What could it be? And peering over the bough of the tree he saw a man on the ground with something long and black in his arms. He gazed down in wonderment. Whatever was that, and how his little leg hurt. Another bang and his ear began to hurt. Suddenly a great fear seized him, he slowly turned and tried to hide round the tree, peering at the ground as he did so. Bang! again, and now his poor little body was stinging all over. He grunted loudly and slowly climbed up the tree, calling Mrs Koala and Blinky as he went. He managed to reach the topmost branch and now turned to see where his family were. Tears were pouring down his poor little face. He brushed them away with his front paws and cried just like a baby. Fortunately Mrs Koala and

They sat patiently waiting for him to wake.

15

Blinky Bill

Blinky Bill were hiding in the leaves, quite motionless, and the shadows of the tree made them appear as part of it. The man with the gun stood and waited a long time, then walked away, whistling as he went—the only sound to be heard in the bush except the cries of a little bear far up in the tree.

All that day and night the little family lay huddled together, not daring to move, or to think of the sweet gum-leaves that hung from the tree inviting them to supper. As the sun rose the birds woke with a great chattering, the earth stirred with the feet of small animals running backwards and forwards; but up in the gum-tree a mother bear and her baby sat staring in surprise at another bear who did not move. They grunted and cried, and even felt him with their soft paws, but he still did not move. All that day and the next night they sat patiently waiting for him to wake, then at last Mrs Bear seemed to understand that her husband was dead. She climbed down the tree, with Blinky following close behind, and went to another tree where they had a good meal of young leaves and tender shoots.

"Why are we eating so much?" Blinky inquired.

"We are going away, dear," Mrs Bear replied. "We must find a tree farther in the bush where those men with guns can't come, and as we may be a long time in finding a suitable home, these leaves will keep us from feeling hungry."

Together the mother and her cub slowly climbed down the tree, and great was their surprise to find Angelina Wallaby waiting for them.

16

A Tragedy

"Where are you going, Mrs Bear?" she asked.

"Far into the bush with Blinky, away from the man with his gun," Mrs Bear replied.

"What will I do?" asked Angelina. "I shall miss Blinky terribly." And her big eyes filled with tears.

"Come with us," grunted Blinky.

"Oh, that will be splendid," said Angelina. "I know a gum-tree far away with a baby in it just like Blinky. Blinky can crawl up on to my back when his legs are tired, and I'll carry him along —you too, Mrs Bear, if you feel the journey too long."

Thanking her the three started away. Mrs Bear turned and gave one sorrowful look at the tree that had been their home for so long. It had been a kind tree, sheltering them through all weathers and feeding them every day of the year, but not strong enough to protect them from tragedy.

After travelling for a mile or more the bears began to feel very tired, as they were not used to walking along the ground. Very rarely they leave the branches of the trees; occasionally one will climb down to feed on some vegetation in the grass; but they feel very strange having to use their four legs to walk with. It is so different to sitting on a limb of a tree, hind paws firmly grasping the branch while the two front paws are busily pulling down tender leaves to their mouths. So it was no wonder when Mrs Koala and Blinky began to limp.

"Let us rest here under this bush," said Angelina, hopping up to a thick scrubby tree. "We can have a sleep, and when the moon is up we will go on."

"I think you are wonderful," said Mrs

17

Koala, and all three lay at the foot of the bush, the two little Koalas glad to rest sore little toes and tired little legs.

In the cool shade they slept until the sun went down, then waking up, and feeling very hungry, Mrs Koala and Blinky climbed a sapling. Blinky rushed ahead as they neared the top and stuffed his mouth as full as full.

"Don't gobble," said Mrs Bear, cuffing his ear.

"They're so juicy," said young Blinky, as he peered over the branch and threw a few leaves down to Angelina.

"They are nice," said Angelina, as she munched them ever so gently. "I have never tasted these leaves before; but we must not stop here any longer. This is strange country, and we have a long way to go."

"I don't want to go," wailed Blinky, "I'm tired."

"Both of you hop on my back and we'll be there in no time. I can leap along in the moonlight like a kangaroo."

After some arguing over the matter, Mrs Bear and Blinky climbed on her back, and away they went. It was great fun. Flop, flop, flop, through the grass, ducking their heads to miss the branches and twigs of low-growing trees, and then racing along through open country.

Many a rabbit looked up in surprise from his supper-table to see the strange sight, and possums screeched in the branches as they looked down at some new kind of wallaby, as they thought. At last, breathless and tired Angelina stopped at the foot of a tall, straight gum-tree. Silver white it stood in the moonlight with branches spread far up in the sky.

"Here is your new home," said Angelina.

"How beautiful," murmured Mrs Bear, as she and Blinky crawled down from their friend's back.

Tears were pouring down his
poor little face.

"It is safe, and you will be very happy here, and Blinky will have a playmate." Angelina flopped on the grass, her long legs sprawled out, and she panted loudly.

"Where are you going to live?" Mrs Bear inquired. "We want you near us, please."

"I'm going to live just round the corner," said Angelina. "I have a friend who is waiting for me."

"Is she a relation?" asked Mrs Bear kindly.

"No!" replied Angelina. "She is a he!" And, blushing, she looked very slowly down at her paws; then suddenly turned and hopped away.

"Dear, dear," grunted Mrs Bear, "the world is full of surprises."

"Now, you young scamp, come here and climb this tree with me," and Blinky scrambled on to his mother's back.

"I think it's quite time you used your own legs," said Mrs Bear. But she made no attempt to shake him off.

Slowly she crawled up. A new tree was no joke, and this one was ever so high and straight. With many grunts she eventually reached a fork in the branches and stopped to take in her surroundings. Everything seemed very quiet, but her eyes glistened as she looked at the young gum-tips. A young cub to feed was a matter of no light concern, and he was so particular. Only the youngest leaves he ate.

Blinky was the first to discover other tenants in the tree.

"Look, mother," he whispered. "There's a litle bear, just like me."

Sure enough, peeping at them from between leaves above their heads, two funny eyes and a small black nose could be seen.

A Tragedy

"Now, no quarrelling!" said Mrs Bear sternly. "I've had enough for one day, and I want peace."

Another climb and they came to a branch where sat Master Bear.

"Hulloa," called Blinky.

"Hullo," replied the other.

"Where's your mother?" Mrs Bear asked. "Tell her I would like to speak with her."

He crawled up the tree slowly. Then many grunts were heard to come from that direction until Mother Bear looked down and called in high-pitched grunts:

"Come up, and bring your son to tea."

It did not take Mrs Koala and Blinky long to find the way, and there all night the little bears ate and gossiped. Mrs Koala told her story, and it was agreed that she and Blinky should have the branch two limbs higher up for their new home. Very carefully she told Blinky he must behave as a good little cub should: "Don't rush about; lift your feet when you walk; don't slide down the boughs; and don't drop your food over the side of the tree as Mrs Bear below us might object."

"I'll be a good cub," said Blinky very seriously, and straightaway started to nibble some young leaves.

She brought her young son Snubby with her.

During the evening Mrs Koala's friend came up to see how she and Blinky liked their new home. She brought her young son, Snubby, with her, and a dear little chap he was. About the same age as Blinky, and in fact so like him that it was hard to tell the two apart.

21

Blinky Bill

"Now you two young eucalyptus pots, run off and have a game," said Snubby's mother. "I want to talk to Mrs Koala."

Blinky and Snubby needed no second bidding, and were up the branches playing and climbing in the most dangerous corners in no time.

"You have not told me your name," said Mrs Koala to her friend.

"My name is Mrs Grunty."

"Oh, what a nice name. I'm sure you must be proud of it," said Mrs Koala.

"Well, no—not exactly," said Mrs Grunty. "I got the name while I was in Queensland."

"Good gracious! Where is that?" asked Mrs Koala.

"Have you never heard of it? Is it possible?" said Mrs Grunty. And she looked more surprised than ever. "Well, I must tell you my experiences. I was taken from my mother when I was about six months old, by a man who was trapping bears. I don't know how I escaped from being killed like all my relations; but I heard the man say to his friend as he caught me and popped me in a sack: 'This little fellow's a pretty one and I've been promised a ten-bob note for a baby'. The sack was very dark inside and I felt very frightened as I was slung over a horse's side and carried for many miles in this manner. I knew when we left the bush track, because the smell of the gum-trees faded away; and all I could smell for many miles after seemed to be horse. Sometimes he snorted and I could have jumped out of the sack with fright if there had been a hole to jump through. After many hours we stopped, and I was taken out of the sack and handed to a lady and a little girl who were waiting outside a big house by the roadside.

" 'Isn't he a darling!' said the little girl as she patted me. None of them seemed to think I might be a little girl. They all called me 'he'.

A Tragedy

I was squeezed and hugged and petted; and needless to tell you Mrs Koala, I scrambled up her arm and on to her shoulder. It was the nearest thing to a gum-tree I could see; but, alas, no gum-leaves grew there—only funny stuff all round me called hair. The little girl's mother and father said I looked 'so surprised'. Well now, Mrs Koala, wouldn't any bear be surprised to find herself up a gum-tree that talked?"

Mrs Koala was too amazed to reply. She just grunted.

"The next thing that happened," continued Mrs Grunty, "was to place me on a thing they called a cushion. It certainly was soft and cosy—but where was my snug tree-corner I wondered, and I also felt very hungry.

" 'Oh, I forgot to ask the trapper for leaves for the pet,' said the lady.

" 'Give him some cake,' said the man.

"They offered me some dreadful looking stuff, and of course I could not eat it, and I began to cry for my gum-tips. Then the little girl said perhaps I would like bread and milk, and she ran away to get it. I was so hungry that I ate a little and then fell asleep, as the jogging about on the horse had made my body ache and I felt very tired. They placed me in a box with a bear just like me, only he didn't breathe and his eyes didn't blink, and he had no smell of eucalyptus; but he was soft and cuddly like my mother. I woke in the morning, and what do you think they brought me for breakfast? Bananas!"

"How shocking!" gasped Mrs Koala. "And still no leaves?"

"No leaves," sighed Mrs Grunty. "And as the day went by they became concerned about me. They offered me cheese, lollies, and even pudding to add to my sorrowful plight. I heard the little girl's father talking about something he read in a paper in which it said:

Blinky Bill

'During the year 1920 to 1921, two hundred and five thousand six hundred and seventy-nine koalas were killed and their skins sold to the fur market, under the name of wombat'."

Hearing this Mrs Koala gave a jump with fright and nearly fell off her perch.

"Oh! how dreadful! It is only a short time ago that my husband was shot. And we are supposed to be protected and allowed to live. What will I do if Blinky is killed?"

"You need not worry," said Mrs Grunty, patting her paw in a comforting way. "We are safe here. No man ever comes into  this part of the bush. But I must tell you the rest of my story. These people were really trying to be kind to me. They did not wish to lose me, but it was the worst kind of kindness. As you know, I would die very quickly if I had no gum-leaves to feed on. After two more days of tempting me with everything they could think of, they became alarmed and decided I must go back to the bush.

"'We would never forgive ourselves, if the dear wee thing died,' the mother and father said. But the little girl began to cry. She brought me her best dolly and put it in my arms to try and comfort me, but I felt too sick and hungry to take any notice of it.

"That night when she was asleep, her father put me in the sack again and once more I was on a horse's back, but he rode with me this time and rode all through the night. Just as day was breaking I smelled the bush and, oh, the gum-trees! Already I felt better, for I knew I was home again. Very soon the horse stopped and once more I was taken from the sack. I blinked my eyes, scarcely able to believe that I was in my own world again.

A Tragedy

"The little girl's father put me down on the ground at the foot of a tall gum.

"'There you are, little fellow!' he said. 'I hope you are happy now. And I'll do my best to see no more of you are trapped. So long!' And staying just long enough to see me on my way up the tree, he turned on his horse and rode through the bush."

"And how did you find your way home?" asked Mrs Koala.

"It took me a long time, as I was very weak," said Mrs Grunty, "and I had to find our own white gum-tree, as you know. But I travelled gradually, at night-time, and went on travelling until I found this very tree, which I liked so much that I stayed here. And besides," she gave a little giggle, "Mr Grunty happened to be in the branches."

It was great fun.

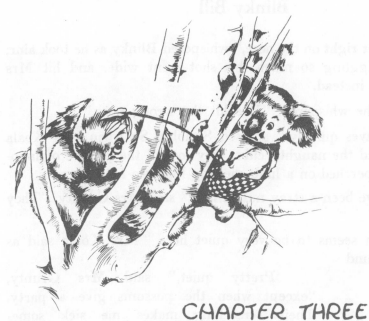

CHAPTER THREE
Naughty Escapades

MRS GRUNTY'S story was interrupted by a sharp whack on the nose.

"Good heavens! What's that?" she cried, rubbing the sore spot with her paw.

"Those young imps are fighting already," said Mrs Koala, peering up above at the branches.

But Mrs Koala was wrong. Blinky and Snubby were having a lovely game, dodging in and out the leaves, and pelting everything visible with gum-nuts.

"Let's have a shot at mother," whispered Blinky, his beady eyes twinkling with mischief.

"You go first," said Snubby under his breath.

27

"I'll hit her right on the nose," whispered Blinky as he took aim; but he was giggling so much, his shot went wide, and hit Mrs Grunty's nose instead.

"O-o-h!" he whispered. "I've hit the wrong nose."

"Chew leaves quickly," advised Snubby. So when Mrs Koala eventually spied the naughty cubs, they looked the picture of innocence, quietly perched on a limb chewing like two little cherubs.

"Must have been a stray nut falling," said Mrs Grunty. "They do sometimes."

"The bush seems to be very quiet here," Mrs Koala said as she looked around

"Pretty quiet," said Mrs Grunty, "except when the possums give a party. Their screeching makes me sick sometimes, such a lot of jabbering and rushing about. What for, I don't know. They are not nearly so rare as we are. Do you know, we are the only bears in this bush for miles around?"

"Can it be true?" Mrs Koala murmured in surprise. "You see, I've never been one to travel. I am content to stay in the same tree for a very long time."

"I've lived in the district for ten years," said Mrs Grunty, "and you and Blinky are the only bears I've seen during that time. I remember well the little girl's father telling her when they first saw me that not so many years ago the bush was alive with us bears from Queensland to the south of Victoria. Now, we are so rare that we have become a curiosity, something to be put in zoos, for children to see; and actually in museums. I believe our grandparents sit there in glass cases, stuffed with something inside to make them appear alive, and, oh dear, glass eyes. In New South

Naughty Escapades

Wales, I think we could wander for miles from one corner to another and never meet a bear. I don't know why we were all killed. As you know, we don't eat the farmers' crops or ruin their orchards. All we asked for were our own gum-trees."

Mrs Koala moved nervously. "I hope we are safe here," she whimpered. "How are we to know when a man may come along with a gun?"

"I know we are safe," said Mrs Grunty contentedly. "The nearest human being to us is a lady who keeps a store a good many miles away. Sometimes I have ventured out to peep at the motor cars as they rush along the road, and I've heard men asking her: 'Are there any possums or bears in this bush?'"

"'No!' she says in a snappy voice. 'Only snakes!'"

"Snakes!" cried Mrs Koala. "Where?"

"Oh, they are quite harmless, if left alone. But of course, if animals and humans go poking about them, they naturally become very angry. I've passed many in the bush; but I mind my own business, and they take no notice of me."

The days and nights came and went, and Blinky grew into a strong bear. Always up to some mischief, he kept the older bears in a constant state of watchfulness. He was very venturesome and scrambled up to the highest twig on the tree, or out to the farthest branch, scrapping and hugging his playmate or grabbing a nice tender leaf from him just as it was about to pop into Snubby's mouth.

One night Mrs Koala and Mrs Grunty decided to go for a walk. They gathered their cubs together and in a stern voice Mrs Koala gave her orders

"I'm going for a walk over the hill, Blinky, and don't you

move out of this tree. No skylarking and romping while I'm away; and be good to Snubby."

"Yes, mother," said Blinky demurely, "I'll mind Snubby till you come back."

So Mrs Koala and Mrs Grunty climbed down the tree and, after ambling along the ground in a comical way, they disappeared over the rise of the hill.

Blinky had been watching their progress and he also had heard Mrs Grunty telling his mother about the store on the road where the motor cars went past, and he had a great longing to see these things.

"Stuck in a tree all the time!" he grunted. "I'm for adventure, snakes or no snakes. I'm not afraid."

"What are you saying?" inquired Snubby in a tone of wonder.

"I'm going to see those motor cars and the store," said Blinky in a bold voice.

"Oh! you can't," said Snubby, quite frightened at the idea. "Our mothers will be very angry, and besides you'll get lost!"

"I'm going!" said naughty Blinky in a bold voice, "and you may come too if you like."

"No! I couldn't," said Snubby in a terrified whisper. "Mrs Snake might chase us."

"If we don't poke faces at her, she won't," said Blinky. "I'm going."

"*Please* don't go, Blinky," implored Snubby.

"Cry-baby," mocked Blinky. "Just show me which way the road lies."

"Over there," said little Snubby, pointing his paw to the direction.

"I'll be back in no time; and while I'm away, don't fall out of the tree." And Blinky started down the tree with a very brave look in his eye.

He was soft and cuddly —
like my mother.

Blinky Bill

At the foot of the tree some of the braveness left him. Everything was so strange and the world seemed so large. Even the bushes appeared to look like big trees, and he fancied he could see all kinds of strange faces looking at him round the corners and through the grass. A cricket popped up, just at his feet. Blinky stood still with fright, his heart going pit-a-pat at a great rate.

"Good evening, young bear, and where do you think you're going?" the cricket inquired.

"To see the motor cars and the store," Blinky replied in a very subdued tone.

"Great hoppers!" said the cricket. "A very bold lad, that's what I think you are."

"A fellow can't stay at home all the time," replied Blinky.

"Well, take care you don't come to harm!" And the cricket hopped on its way.

"Cheek," muttered Blinky to himself. "Why can't a bear go and see motor cars?"

On he went, sometimes stopping to nibble at a plant that looked extra sweet. It was a great adventure to taste something new and see and smell the bush flowers. After travelling many miles he began to feel tired, so looked around for a gum-tree where a little bear could have a nap in safety.

Finding just the kind he wanted, up he climbed, and there, in a cosy fork between two large branches, he cuddled up and went to sleep, his head snuggled down on his tummy, and his two front paws folded over his ears. He looked just like a ball of fur, but to anyone trying to spy him in that tree—well, it was impossible. Towards daylight he opened his eyes, and was a little surprised to find himself in a strange land. He had to think quite hard for a time to find out where he really was, then remembering he was on an adventure, he snatched a few leaves and gobbled them up in a great haste, for he wanted to travel before the sun rose too high in the sky. Very carefully he climbed down the tree, as a slip would mean a broken leg or arm, and Mr Blinky knew how to use those strong claws of his. He spread them out in a masterful way, not losing his grip with one leg until he was sure of the other. Once on the ground, he gambolled along just like a toy bear on being wound up with a key.

As the sun climbed higher in the sky he found the tall trees growing thinner, farther apart, and more open ground, also the bush tracks branched off into other tracks. It was puzzling to know which to take, but he kept in mind the direction Snubby had pointed. Another rest during the midday and he felt that his journey must be nearing its end. He could now hear strange noises, and smell the dust.

"I must be near the motor cars and store," he thought as slowly he crawled up a tree to see what was in view.

There just ahead of him was the road, and that surely must be the store.

"What a funny place," thought Blinky.

Down he came, out of the tree, and toddled to the edge of the bush. There he lay in the scrub, waiting to see all the wonders of the outside world. The sun was setting and something came rushing along the road with two bright lights twinkling. Astonished, Blinky gazed at it. Bu-r-r-r and it was gone, leaving behind a cloud of red dust that nearly blinded him.

"If that's a motor car, I'm sorry I came," said Blinky slowly, as he brushed the dust from his nose.

Peeping through the bushes again he saw lights in the store and some strange being moving about inside. Waiting until all was quiet, he walked across the roadway. Here was adventure indeed, and just the smallest quake of fear ran through him. Glancing over his shoulder he looked to see how far the bush lay behind, in case he needed to run back at any moment, and then walked right on to the veranda. Over the door were large letters that looked like this:

MISS PIMM
REFRESHMENTS

Puzzled, he gazed at everything, never once thinking of his home that lay many miles behind him. He poked his little nose round the doorway. No one was about, and what a lovely lot of new things to see. Rows and rows of strange things in tins and jars.

Bottles on a shelf filled with pretty colours. Some marked "Raspberry" and others "Orange". And good gracious! there were some gum-tips in a bottle standing on the counter.

"I must eat those," said Blinky to himself, "they look very juicy."

Softly he scrambled on to a box, and then another climb, and he stood on the counter.

Looking round all the time to see that no one came unawares, he tiptoed to the gum-tips. From his position behind the bottle he could see Miss Pimm moving about in her kitchen, and judging by the smells that reached his nose she was cooking her dinner. He ate and ate and ate those gum-tips. Such a wonderful "tuck-in" he had. His tummy grew very round until at last he found he could see Miss Pimm very clearly, as only a few stalks stuck out of the neck of the bottle. They looked very strange standing there, without a leaf to show, and a fat little bear gazing through them all the while. Next to him stood some big jars of sweets. All labelled in the same strange writing: "Boiled Lollies", "Ginger", "Chocolates", "Caramels", Peppermints".

Naughty Escapades

"They look nice," thought Blinky, as he touched the jar with his paws. "P-e-p-p-e-r-m-i-n-t-s. Perhaps they are really gum-leaves," he thought, and very quietly lifted the lid. His claws were handy for more things than climbing gum-trees.

He scooped a pawful out of the jar, and cautiously tasted one. Finding it hot and very like some plants he had tasted in the bush, he ate more. He went on eating Miss Pimm's peppermints and put in his paw to gather more from the jar. Just as he did so, the lid on which he had been standing slipped from under him, and down it rolled with a terrible thump and bang.

Miss Pimm came rushing through the house.

"What a smell of eucalyptus! I must have upset a bottle," she cried to someone in the kitchen.

Blinky got a dreadful fright. He was too frightened to move and just sat there and blinked, one paw in the peppermint jar and the other in his mouth.

"Oh, you robber!" shrieked Miss Pimm, as she caught sight of him. "Stealing my peppermints. I'll teach you—you young cub," and she grasped a ruler that lay on the shelf.

"It's life or death," thought Blinky very quickly, and made a dart off the counter and round the corner, right into a large tin of biscuits. Fortunately the tin was nearly empty, so there was plenty of room to hide.

"You young scallawag," cried Miss Pimm, "wait until I catch you. All my gum-tips gone as well." This seemed to put new vigour into her actions and she fairly flew round the shop. To Blinky, hiding away in the biscuit tin she sounded more like an elephant rushing round than anything else. Round the corner she came and then, catching sight of Blinky in the tin, she banged the lid down with an awful crash.

"I've got you now, you young thief,"

35

"Good Heavens!
What was that?"
Mrs. Grunty cried.

she called out triumphantly. "You won't get out of there in a hurry, and to make sure of you, I'll get a box to put you in."

Blinky was breathless. Whatever was going to happen? Would he be killed or taken to one of those zoos that Mrs Grunty spoke about?

I must get out of here, he thought, and waste no time about it.

Listening with his ear to the side of the tin, he heard Miss Pimm's footsteps going towards the kitchen, then pushing open the lid a little way with his head he peeped out. Everything was safe. She was still away, but he could hear her talking and rummaging about outside. Quickly he climbed out of the tin and was walking round the back of the counter looking for a good place to hide when he heard Miss Pimm's footsteps coming back again.

"Oh dear, what shall I do?" he panted. "She'll catch me for sure this time." He dived into a sack of potatoes just as she came through the doorway.

"You'll stay in this box now, young man," said Miss Pimm, "and I'll sell you to the first person who wants a young thief." She tramped round to the biscuit tin. Imagine her rage when she found the tin open and no bear there.

"He's the devil himself," she cried, and started to open every tin she could find. Next she looked round the boxes of fruit, and under the counter, then sniffing loudly, she came to the sack of potatoes. "So you'd make all my potatoes taste of eucalyptus. Well, we'll see about that. Where's my box?" She rushed over to the door to get the box, and at the same moment Blinky jumped out of the sack of potatoes. But she saw him. Round the counter she came, the box under her arm, and round the other way rushed Blinky.

"Stop! Stop! I tell you," she screamed. But Blinky had no idea of stopping. He popped in and out of corners, over tins, under bags, and Miss Pimm after him. It was a terrible scuttle and the whole shop seemed to shake. Bottles and tins rattled on the shelves, the door banged, papers flew everywhere, and in the middle of all the din Miss Pimm tripped over a broom that was standing against the counter. Down she fell, box and all. The clatter was dreadful and her cries were worse. Blinky was terrified. How he wished a gum-tree would spring up through the floor. Suddenly, all in a twinkling, he saw a big bin standing open beside him and without any thought of what might be inside, he climbed up the side and flopped in. It was half full of oatmeal.

Using both paws as quickly as he could, he scratched a hole in the oatmeal, wriggled and wriggled down as far as he could until he was quite hidden: all that could be seen was a little black nose breathing very quickly. He kept his eyes closed very tightly, and felt very uncomfortable all over: but he was safe at last.

Miss Pimm slowly picked herself up. Her side was hurt and her leg was bruised. The box was broken and also the broom handle. She seemed quite dazed and felt her head. Then, holding on to the counter with one hand she limped round the back of it once more.

"You'll die this time, when I get you," and she seemed to choke the words out.

Every tin, every sack, and every box was moved and examined, but no bear was to be found. She didn't stop to have her tea, but went on searching, hour after hour, and all the store had to be tidied up again. After a very long time she locked the door leading on to the roadway, and Blinky, feeling the benefit of his rest and becoming bolder each minute, peeped over the top of the

He ate – and ate – and ate
those gum-tips.

oatmeal bin. He saw Miss Pimm taking a little packet from a case marked "A.S.P.R.O." He popped down again as he felt quite safe in the bin, but he listened with his large ears to any sound she made.

Presently the lights went out, and after mumbling to herself about the "young cub", she went through to the kitchen. Blinky could see the moon shining through the window-panes and he very, very quietly and gently crawled out of the bin. A shower of oatmeal flew over the floor as he landed on his feet and shook his coat and ears, so that oatmeal was everywhere. Right on to the window-ledge he climbed, trod all over the apples in the window that Miss Pimm had so carefully polished, and sat down for a few minutes on a box of chocolates, then noticing more peppermints in the window he pushed a pawful into

He sat down for a few minutes on a box of chocolates.

his mouth and munched away in great content. The window was open half way up so he climbed up the side and sat on the open sill, feeling very brave and happy. What a tale he would have to tell Snubby when he reached home.

"Click!" The light in the store was on.

Blinky wasted no more time on thoughts. He was off that window-ledge and across the road in a few seconds. He reached

Naughty Escapades

the edge of the bush safely and
turned round to see what was happening. Miss Pimm stood in front
of the store with a big policeman,
pointing to the open window, and
then they looked across the roadway to the bush where Blinky lay
hidden behind a tree.

"Well, it's a pity he got
away," Blinky heard the policeman say, "as the Zoo would have
paid you well to have had that
young bear. I didn't know there
were any about here; and I've lived
in the district for thirty years."

"I'd have given him gladly to the Zoo and no payment in
return," said Miss Pimm savagely, "if they had offered to replace
the peppermints and oatmeal."

The next day when some motorists stopped at Miss Pimm's
store and bought some biscuits, they wondered why the biscuits had
such a strong taste of eucalyptus.

Blinky now felt a "man of the world"; but he thought it wise
to go home before any more adventures came his way. So walking
along and running sometimes as fast as his funny little legs would
take him, he came to the tall tree where he had rested the night
before.

Climbing up to the same branch he was asleep in no time and
slept all through the night until the birds woke him at dawn, with
their chattering. Two kookaburras flew into the tree where he lay
and laughed very loudly as they saw Blinky curled up in the corner.

"I'll tell Jacko, if you laugh at me," he said, in a loud voice.
"He's my godfather."

"We were only laughing at the white stuff on your nose," the
kookaburras explained. "It looks so funny." Blinky rubbed his

nose with his paw, and found it still covered with oatmeal, then grunting angrily he stood up and gave himself a shake. "I must be going," he said. And down the tree he climbed and on to the ground again.

He wondered if he had been away from home very long, and began to feel a little uncomfortable about his greeting when he did arrive. Would mother be very angry? Perhaps she was still away with Mrs Grunty. But his fears did not last very long, as a bee flew across his pathway, and he became very curious about that bee. It flew to a flower to gather the pollen. Blinky trotted along to see what it was doing and watched very closely as the bee buzzed about dipping its small head into the heart of the flower. Something warned him not to touch it; but being a little boy bear, he just couldn't watch any longer without giving a poke. So out came his paw, and he reached to pat it. He tried to play with it; but the bee objected, and with a loud buzz stung him right on the nose. Oh, how he cried, and danced about, rubbing his nose with his paws. He ran on blindly, not looking to see where he was going, and after some minutes, when the pain stopped, he found he had lost his way. He had taken a wrong turning on the bush track, and now—what would happen?

Blinky sat down to think things over. While he was puzzling his brain, and wondering which way to turn, a kind little green lizard peeped through the grass and said in a very small voice:

"What's the matter, Blinky? You look very sorry for yourself!"

"I'm lost," replied Blinky, "and I don't know how to find my way home."

42

Naughty Escapades

"I know where you live," said the lizard joyfully. "You follow me, and I'll lead the way."

"I'm so glad I met you," Blinky replied. And, as the lizard walked ahead, he followed, never taking his eyes off her. In and out of the grass and under bushes she ran at an amazing speed, until they reached the path again.

"You're safe now," she said, turning to Blinky, "keep straight ahead and your gum-tree is not far away."

"I know where you live." said the lizard joyfully.

"Thank you, Miss Lizard," said Blinky politely. "I must hurry as my mother is waiting for me."

On he ran. It seemed a long way to him, and how he wished Angelina would hop along and take him on her back.

As he came to the top of the hill, he saw his home down in the hollow, and he was quite sure he could hear his mother calling for him.

Hurrying along, faster than ever, he now heard grunts and cries, and his heart went pit-a-pat as though it would jump out of his skin.

Suddenly his mother saw him. She grunted loudly with joy, and Mrs Grunty and Snubby joined in the chorus.

"I'm here, mother," Blinky called. "I'm at the foot of the tree."

"Oh, you naughty cub. Where have you been? Just wait until you climb up the tree——"

"Don't smack me, mother," Blinky whimpered. "I'll never run away again."

Bit by bit he climbed the tree, all the time imploring his mother not to spank him. He was so long in reaching the branch where Mrs Koala and Mrs Grunty and Snubby were waiting, and they were so pleased to see him safely home, that Mrs Koala forgot to spank him. She hugged him and petted him and Snubby laughed and danced on the branch. It was good to be home, but Blinky still wondered if his mother would remember to punish him. But she didn't. She did not forget. Mother's don't do those things, but she wanted Blinky to think she did.

"Where have you been all this time?" she inquired.

"I saw Miss Pimm and a big policeman," Blinky said in a loud voice. "And I ate Miss Pimm's peppermints."

"Wonder it did not kill the young lubber," said Mrs Grunty.

Snubby's eyes nearly fell out of his head as he listened to Blinky's story, when later on in the evening they sat together in the fork of the tree whispering and giggling as Blinky told him all about his adventures. When at last he cuddled up and went to sleep, close to his mother, Mrs Koala could be seen rubbing a gum-leaf over a very swollen little nose.

CHAPTER FOUR
Frog Hollow

NOW a good little bear would have been quite contented to live for ever quietly and safely up in his tree, after exciting adventures like those of Blinky's—but not he! As the weeks went past he became tired of climbing and playing on the same branches, and even. grew tired of Snubby. He quarrelled, and kicked, and sometimes, I'm sorry to say, actually bit his playmate's nose. Of course Snubby immediately cried, and Blinky teased him all the more.

Poor Mrs Koala had a very trying time in keeping the peace. Sometimes Mrs Grunty got quite snappy and wouldn't speak, which upset Mrs Koala very much, as she knew it was all Blinky's fault.

"That boy of yours will come to no good!" said Mrs Grunty one day. "If he was mine, I'd try a little of the stick around his hind parts."

Blinky Bill

"What am I to do?" sighed Mrs Koala. "I can't smack him all the time. Where he gets this wild manner of his from I don't know. I believe his great-grandfather was very wild—on his father's side of course. My people were always very quiet."

"Well, most probably he'll grow out of it, if he doesn't fall out of it," said Mrs Grunty. "Have one of these leaves and forget all about it." So the mother bears patched up their little differences, until naughty Blinky did something extra bad and mischievous; then all the trouble started again. Mrs Grunty loved to have her noonday snooze, and became very irritable if she did not get it, or was disturbed during that time.

"A mother must have a few minutes to herself, otherwise she becomes old and wrinkled, and goodness knows my nose is funny enough without lines round it," she mumbled away, as she crawled to her favourite corner.

Sometimes just as she got to sleep, all nicely curled up, and was dreaming of peaceful things, Mr Blinky would creep along the branch, and nip her ear, or poke her side with his paw.

"Go away, go away, or I'll eat you!" Mrs Grunty would growl as she reached out to cuff his ear, but Blinky was always too quick for her and would dodge behind the tree.

Frog Hollow

"Impertinent young fellow," Mrs Grunty would mumble as she dozed off again.

One day, never to be forgotten, she was awakened from her snooze by muffled giggles and grunts. Cautiously she opened one eye slowly and peeped around. What was that peculiar feeling in her ears? Brushing her head quickly with her paws she found a bunch of gum-tips poking out from each ear. It was too much for Mrs Grunty, and she decided to take action quickly. Blinky by this time was far up on a topmost branch, safely away from angry mothers.

"Come down at once," commanded Mrs Grunty and Mrs Koala together.

But Blinky pretended he was deaf and took no notice of their angry calls.

"Blinky, come down this minute!" Mrs Koala demanded.

"I'll go up and get him," said Mrs Grunty in a determined voice. "No bear of that age will get the better of me." And she stamped a hind leg on the tree to show that she really meant it.

Blinky began to feel things were getting a little uncomfortable, and he really didn't want to go on eating so many leaves all at once, so he decided to face the enemy.

"Are you looking for some nice young leaves, Mrs Grunty?" he inquired in a polite voice.

"No!" snapped Mrs Grunty, "I'm looking for a bad young bear!"

"Snubby's not up here," Blinky replied in an innocent tone.

"Now, no cheek," grunted Mrs Grunty, "you're bad enough as it is; come down out of that branch!"

"Just wait a minute," Blinky replied, "and I'll bring you some beautiful juicy leaves."

Down she fell —
box and all.

Frog Hollow

"Where are they?" Mrs Grunty asked excitedly, quite forgetting her anger.

"Up here," said Blinky. "Would you like a few?"

"Yes, I would," replied Mrs Grunty. "And bring some for your mother; she has a bad headache."

Blinky gathered the very freshest tips he could find and, chatting gaily all the while (for he was a cunning young bear), he came down the tree and held them out to Mrs Grunty."

"You're a dear little bear!" said Mrs Grunty as she nibbled the leaves. "I'd be proud to have a son like you."

Naughty Blinky stood behind her back and screwed up his nose at her, and Snubby, who was watching from a branch close by, gave a loud, squealing grunt.

"Well, well, how kind of Blinky!" said Mrs Koala, as she munched the leaves with her friend. "He is a thoughtful son."

But life seemed very monotonous to Blinky. He knew every branch, twig, and leaf of that tree off by heart, and Snubby never seemed to think of any new games, so he decided to start on another adventure. The more he thought of it, the braver he grew, until one evening, when the moon shone extra brightly, and the leaves looked silvery-green, he decided the time had come to make a start. His mother and Mrs Grunty and Snubby were sitting together away out on a distant branch, quite out of view, so stealthily and quickly Blinky slid down the tree and on to the ground. "Ha, ha, it's good to be away again," he said to himself as he looked around.

49

How pretty everything looked in the moonlight, and the dew on the grass and leaves sparkled so brightly.

"I love mother and Snubby very much," Blinky murmured; "but they don't seem to think I'm grown up and want to see things. And what a funny bear Snubby is. I'm beginning to think he must be a girl, as he never wants to go adventuring."

"Hi, there!" called a loud voice from somewhere in the bushes. "What do you think you're doing down here?"

"Who are you?" panted Blinky with fright, for certainly he didn't expect anything to happen so soon.

"Who am I? Come over here and see," came the reply in a gruff voice.

"You won't eat me, will you?" Blinky asked in a frightened voice.

"Eat a bear. Ha, ha! Well I've never tasted one, and I'm not going to start now. I'm not too fond of swallowing fur and eucalyptus in one mouthful."

And just as he said those words Mr Wombat shuffled out of the bushes.

"Oh!" gasped Blinky, "what a big fellow you are! What's your name?"

To a stranger like you —
I am Mr Wombat.

"The cheeky young rabs call me 'Womby'; but to a stranger like you I am *Mr Wombat*."

"Where do you live?" Blinky inquired, still just a little nervous at seeing so large an animal standing right in front of him.

"That's a secret," replied Mr Wombat. "But if you know

"That boy of yours will come to no good" said Mrs. Grunty.

how to keep quiet about those things I'll take you to see my home."

"I won't tell a soul, Mr Wombat," Blinky whispered.

"Very good! Well, come this way," said Mr Wombat. He led Blinky through the thick undergrowth, crashing the bracken down with his sturdy legs, and grunting loudly as he went. It was rather difficult for Blinky to keep pace with him, as he went at such a rate; but he paused now and then to give a glance over his shoulder and waited for his little friend to catch up with his steps.

The bush grew thicker, but presently Blinky noticed the ground had a "dug-up" look about it. Roots of bushes had been undermined, plants eaten down to the ground, and altogether everything looked very untidy.

Right ahead a very large tree grew up to the sky, and Blinky thought he had never seen such a big gum. The trunk was enormous and the roots spread out in all directions.

"This is my home," said Mr Wombat proudly. "Don't you think it fine?"

"Yes," replied Blinky. "It's a very grand place. But how do you climb that huge trunk?"

"Climb!" said Mr Wombat scornfully, "I've no need to do any stunts here. I live under the roots."

"Oh!" gasped Blinky, "not in that big black hole?"

"Yes! That's my home," replied Mr Wombat. "And the rain can come down as hard as it likes and the wind blow and shake the tree as long as it likes; but I just lie here underneath, safer than all the bears up in the trees.

"Come in and have a look round.

Frog Hollow

Everything's lovely and dark; and there's a very nice muddy smell inside."

"I don't think I'll come in, Mr Wombat," said Blinky in a quiet voice. "I'm in rather a hurry. But if you don't mind I'll sit down on the ground for a few minutes to rest my legs."

"Please yourself," said Mr Wombat rather gruffly. But seeing Blinky's startled eyes, he felt sorry for the little bear and offered to hunt round for a few shoots of plants to eat.

"I'm not hungry," Blinky said. "But I wish you would tell me all about that big black hole," pointing to Mr Wombat's home.

Mr Wombat at once came and sat down beside Blinky and started to tell him the story.

"Well," he began, "I've lived here for many years now. Long ago I lived out in the open near Farmer Brown's house; but it became too dangerous. He was a bad-tempered man, and had no time for a wombat. He sowed his fields full of potatoes and peas, and juicy carrots and turnips, then expected a wombat to look at them and not come near."

"How silly!" interrupted Blinky. "I'd have eaten all his peas up in one mouthful."

Mr Wombat turned suddenly to have a look at Blinky's mouth, then shrugged his shoulders and went on with his story.

"Yes, he was silly. He even fenced his paddocks with very strong wire, and didn't I laugh to myself as I lay behind an old tree-stump hearing men digging in the hot sunshine, then ramming down posts and nailing wire all round them."

"What did you do?" Blinky inquired.

"I waited until the night came, as I'm as blind as a bat during the day, then I crept silently over to the new fence, and had a look at it. Poof! I burrowed under it in a few minutes and had a great supper of potato roots; then just to show Farmer Brown how strong I was, I burrowed another hole from the inside of the fence to get out again. In the morning as I lay in bed I heard Farmer Brown and his men shouting loudly and using very strange words.

"One night I had a narrow escape. Carefully treading over the ground, I had just reached my favourite roots, when, snap! something caught the tip of my toe. I howled with pain and rage. What new trick was this of Farmer Brown's? Then to make matters worse men came running from all directions, shouting and calling at the top of their voices. Dear me, how excited they were—and all over a wombat in a potato patch!"

"What did you do?" asked Blinky breathlessly.

"Huh! I just gave a tug at my paw, and out it came. I lost a toenail—but what's that! Then the excitement rose. Guns began to crack and a bullet flew past me very close to my ear—too close for my liking. Fortunately for me it was a dark night, with only the stars overhead, and luckily I remembered just where my burrow was under the fence. I raced along, wild calls coming behind me and heavy boots thudding the ground. But I won! Under the fence I rushed; out the other side, and into the bush I raced. I did not stop at my home; but kept running for miles, as far away from Farmer Brown as I could manage. When I finally fell down exhausted, my foot was causing me a great deal of pain, so I licked it for a long time and then fell asleep. After that adventure I decided to look for a new home, and here I am."

"Well, you're safe here, Mr Wombat," said Blinky. "And if I were you I'd stay here and never wander again."

"I'm safe enough," replied Mr Wombat. "But the food is not up to much, and pretty dry in the summer; but I manage to scrape along. I'm not in fear of my life like my grandparents were."

"Why, what happened to them?" Blinky asked anxiously.

"They lived up in the north-west," said Mr Wombat, "a wild place if you like! The black people there used to hunt them with yam-sticks. Poor grandad and grandma were in constant danger of being killed."

"How?" asked Blinky.

"Well," continued Mr Wombat, "the black people would go out in hunting parties and when a wombat-hole was found a boy was usually chosen to go down feet first. As he wriggled his way down the burrow he tapped on the roof of the tunnel with his hands. Those above the ground were listening and followed the taps as he went, until at last when the boy's feet touched a wombat, he would give a signal and then the men above would quickly dig down into the earth and right on to the wombat. A few moments and he was dead. No chance of escape at all——"

"It's just as well for you, Mr Wombat, there are no black fellows here," said Blinky.

"And just as well for you too!" replied his new friend. "But where are you going, anyway? You haven't told me yet."

"Well, I don't know," Blinky said in a doubtful tone. "Do you know of any adventures round here?"

"Adventures! What do you, mean exactly?" Mr Wombat asked.

"Oh, you know—things to see—not gum-leaves all the time," replied Blinky.

"Ho, ho," laughed Mr Wombat. "So you're looking for new sights, are you? Well, now I come to think of it, there's Mrs Spotty's school down in the hollow."

"I don't think I'll come in Mr. Wombat."
said Blinky in a quiet voice.

Frog Hollow

"Who is Mrs Spotty?" Blinky asked.

"Mrs Spotty Frog. She has a boarding-school for young frogs and tadpoles. A very select school, so I'm told, and there's lots to be seen if you happen to pass that way."

"I'll go that way, Mr Wombat," said Blinky with a smile. "Is it down this track?"

"Yes, follow your nose, and you can't miss the place. You'll hear it long before you come to it." And Mr Wombat grunted with disapproval.

So bidding him good-bye, Blinky started down the track towards Frog Hollow.

It was not a great distance, and before very long sounds of croaking and gurgling reached his ears. Scrambling along, he came to a clearing in the bush, and what a sight met his eyes! He held his breath in astonishment. There, right in front of him was a large pool, surrounded with bells and every bush flower he had ever seen. It was a green pool with water-lilies floating on the surface and round the edges brown and green rushes stood very erect: but strangest of all—hundreds and hundreds of frogs. All sizes, from the babies upwards, were squatting on the lily-leaves, or poking their heads just through the green water. The noise was deafening. Every frog croaked. Big frogs with deep throaty croaks, smaller ones with a shrill note, and baby frogs piping in unison. On a large leaf in the centre of the pool Mrs Spotty waved her leg. Every frog watched her with the greatest attention.

"One, two, three," she called, and waved her leg in a downward motion. The croaks came loud and long.

 "Stop!" she called in a shrill voice. Instantly the frogs were silent.

"Miss Greenlegs, fourth from the left in the back row, you're flat. Flat as a lily-leaf. Take your note and try it alone."

Blinky Bill

Turning to a large frog that sat a little to the right of her, she waved her leg.

He drew a straw across a blade of grass and listened intently, his head bent sideways against the grass. A tiny note floated across the pool and, reaching Miss Greenlegs's ears, she puffed out her throat and gave a beautiful croak. It was clearness itself.

"Excellent," exclaimed Mrs Spotty. "Now, all together please." And again she waved her leg.

"Croak, croak, croak," every frog puffed and rolled his eyes in a wonderful way.

Blinky was spellbound. Slowly he tiptoed nearer to the pool. But a twig snapped under his feet. Instantly every frog dived into the water. Not a sound was heard, and only a few ripples and bubbles broke the surface of the pool. Blinky gazed and gazed. Where have they gone? he thought, and ran down as fast as his legs would carry him to the reedy bank. Not a frog was in sight. But he felt that somewhere down in that pool eyes were watching him very closely. He kept perfectly still, hardly daring to breathe, watching a few bubbles floating to the surface only to burst and leave nothing at all. It seemed hours to Blinky before he saw a green body silently lift itself out of the water and slide on to a lily-leaf where Mrs Spotty had stood. The big frog eyed

The big frog eyed Blinky curiously.

Blinky curiously, never moving and ready to slip back again into the water at a moment's notice.

"Are you Mrs Spotty?" Blinky quietly inquired.

Frog Hollow

"Yes, that's me," came the reply. "What do you want?"

"I came to see your school and hear the frogs sing, and I wish you'd let me come to school too," said Blinky plaintively.

"We don't have bears in our school as a rule," said Mrs Spotty; "but I've no objection to you joining the class if you behave yourself. Have you been to school before?"

"No, Mrs Spotty," Blinky replied, "but I've travelled quite a long way."

"Can you play leap-frog and swim?" asked Mrs Spotty.

"No, I can't do any of those things," Blinky replied, "but I can climb gum-trees."

Mrs Spotty's eyes looked more like those motor-car lights down by Miss Pimm's store than anything else he had ever seen, Blinky thought; and they were such poppy ones too.

"Can you jump?" she asked.

"Yes," said Blinky joyfully, "I can jump very high."

"How high?" asked Mrs Spotty.

"Oh, as high as a tree," Blinky replied.

"Well, I think you may be of assistance to me in teaching the tadpoles how to jump. Come over to me, while I have a good look at you. But stop!" and Mrs Spotty turned three shades paler in green. Balancing herself on the edge of the leaf she looked at Blinky and said in a very slow voice:

"Do you eat frogs?"

Blinky Bill

"I've never tasted them, so I don't know," Blinky replied.

"Well, don't start," Mrs Spotty said in a cross voice. "Now you may come over and sit on the leaf beside me."

"I can't swim. I told you I couldn't," Blinky wailed.

"Oh, well, sit on the bank and watch me put the class through their paces. By the way, what's that funny looking thing in the middle of your face?"

"That's my nose," Blinky replied, trying to look very unconcerned.

"A queer looking nose," said Mrs Spotty rudely. "But never mind, I'll call the class for the swimming lessons."

She gave three loud croaks, and at once dozens and dozens of frogs popped up from beneath the water and out from the rushes. They eyed Blinky nervously, until Mrs Spotty told them he did not eat frogs.

"Now, you young gentlemen with the slender legs, take your places ready for the diving.

"Don't push and crowd, it's very rude and if I find any frog standing on another's tail or causing an unprepared-for jump, I'll punish him severely."

The frogs arranged themselves on the leaves and waited for the word to start. A great commotion was taking place up in the shallow end of the pool, and Mrs Spotty looked sternly in that direction.

"Tadpoles!" she cried, "stop that mud-larking and pay attention to your lesson."

"Now! One, two, three—Dive!" she called at the top of her voice, and dozens of green slippery legs flew through the air and into the pool.

"Too much splashing!" Mrs Spotty declared. "Again: one, two, three—Dive!" And once more the green legs and bodies sprang into the pool.

Frog Hollow

"That's better. Now for a swim." And leaning over the leaf she called her directions to the frogs.

"Scissors! Scissors! Scissors!" she cried as they swam round her leaf, and back again to the starting-point.

"Now for the Tads." And Mrs Spotty lined them up in a row, the fattest ones to the front and the tiny ones at the back.

They behaved like young outlaws—pushing and wriggling and flipping about in a very bold way.

"Not so much of that tail waggling; and, Jimmy Tadpole, don't use your tummy for pushing. Oh! dear, I'm sure I'll never make ladies and gentlemen of you," sighed Mrs Spotty. "You're the most brazen lot of Tads I've ever had in my school."

But the tadpoles didn't care, all they thought about was swimming.

Mrs Spotty gave them their lesson and sent them back again to their own end of the pool, much to the relief of the frogs, as no self-respecting gentleman could swim in the same place as a tadpole.

Blinky by this time had come right to the edge of the pond, and was enjoying himself immensely, until an extra large frog suddenly leaped right on his back.

"Oh, oh, you gave me such a fright!" Blinky cried. "Get down please. I'm not a log!"

The frog took no notice whatever, but hopped on his head instead. Blinky touched him with his paw, and jumped with fright. He was so cold and slippery—not a scrap like touching Snubby.

"Get down at once!" called Mrs Spotty in a stern voice. And to Blinky's further

61

surprise the frog went helter skelter down his nose and into the water.

"Let's use his nose for a spring-board," the frog called out at the top of his voice.

The very thought of such a thing sent shudders down Blinky's back. Just imagine hundreds of frogs sliding down his nose, one after the other!

"You'll do no such thing!" retorted Blinky indignantly.

"Well let's use his back for leap-frog," another cried.

"I don't mind that," said Blinky, "as long as I have a turn too. I could jump over one of your backs."

"That is a fair thing," said Mrs Spotty. "Now get in places, please."

One after the other the frogs lined up behind Blinky croaking and hopping about, treading on one another's toes and goggling their eyes with excitement.

"Bend down, please," Mrs Spotty called to Blinky. He bent over, making sure his nose was well out of the way.

"Flip—flop—" and the frogs started, one behind the other, jump after jump; and the highest hops were greeted with croaks from the onlookers.

"I wish you'd warm your toes first," said Blinky. But still they came. Flip-flop-flip-flop.

When the last frog had jumped over his back, Blinky raised his head.

"It's my turn now," he cried. "And I want to jump over the biggest frog of all."

Mrs Spotty's pupils looked rather nervous and eyed one another to see which was the largest.

"Go on, Fatty," they called to one big fellow. "You know, you had more mosquitoes for tea than anyone else."

Frog Hollow

Fatty looked very uncomfortable and glanced at his tummy. "It's not mosquitoes," he said crossly, "it's muscles——"

Plonk! right on top of Mrs. Spotty.

"All the better," called Mrs Spotty. "Stand over here and be ready."

Fatty frog hopped beside Mrs Spotty and stood there quaking. What if he slipped! That bear on top of him would be nothing to laugh about.

Blinky stood ready, and Mrs Spotty, who was standing in front of Fatty, called out in a loud croak:

"Ready! Go!"

Blinky made a funny little run, then a few stumbles and with a grunt he flopped over Fatty, and plonk! right on top of Mrs Spotty. She fell with a dreadful thud, and tried to croak; but she was smothered in fur.

Blinky rolled over and over with laughter. When he managed to stand up—there he saw a very flat looking frog that had once been Mrs Spotty.

"Oh, I've killed her!" he cried in a frightened voice. "Come and pick her up!"

All the pupils hopped to Mrs Spotty's assistance. She certainly did look flat; but her throat was puffing and one eye moved a little.

Blinky Bill

"Water! water!" the big frogs called as they dragged her to the edge of the pool.

"Push her in!" cried naughty Blinky, and before any frog had time to think, he gave her a push with his paw, and in she went, head first.

"Now you've done it!" called the frogs in cries of horror. "We'll tell the policeman."

"Policeman," thought Blinky, "where have I heard that name?" And then he remembered Miss Pimm's store.

In the excitement, while the frogs were hopping about and trying to rescue Mrs Spotty, he hurried away to the edge of the bush. Peeping behind a log he saw the frogs hunting everywhere for him; under leaves, behind the rushes and even down in the pool.

CHAPTER FIVE

The Rabbits' Party

"**I** THINK I'd better be going home," thought Blinky. "Anyway I'm not sorry for Mrs Spotty, she had such googly eyes."

He glanced at the sky and noticed the moon was sinking, so thought it time to make haste, as perhaps his mother may be looking for him by now. Past the gum-trees and thick bushes he scrambled, and just as he reached a clearing in the trees he paused to listen.

"The crickets are busy to-night," he thought as their chirruping came through the bush. "I'll just see what they're up to."

Quietly he tiptoed into the grass, and suddenly stood quite still. In front of him, not many yards away the crickets were holding a cricket match.

Blinky chuckled as he looked at them. The batsman had a leaf for his bat, while the bowler had a spider's cocoon for a ball. They were too interested in their game to notice Blinky; but he missed nothing. A deafening chirruping rent the air. Most of the spectators were perched on the blades of grass, as high

The batsman had a leaf for a bat.

up as they could climb, and were waving their legs in the air, and shaking the grass they stood on.

"He's bumping the ball!" they shrieked in cricket voices.

"Pull him out! Pull him out," they shouted, and at once the umpire hopped over to the bowler and soundly boxed his ears with his front leg.

The bowler lost his temper, and jumped on the cricket ball, breaking it in pieces.

"Shame! Shame!" shouted the crickets. And in the next instant they surged on to the ground. Springing in the air they pounced on him and gave him a terrible kicking; and as Blinky turned to walk away he saw them piling earth on top of the bowler.

"I must hurry now, as I'm sure it's

"Did you pull my tail?"
Madam Hare demanded.

getting late," he thought, and he was beginning to feel very shaky. What if his mother found he was missing. That Mrs Grunty could be very cross at times, and she might persuade his mother to use a stick round his hind parts, as she once suggested. In his haste he stumbled over a stone and hurt his foot, so sat down to wait until the pain left him. Just behind the stump he was sitting on, a rabbit had made her home, and as she came scurrying through the grass she did not notice Blinky sitting so quietly. Between her teeth she carried some flannel flowers and a sprig of boronia.

"Good evening," said Blinky.

"Oh! What a fright you gave me!" whispered the rabbit. "I know who you are all the same."

"Who?" asked Blinky.

"You're Blinky Bill, and my mother knows your mother," said the rabbit.

"Then you are only a bunny," said Blinkly gladly. "How old are you and where do you live?"

"I'm one year old, and I live in that burrow right behind this log."

"What's your name?" Blinky asked.

"Bobbin!" the bunny replied.

"That's a silly name," said Blinky quite rudely.

"That's my christened name, and my mother says it is very suitable for me."

"What does suitable mean?" Blinky asked.

"Well, mother says I'm always bobbin' about, and never still. I make her quite nervy at times."

The Rabbits' Party

"What does she do when you run away?" Blinky asked rather anxiously.

"Run away!" said Bobbin, looking very surprised. "I never run away. Only bad children do that!"

"Well, where have you been, and why have you those flowers? You look very stupid carrying them in your mouth," Blinky remarked.

"I've been gathering flowers for the birthday party," replied Bobbin; "and how can I carry them without breaking their petals, if I don't hold them between my teeth?"

"Haven't you a pouch or a pocket somewhere?" Blinky retorted. "But am I mistaken? Did you mention a birthday party?"

"Yes," said Bobbin excitedly. "It's my brother's party, and ever so many friends are coming, and there's lots and lots to eat. Thistle cakes, with the prickles all over the tops; dandelion milk, lovely and frothy, that's to be drunk through a grass straw; daisy creams with pink edges; and, oh! best of all, buttercups, full of butter. And I nearly forgot—gum-leaves to chew, for those who like chewing-gum. Then last of all, there's grass salad for the mothers and fathers."

Bobbin hopped about with glee and twitched her ears in a most surprising manner, while Blinky's eyes bulged with excitement.

"Could *I* come to the party?" he inquired breathlessly.

"You haven't a present to bring!" Bobbin answered.

"I know that," replied Blinky sorrowfully; "but I'll let them play with my ears if they like."

Bobbin looked at his ears and considered the matter for a moment.

"Do you eat frogs?"
Mrs Spotty asked.

The Rabbits' Party

"Well, perhaps that will do," she replied. "We could hide the peanut in them when we play 'hunt the slipper'."

It sounded rather a muddle to Blinky; but he was prepared to take any risks if only he could get to the party.

"Could we go now?" he inquired anxiously.

"Yes, but wipe your feet on the grass, before we go inside, as mother's been cleaning all night long," Bobbin advised.

Blinky did as he was told, and followed Bobbin through the doorway. Fortunately for him the burrow was a large one, so he had no difficulty in crawling along.

"Isn't it dark!" he said in a frightened voice.

"You'll soon get used to that," Bobbin replied cheerfully, as she padded ahead. "Do you hear the scraping and thumping? That's the party," she said excitedly.

"What are they doing?" Blinky asked.

"Dancing!" Bobbin replied. "Let's hurry . . ."

In and out of passages they ran, round corners, up and down, and at last came to a large cave. The floor and the walls were bare earth, but over the ground a carpet of grass was spread, and the ceiling was bright with flowers. From the centre a bunch of Christmas bells hung, and directly underneath, the table was spread with all the party cakes and drinks. In the middle of the table a birthday cake stood, glittering with dewdrops that fell from the flowers surrounding it. It was made from corn husks and thistledown, so you can imagine how crunchy it must have tasted.

As Blinky and Bobbin appeared the guests stood and gazed in wonderment; their large brown eyes opened very widely and nervous noses sniffed the air.

"Here's Blinky Bill," Bobbin called as she hopped to the middle of the cave, "and he's come to see the party."

Blinky Bill

"You're very welcome, I'm sure," kind Mrs Rabbit said, as she took Blinky's paw. "Come along and meet my friends. This is Madam Hare; shake paws with her. She is very shy, but is an old friend of mine; and this is Brer Rabbit, my husband, who is a great hunter; and here is Bunchy, my son, whose birthday it is." Each one shook paws with Blinky, and he wondered if it would ever come to an end, and the party start, as he was feeling very hungry and wanted to taste those gum-tips. Bunchy thought it great fun to have a bear at his party and followed Blinky wherever he went.

"You've lost your tail!" he said in surprise as he hopped round him.

"Don't wear a tail," Blinky mumbled.

"Why does everyone pass remarks about my tail or my nose," he wondered.

"Tea's ready," Mrs Rabbit called. And everyone made a rush for the table.

"Don't rush, and don't grab," Brer Rabbit thundered in a loud voice.

Madam Hare may have been shy, but Blinky noticed she reached the table as soon as he, and rather rudely pushed her way right beside Brer Rabbit.

"The bold hussy," someone whispered and gave her tail a nip.

She gave a little scream and spitefully bit the ear of the rabbit who sat next to her; but it wasn't Brer Rabbit's ear.

"Order! Order!" Brer Rabbit commanded. "This is a party, and no fighting, please. If your tails are in the way, sit on them."

The party went on pleasantly after that command. Everyone nibbled and munched, except Blinky who forgot his manners completely and gobbled the gum-leaves as fast as he could. It was just as well nobody else liked them, for in a very short time they had all vanished. The cake was a great success and Bunchy handed a piece to each guest, quickly taking a nibble from one or two when nobody was looking.

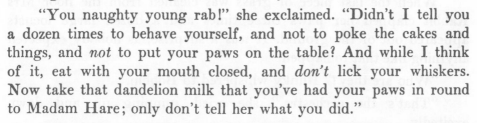

His mother gave him a sharp nip on the ear when she found him poking his paw in the dandelion milk, and slyly sucking it when he thought he was safely hidden from view.

"You naughty young rab!" she exclaimed. "Didn't I tell you a dozen times to behave yourself, and not to poke the cakes and things, and *not* to put your paws on the table? And while I think of it, eat with your mouth closed, and *don't* lick your whiskers. Now take that dandelion milk that you've had your paws in round to Madam Hare; only don't tell her what you did."

"No, mother," said Bunchy obediently, and he hopped to Madam Hare and handed her the milk.

"You dear little rab!" she cried in a very high voice. "I *do* like dandelion milk."

"So do I," remarked Bunchy as he hopped away.

"What's that? What's that?" said Brer Rabbit in between mouthfuls of grass salad.

"Father, you're speaking with your mouth full; and it's so bad for the children to see," gently reprimanded Mrs Rabbit, much to Blinky's amusement, as his mother had often corrected him for exactly the same thing.

"Can't we have games, Mrs Rabbit?" he asked when at last he sat before an empty plate.

"Games and dancing—that's the idea," roared Brer Rabbit. "Clear the floor."

73

Everyone helped, and Blinky gave Madam Hare's tail another pull as he passed her with an armful of grass.

"Dear, dear, I think there are rats about," she said in an injured tone. "My poor tail has been pulled again, and you all know it's moulting time. I'll catch a dreadful cold is I lose any more fur."

Nobody seemed to take any notice of Madam Hare's complaints, and Blinky and Bunchy both agreed to give it another pull later on in the evening.

When the last piece of grass was cleaned from the floor Mrs Rabbit clapped her paws three times and a dozen large locusts appeared out of the ground. It *was* a surprise, as nobody expected anything like that to happen.

"Who are they?" Blinky whispered to Bobbin.

"That's the orchestra," she cried jumping up and down excitedly.

Each locust walked to a corner of the cave and quietly sat down with an expectant look on his face. The conductor, who was a "double drummer", scraped his hind legs on his wings. "Gurra-gurra-gurra" came the vibrating notes. That was the signal, and instantly all the other locusts started scraping their legs.

Girr!!

Girr!!

Girr!!

Gurra!!

Gurra!!

Gurra!!

"Girr—girr—girr—gurra—gurra—gurra." The cave echoed with the drumming noise and beads of perspiration rolled down the conductor's face as he worked himself up (or down, to

The Rabbits' Party

 be correct) to a slow deep "Gurra". The air throbbed with the music. It was really inspiring, and soft furry rabbit feet began to thump the ground. Lady rabbits looked coyly at the gentlemen, and odd little twitches of the ears and twinks of the whiskers were to be noticed.

"Take your partners for 'The Bunny Hug'," Brer Rabbit called in a deep voice.

There was a scampering and rushing, as each rabbit grabbed a partner. Madam Hare didn't even wait to be asked to dance, but seized Brer Rabbit in her arms and began rolling from one side to the other, also jerking her arms up and down in a forward manner.

"That Madam Hare is not as shy as I thought she was," murmured Mrs Rabbit as she was led away by an elderly partner.

Blinky was delighted. His very first dance. Now he would have something to tell Snubby when he reached home. Taking Bobbin in his paws he rolled from one side to the other, just like Madam Hare, whom he kept watching closely.

"You're treading on my toes," whimpered Bobbin.

Blinky looked down at her paws quite alarmed.

"Your toe-nails are too long," he said rudely.

"They're not!" Bobbin replied indignantly. "How could I dig burrows with short toe-nails?"

"I forgot," said Blinky politely. "But look out, here comes Madam Hare, and I'm going to pull her tail again."

Bobbin began to giggle, as she did not like Madam Hare a bit. She "showed off" such a lot.

As the dancers neared Blinky he cautiously grabbed Madam Hare's tail and gave it a very hard pull, so hard in fact that a pawful of fur flew into the air.

Before Madam Hare knew what she was doing, she boxed Brer Rabbit's ears. He was astonished, and looked very pained.

"Did you pull my tail?" Madam Hare demanded in an angry voice.

"Certainly not!" Brer Rabbit replied. "And I'm not going to dance any longer with you."

That was the end of everything for Madam Hare. She hopped right into the middle of the floor and kicked every one as they passed in their dance. It was the beginning of a wild fight. Fur flew through the air, teeth gnashed. And, oh, the savage kicks! Everyone kicked, and the dust began to make them sneeze and cough. The orchestra made a gallant attempt to soothe the ruffled dancers, and dinned louder than ever; but the scuffle grew worse.

Bobbin thought it time to tell her father who it really was that had caused all the trouble. When Brer Rabbit heard her story he at once made for the culprit.

Blinky saw him coming and tried to hide; but Brer Rabbit never moved his eyes from that young bear. Tapping another big rabbit on the shoulder he asked for his assistance and together they grabbed Blinky, firmly holding his front paws. Blinky kicked with his hind legs as hard as he could, but he was handicapped.

"Let go!" he screamed. "You're hurting me."

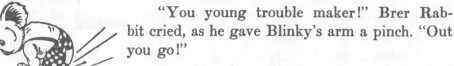

"You young trouble maker!" Brer Rabbit cried, as he gave Blinky's arm a pinch. "Out you go!"

By this time all the other rabbits had

"Come down here!"
Mrs. Koala ordered.

ceased fighting and stood watching the excitement. The orchestra kept playing and an angry note crept into their drumming.

"I've a good mind to take the young bounder to old Mother Ferrit," Brer Rabbit exclaimed.

"No, don't do that," called out Madam Hare. "Let me punish the young rascal."

Blinky shivered with fear. Madam Hare had such big feet and could give a very big kick. How he wished he had a tail round his hind parts. Scowling and showing her teeth Madam Hare pounced on Blinky.

"You little wretch!" she screamed, "you've ruined my tail, and its moulting time. I'll have none for a long time now."

"You're a bully, and I'm glad I did it," roared Blinky trying to kick her.

"Hold his arms!" Madam Hare commanded, as she turned her back to Blinky; then quickly looking over her shoulder she measured her distance.

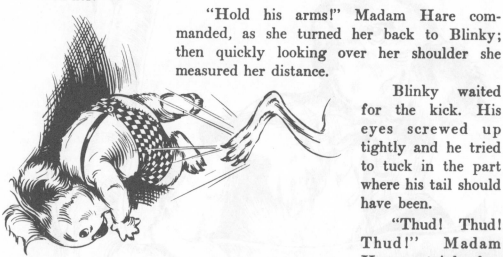

Madam Hare gave him a parting Kick as he shot through the doorway—

Blinky waited for the kick. His eyes screwed up tightly and he tried to tuck in the part where his tail should have been.

"Thud! Thud! Thud!" Madam Hare certainly forgot to be shy.

"Oh! Oh!" wailed Blinky, "Stop! Stop!"

78

The Rabbits' Party

Roars of laughter came from all the rabbits.

"Throw him out! Throw him out!" they called loudly.

Blinky was pushed towards the opening of the cave and Madam Hare gave him a parting kick as he shot through the doorway.

He landed on his paws quite ten feet away. But thank goodness he was safe from the angry rabbits and Madam Hare.

He shook himself and gently patted the place where the kicks had struck.

"Savage animal!" he called at the top of his voice; and at once a head appeared in the opening.

"Chase him! Chase him!" the rabbits cried; but Blinky did not wait to be chased. He was running as fast as he could, colliding with corners, bumping his head and snubbing his nose.

Panting, he reached the entrance of the burrow; but oh! horror of horrors, Madam Hare's large feet came thudding behind him.

"I'll catch you; I'll catch you!" she called. "And off to Mrs Ferrit you'll go!"

Blinky nearly fainted with fright. He felt quite giddy, and his breath seemed to catch in his throat.

His heart pounded and thumped and his legs would *not* go fast enough.

Out into the moonlight he raced, crying and whimpering, stopping just a moment to look behind to see where that Madam Hare was.

Now her head came through the burrow and on she raced.

"Save me! Save me!" Blinky called at the top of his voice; but he hadn't the faintest idea who could rescue him.

79

Blinky Bill

Suddenly the branches cracked and a brown form came hurriedly hopping through the undergrowth. It was Angelina Wallaby.

"Quick! Quick! Angelina," Blinky called. "Madam Hare's going to take me to Mrs Ferrit."

"Is she? Well, she's not," said Angelina in a determined voice. "Here! hop on my back as quickly as you can. Hurry up. She's coming!"

Blinky scrambled on to Angelina's back as quick as winking, and before he'd settled down safely she gave a hop and away they went.

Madam Hare was stupid enough to think she could hop as quickly as Angelina and she plunged through the bushes calling wildly; but Angelina's hops were too long for her, and very soon Madam Hare gave up the chase.

She looked a sorry sight with her stumpy tail showing bone, where only a few hours ago a beautiful white tuft reposed, her whiskers were bent and broken, and her ears hung limply sideways. Her coat, that had taken hours to polish and brush, was covered with dust and tiny twigs, and her eyes were blood-shot.

She flung herself on the ground and kicked the dust in temper. If only she could have seen Blinky at that moment, she would have eaten anything that chanced to pass her by, for he was having a beautiful ride, flying along on Angelina's back—not caring tuppence for Madam Hare and her tail.

"Lucky for you, Master Blinky, I happened to be out looking for supper," said Angelina in between hops.

"I'm so glad, dear Angelina, you came along. That Madam Hare has a very nasty temper."

The Rabbits' Party

"And what about your mother's when you arrive home?" chuckled Angelina.

"Do you think she'll be very angry?" Blinky inquired, quite frightened at the thought of it now.

"She's ramping," exclaimed Angelina, "and so is Mrs Grunty."

"What will I do?" asked Blinky in a whisper.

"Oh, tell the truth!" said Angelina. "If she spanks you, well—you know you really deserve it."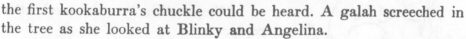

Things must be pretty bad at home thought Blinky when Angelina speaks like that. However, if he was to have a spanking, the sooner it was over the better. Very soon Angelina hopped to the bottom of the tree where Blinky lived. The moon had sunk behind the hill, and the first kookaburra's chuckle could be heard. A galah screeched in the tree as she looked at Blinky and Angelina.

"Stop that noise!" Blinky grunted as he shook his paw at her.

Everything was extraordinarily still. No Mrs Koala was to be seen, no Mrs Grunty and no Snubby.

"They must be asleep!" Angelina whispered in a low voice. "Climb up to your bed quickly and don't make a noise."

"All right, Angelina," Blinky replied. "Good night, and thank you for saving me."

"Good night," Angelina purred. "Keep sitting if your mother spanks you." After giving this good advice she hopped away into the bush.

Blinky climbed quietly—ever so quietly up the tree.

He peeped over the branch where his mother usually slept. There she was, and Mrs Grunty with Snubby too, all curled up together, sound asleep, with their noses snuggly tucked down on their tummies.

Up past them Blinky climbed, hardly daring to breathe, and he kept climbing until he reached the highest branch, then, too tired to think any more about a spanking, he fell asleep.

Mrs Koala awoke when the sun peeped over the hill. "Oh, dear," she sighed, "that naughty Blinky! I wonder where he is. Now I'll have to start hunting for him, and when I *do* find the young cub he'll know all about it."

Peering up among the branches to see if any leaves would tempt her for breakfast, she was astonished to see a furry body that looked very much like her son.

"Blinky!" she called in a stern voice, "is that you?"

"Yes, mother," came a meek little reply.

"Come down here!" she ordered.

Blinky thought it wise to do as he was told, so slowly climbed down to his mother.

"Where have you been?" Mrs Koala demanded.

"Looking for some leaves," Blinky replied, his nose quivering with fright.

"Now, no stories, my son, where have you been?"

Blinky had never seen his mother look so angry, so he decided to tell the truth.

By this time Mrs Grunty and Snubby were awake and sat staring with eyes of amazement.

"Smack him!" Mrs Grunty exclaimed.

The Rabbits' Party

"Wait till I hear his story," Mrs Koala replied, and she felt rather annoyed with Mrs Grunty, as it was not her business to tell her what to do with her own son.

Blinky told his story, keeping several parts to himself, about pushing Mrs Spotty in the pool, and grabbing Madam Hare's tail.

"Very well, Blinky," Mrs Koala said when he had finished his tale, "you are going to boarding-school after this."

"Not Mrs Spotty's?" Blinky asked in a frightened voice.

"Not Mrs Spotty's?" Blinky asked in a frightened voice.
"No!" Mrs Koala replied, "you'll go to Mrs Magpie's!"

Just as this book was going to press,
the publisher asked me for another
drawing of Blinky Bill. I wrote to
Blinky asking for his latest portrait
and this is what he sent me.

BLINKY BILL GROWS UP

"I'm grown up now."

CONTENTS

CONTENTS

CHAPTER I

Blinky Runs Away

M^RS KOALA and Mrs Grunty had talked matters over for nearly a whole night, and towards the dawn had decided upon a plan.

"You know, my dear," said Mrs Grunty, "Blinky needs a firm hand over him now that he has grown up; and who could you find better than Mrs Magpie to give him just the discipline that all young bears require?"

Mrs Grunty used all her powers of persuasion. She secretly longed to give Blinky a good smack occasionally, and at times found her right paw fairly itching to be used hard on that naughty bear's pants.

"And you know, Mrs Koala," she continued, "Snubby is a different child since Blinky came here. He was always so good and obedient before, but now——" and she sighed deeply, right down in her bear tummy.

"Well," replied Mrs Koala, "I wouldn't change Blinky for fifteen Snubbies." And she gave a decided sniff.

"Of course not! I quite see your side of the question," Mrs Grunty answered. "But this everlasting mending of pants and cleaning of ears, while all the time wondering when I'll get a hit on the nose again with a gum-nut.—Well, it's too much for any mother bear."

"But think of all the lovely gum-tips Blinky has brought you to eat," said Mrs Koala, bristling with indignation. "All the same, I must admit he has been very trying lately. I sometimes think it is the new pair of knickerbockers that is to blame, because he's been twice as naughty ever since the day he first put them on."

"Then take them off again," growled Mrs Grunty. "They're always hanging half-way down his legs, never fastened as they should be. If there's one thing I can't stand it's knickerbockers half-mast."

"Oh, I don't mind that so much," Mrs Koala replied. "Every real bear at that age seems to wear them that way; but he loses the buttons, and I can't find any at all now."

"We don't seem to be any further ahead in our discussion," said Mrs Grunty coldly.

"If I send Blinky to Mrs Magpie's school for a month, perhaps he'll return a little quieter," Mrs Koala said sorrowfully. "But you'll never make a man of Snubby!"

"What did you say!" Mrs Grunty exclaimed snappily.

"You'll never make a man of Snubby!" and Mrs Koala glared as she repeated her remark.

"Come, come, my dear, we must not quarrel over our children," said Mrs Grunty kindly. "After all it will do Blinky no harm and give you a good rest."

So it was decided. Blinky was to be packed off to Mrs Magpie's school the next evening and the two mother bears became friends again.

Up in the gum-tree snuggled together, two little bears had listened to all this with big ears opened wide.

"Did you hear that, Snubby?" Blinky asked with wide open eyes. "I'm to be sent to Mrs Magpie's!"

'I tell you, I'm not going to school, now or never.'

"How dreadful! She'll peck you ever so hard," Snubby whispered.

"She won't, 'cause I won't go!" Blinky boldly replied.

"You'll have to. Your mother will make you," Snubby answered.

"I'm nearly as big as she is; and besides I'm grown up now. Look at my bockers!" And Blinky proudly pulled them a little farther down his short stubby legs.

"I wish my mother would make me a pair of bockers," sighed Snubby.

"I'll leave you mine, 'cause I won't be wearing them again," Blinky replied.

"Oh, you can't go to school undressed!" And Snubby looked very shocked.

I know where the flying squirrel plays.

"I tell you, I'm not going to school, now or *never*. I'm going to run away; but I think I'll take my bockers with me as you'd look silly in them." With that Blinky puffed out his tummy till a few stitches gave way.

"Where are you going?" Snubby inquired in a frightened voice.

"Oh, just away, over there." And Blinky waved a little paw in all directions.

"That's where the men are!" Snubby whispered, holding his breath.

"And adventures, too," Blinky replied excitedly.

Blinky Runs Away

"I know where Mr Smifkins's farm is and I know where Mr Willie Wagtail lives, and where the flying squirrel plays, and lots of other things, and best of all where the lyre-bird dances. I'll go and see all these things, while you're up here in the gum-tree just eating leaves all night long and listening to old Mrs Grunty growling."

Snubby longed to go too, but he was such a good little bear. When he thought of all that Blinky said, his heart went pit-a-pat so loudly that he became frightened at the very thought of running away. Much better to be safe in a tree even if his mother did growl sometimes. But he knew he would miss his playmate and tears slowly trickled down his little face.

"How could you wear bockers when you're crying?" said Blinky scornfully.

Snubby brushed the tears away with his paw.

"I don't think I'm crying," he said bravely. "Mother's eyes go like that when she has lost her glasses.

"What will you eat while you're away, and where will you sleep?"

"There are juicy plants to find and I'll sleep in a tree; but if I get to Mr Smifkins's place I'll find a cosy corner in his house. But I can't tell you any more just now—it's wasting time. The sun will be up soon and I must hide before mother finds I'm gone. Just watch how quickly I slide down this tree."

The naughty bear climbed down past Mrs Koala and Mrs Grunty, who were snoozing in a corner. Quickly and silently he slid to the ground leaving a patch of his bockers on the last branch as he went. He looked very funny, pattering over the ground, one leg of his bockers torn and draggled. But he didn't care a fig—anything was better than Mrs Magpie's school.

"The old pecker!" he mumbled to himself as he trotted along. "And it's all through Mrs Grunty. I wish I'd hidden her glasses before I left!"

Blinky Bill Grows Up

The sun peeped through the bush warming the leaves on Blinky's pathway, and shy little lizards poked their heads out from under the stones, surprised to find a bear wandering through their bushland.

Blinky began to stumble, and his knickerbockers caught in every bramble and twig on the way. At last, feeling so tired, he decided to find a suitable tree for a sleep.

A large gum stood straight in his pathway, just the kind made for bears. Smooth and tall, protecting branches high up from the ground, and hundreds of leaves to shelter a little chap like himself. Struggling along he reached the foot of the tree and began to climb. He was an expert climber, much stronger now than when we first knew him, and his claws were longer so that his grip on the trunk of the tree was very sure and strong. Up and up he climbed and had almost reached the top when he heard a great commotion.

"Goodness! What's that!" he exclaimed. "Sounds like Mrs Grunty again," and pausing just under a branch he peeped round the bough to see what all the noise was about.

Feathers were flying in all directions, pecks and squawks disturbed the morning air and the leaves of the tree trembled with fright. Strangest of all, rows and rows of little dead birds hung from the twigs. It looked like a jeweller's shop. The sun caught the bright colours of beautiful feathers on the breasts and wings of tiny feathered folk. Little heads hung down with dull eyes that had glistened only a short time before, and teeny claws curled up —gripping nothing. Tears came to Blinky's eyes. Something terrible had happened. The bush he knew was so kind, everything was alive and sparkling, rustling with life and twittering with gladness; but here everything was still and songless, except for the dreadful fight that was in progress. Two butcher-birds were fighting savagely, each trying to knock the other out of the tree. At last Blinky could not bear to look on any longer.

"Here, you two birds," he shouted, "stop fighting and pecking one another."

He really felt terribly brave, but was surprised to hear his own voice sounding so loud.

"Oh, it's funny nose!" called out one of the butcher-birds.

"What do you think you're doing in our tree?"

Blinky thought very quickly for a moment, then, summoning up all his courage, replied:

"I just called to show you my knickerbockers!"

"Is that the name of the funny looking thing on your face?" called back the rude butcher-birds again.

This was too much for Blinky. He scrambled on to the branch where the birds stood, and glared at them savagely.

"I might have a funny nose," he cried, "but I've got very sharp claws."

The butcher-birds twittered and trembled. Their hooked beaks opened with fright and they clung to the tree very tightly.

"What's all the noise about?" Blinky demanded in a gruff tone.

"Well, you see—it's this way," the largest bird began. "Mrs Pos-

"Look at me—no tail—no whiskers"

95

"What's all the noise about?"
Blinky demanded in a gruff
tone.

sum is holding a bazaar in aid of the poor rabbits who came through the bush-fire. Their homes have been wiped out and all the grass burnt, so that there is no food. Some even had their whiskers and tails singed."

"They shouldn't have whiskers and tails," Blinky remarked. "Look at me—no tail—no whiskers. Tails are stupid things," he said rudely, gazing at the butcher-birds' tails. "Always getting in the way and making animals squeak and yelp when they're trodden on. And, besides, think of the extra washing to be done; as it is my ears take an awful time to clean."

"What polish do you use for your nose?" the butcher-birds asked.

"No polish," Blinky grunted, "only paws." But feeling the conversation was becoming personal he asked more about the bazaar.

"Where is the bazaar to be held?"

"Down in the gully," both birds echoed.

"What's a bazaar, anyway?" Blinky asked, pretending not to be very interested.

"We all sell things and make things, and there's lots to see and hear. Last bazaar Mrs Thrush sang for us, and Gertrude Spider spun her finest web and showed us how to catch flies, and Mrs Spotty Frog's pupils gave an exhibition of jumping."

"Yes," chimed in the other butcher-bird, "and just to make things more exciting Mrs Snake shed her skin, her very own skin— even the part that covered her eyes!"

"It must have been wonderful!" exclaimed Blinky in wonderment. "And what did you do?"

"We help to supply the supper," said the big bird, "and that's just what we were talking about when you came along."

"It seemed to be an angry talk," Blinky replied.

"It's all your fault!" the little bird piped looking at his companion. "He stole my nicest bird that took me hours and hours to catch."

"Stuff and nonsense!" croaked the big bird. "Look at the fine birds I've caught, and yours was such a teeny thing."

"But it has the brightest feathers," complained the little bird.

"I think you're both very cruel," said Blinky, looking at the rows of dead birds. "If I had a gun I'd shoot you!"

Hearing this, the big bird put back his head and pealed with laughter. Blinky stood amazed. Such beautiful clear flute-like notes rang through the air. There was Mr Butcher-bird, the cruellest of birds, singing as no other bird could sing, except of course, Mrs Thrush. Note after note rang out and his mate joined in the chorus. The trees seemed to hush their rustling leaves to listen to such beautiful music.

When the song had finished all thoughts of unkindness had left Blinky's mind. Everything had its own way of being cruel and kind he thought, and after all he must not say rude things to the butcher-birds as he wanted to see the bazaar.

He sat down in a corner of the tree and presently began to nod his little head. His eyes blinked and wouldn't stay open. The tree was so comfortable and he was so tired. He fell asleep and into dreamland. A dreamland of bears. His mother, Mrs Koala, seemed to be patching bockers, and Mrs Grunty, with her spectacles perched right on the tip of her nose, was shaking her paw and saying over and over again:

"He's a bad lad, that boy of yours—he'll be the death of us all!"

Snubby was there, too, peeping timidly round the back of the tree. He looked different, though; something was wrong with his face. And, as Blinky dreamed, he had another look at Mrs Grunty and his mother. Oh, how funny they looked! Their noses had turned into ears and their ears into noses. "How dreadful!" whispered Blinky to himself. "I wonder if my nose is a nose still?"

"He's a bad lad that boy of yours—
He'll be the death of us all!"

And putting up his paw, he woke up to find himself patting that part of his face in a very doubtful manner.

"Hey! you butcher-birds," he called out, "is my nose still here?"

"Still there!" the big bird replied scornfully, "I should say it was. Who wants to steal that? We don't hang up noses in our tree!"

"Well, don't you dare to touch it!" muttered Blinky angrily. "By the way, when is the bazaar?"

"Tonight!" the birds replied.

"May I come?" Blinky smiled his sweetest smile.

"You'll have to take something or do something if you come, there's no free admittance. Mrs Possum is very strict about that. Last bazaar Percy Bull Ant tried to sneak in by clinging to Mrs Rabbit's tail and only that he nearly lost his balance and fell off and gave Mrs Rabbit such a nip, he'd have sneaked in. Mrs Rabbit gave a tremendous leap, and let out such a squeal, that of course he was discovered."

Mrs Rabbit gave a tremendous leap.

"There you are!" cried Blinky excitedly. "Just what I said about tails. Always in the way."

Blinky Runs Away

"Just as well she *had* a tail or the sting might have been much more serious," the big bird replied. "What would happen to you I'd like to know, if a bull ant stung you where your tail ought to be? Tails are a great comfort at times."

"Oh! I didn't mean to be rude," Blinky quickly answered. "But if Mrs Rabbit hadn't had a tail Percy Bull Ant might have chosen a gum-leaf to hide him."

"Not him!" the butcher-bird scoffed. "Why, he even stood up to fight and waved his front legs at Sergeant Hornet when he was ordered to put him out. Such boldness. It caused so much commotion that Mrs Possum fell in the lucky dip and the Rev. Fluffy Ears had to help her out. There she was, covered in sand from head to foot and some impertinent young fellow, who I really believe was Willie Wagtail, called out at the top of his voice: 'Sweet pretty little creature'. Oh, it was really terrible! And all through Percy Bull Ant trying to get in free!"

"I can't take anything and I can't do anything," said Blinky sorrowfully. "But I could look after the lucky dip for them if they want somebody."

"That's a good idea," said both butcher-birds together. "There'll have to be someone this time to keep an eye on things, and watch most carefully that Mr Wombat does not burrow under the 'dip'. He's a cunning fellow and always has an excuse ready. He walks round and round the refreshment stall, sniffing everything and pretending he doesn't like the look of juicy leaves; and just as Mrs Wallaby thinks he is quite safe and turns her back to have a chat with some friend, he snatches a mouthful of the very best he can see."

"Well, that's settled!" said Blinky gladly. "Now I think I'll have another sleep. I always feel dozy in the daytime, and this corner is so warm and soft. Be sure you wake me in time for the bazaar."

CHAPTER II

The Bazaar

DOWN in the gully hidden from view by tall gum-trees, bank-sias, and tea-trees, right against a huge rock the bazaar was held. Dozens and dozens of birds, insects, and animals, all dressed in their very best, chattering and squeaking, calling and singing, spreading their goods out on the rock, under it, and around it. No little boy or girl could see this wonder show, unless they wandered far off the beaten track, through the tall spear grass, deep, deep in the heart of the bush, away from all noises and people, and far down the valley where the maidenhair fern grows. Then you may be lucky enough to see a bush bazaar. But faces must be clean, hands washed, and hair combed, as every animal and bird has plumed and preened himself and herself to look their very best. But hush! the Rev. Fluffy Ears is ready to make a speech and declare the bazaar open.

He looks splendid! I'm sure he has been hours and hours brushing his ears, they look so silky. There he is perched on the branch of a tree looking down on all the bush folk, as they sit and hop around, trying to find a patch of grass or rock to rest upon. There is very little room left for even a grasshopper to squeeze in, and some grumpy old ladies like Mrs Owl and Miss

The Bazaar

Goanna, glare at the younger ones as they try to find a spare seat. The colours are wonderful. Red and orange and purple berries are clustered in huge piles over the rock. Bright green leaves and the softest brown toadstools lie together. Birds' eggs of every colour imaginable are there in dozens to be sold and right up against them are the little dead birds the butcher-birds have brought. This is the produce store and guarding it with glittering eyes is Mrs Wallaby. Woe betide any creature who tries to steal even a berry. Farther away is a wonderful collection of birds' nests, all shapes and sizes, with a notice standing in the centre:

READY MADE HOMES
SUITABLE FOR FINCHES OR MAGPIES
MIXED FROM THE BEST MUD AND GRASSES
DIRT CHEAP!

Then there were small piles of grit, some red, others black and brown. The notice above these read:

ANTS, TAKE YOUR CHOICE!
THE VERY FINEST GRIT ON THE MARKET
ALL HALF PRICE!

Under the ledge of the rock sat Miss Gertrude Spider with a very patient look on her face. But cunning, crafty eyes spoilt her appearance. Every hair on her legs was shining, and her body was polished like a door-knob. She had dozens and dozens of webs for sale, and knew very well that the fairies and goblins would be her best customers. Such folk dwell in the gullies and wait eagerly their chance of buying new webs for their clothes. Some webs were made of the finest thread (far finer than silk the silk-worm spins) and were glittering with dewdrops. These were the very best and most expensive: only for fairy queens and princesses. Others were just as beautiful, though a little coarser, and

103

o dewdrops. But, as Gertrude said, they will "stand wear
ear". Every now and then she pulled a web, tugging it this
way and that to show how strong it really was. Curly leaves on
the ground were crammed full of flies—some dead, some alive. Others

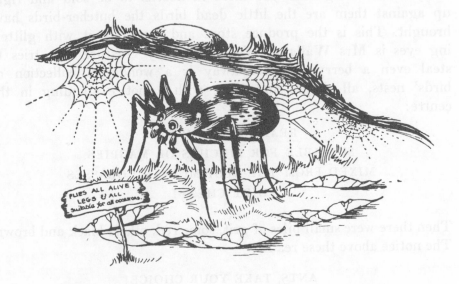

Gertrude's cunning crafty eyes spoilt
her appearance.

held mosquitoes and sand-flies and some even held small beetles.
These were labelled according to their value:

DEAD FLIES—QUITE FRESH, YOUNG AND PLUMP
TAKE SOME HOME FOR SUPPER

Another was labelled:

FLIES ALL ALIVE!
LEGS AND ALL
SUITABLE FOR ALL OCCASIONS

The Bazaar

The beetles had a special notice above them:

BEETLES IN SEASON!
COLOURS NOT CHARGED FOR
WINGS AND NIPPERS SOLD SEPARATELY
BEETLE PIE RECIPE GIVEN FREE

Gertrude Spider had dozens of customers round her stall. But the beetles who had come to see the bazaar stood aside in small groups, whispering in undertones and glancing nervously in her direction. Farther away in a dark musty corner hidden from view by a huge web was her parlour, and she even had the boldness to suggest to small customers that they should "walk into my parlour". Just as if no one knew what *that* meant!

The frogs were in charge of the swimming-pool and had a grand slippery-dip made from a rock covered with slithery moss. Their customers were mostly frog friends, but wild ducks also patronized the slippery-dip. A swoop and a swish and one after another they splashed into the pool, amidst jeering and croaking from the onlookers. The bravest frogs did double-bankers and back somersaults and all kinds of fancy flips and flops. Right across the centre of the pool a branch of a tree rested on either side, and on it squatted a big fat mosquito. This was the greasy pole, and the fellow who was lucky enough to keep his balance while he crossed, had the thought of that fine fat mosquito for a prize.

The mosquito was tied to the branch by the finest spider-web; so he was a prisoner, trembling from head to foot as he watched each new frog take his few steps, lose his balance and go flopping into the pool.

Shh! Shh! There was a sudden silence, and all the bush folk turned to look at the Rev. Fluffy Ears. He waved his paw and flicked his ears, then spoke in a clear dignified tone.

"Ladies and gentlemen, spend all your money at this bazaar,

H

as you know it is in aid of our poor friends who are homeless through the fire. Those who have no money can give their services free. Mrs Possum has worked hard for months to make this bazaar a success, so I hope to see a friendly spirit among you all. Don't spoil things by scratching or kicking your neighbour (as I saw Mrs Magpie and Mrs Peewit doing) or biting and nipping a friend's tail when his back is turned. It is not kind. And above all remember there is to be no stealing."

A flutter in the tree and an angry voice from Mrs Flying Fox prevented Rev. Fluffy Ears from speaking further.

"A nice thing to suggest!" she screamed. "Stealing indeed! As if anyone would do such a thing!"

A painful look came over the Rev. Fluffy Ears' face, he patted his nose, and felt his collar.

"It's an insult! That's what it is," roared Mrs Flying Fox. And she made a lunge at the Rev. Fluffy Ears.

"It's time I interfered," muttered Blinky to himself. Up to the present he had been sitting very quietly in a corner of the tree, too surprised and amazed at everything he saw to speak or even show himself. But he was not going to see another bear get the worst of a fight with all these creatures looking on.

"Stop that!" he commanded at the top of his voice. "Stop at once, or I'll push you out of the tree!"

Mrs Flying Fox darted round to see where the voice came from.

"Oh, it's only you, is it? Another one of the Koala family poking his big nose into other people's affairs." Blinky became very angry, and poor Fluffy Ears began to cry.

"Someone stand below and catch her when I push her off!" he shouted; and before Mrs Flying Fox could believe her ears she was given a kick that sent her flying out of the tree; but to everyone's horror Blinky's bockers caught in a twig just as he gave the kick, and there he hung, suspended in mid-air.

The Bazaar

"Help! Help!" he screamed. "I'm falling."

A rip and a split and Blinky parted from the best part of his knickerbockers. Down he fell—thud, right in the middle of a squealing and kicking crowd. It was not on the programme to find a fat, plump bear squashing and kicking everyone within reach.

"Grab her legs!" Blinky shouted, but no one could get near enough, as he seemed to be raising all the dust it was possible for anyone to do.

"I'll settle this hubbub!" said Percy Bull Ant, blowing out his chest and advancing cautiously with his two front legs waving threateningly. Edging round the fighters he managed at last to get a grip on Blinky's paw. Nip, nip, nip he bit with all his might. Blinky gave a spring in the air and came down right on top of Mrs Possum.

Mrs Possum bit him savagely and naughty Blinky at once kicked her, scratching and ripping her best hat to shreds.

"Oh!" wailed Mrs Possum. "Look at my hat, my very best hat!"

"It wasn't his fault; it's all through Mrs Flying Fox."

Here was Angelina Wallaby of all people, and you can imagine how pleased Blinky was to see her.

"Oh! dear Angelina. Where did you come from?"

"I happened to be watching you from the bush, and when I saw you fall, I thought it high time I came along to save you. Just look at your best bockers! What will your mother say?"

"I-I don't know," Blinky said nervously, feeling the back of his pants.

"Is it a *very* large hole, Angelina?"

"It's so large, that you've no bockers at the back at all!"

"Serve you right! I hope you get a good smacking when you arrive home. *I hope your mother wallops you.*"

"You!" Blinky exclaimed, too surprised for further words.

Guarding it with glittering
eyes is Mrs. Wallaby.

The Bazaar

It was Mrs Flying Fox speaking. She grinned spitefully at Blinky. Certainly, she was bruised after her bump on the ground; but what's a bump or two, and now, there she stood as cheeky as ever. . . .

"It's time to start the lucky-dip," called out Blinky, and trotted over to his stall.

The lucky-dip was a wonderful attraction. A burnt-out stump of a great gum-tree was filled with marvellous things, all tied up in gum-leaves. Everyone who wanted a dip had first to place a present at Blinky's feet, and a row of bull ants kept guard over these.

The first customer was Miss Silver-eye.

"Please may I have a dip?" she inquired.

"Where's your present?" asked Blinky.

"Here it is!" she piped as she placed a beautiful red berry at his feet.

"Hurry up and have your

"Here it is!" she said, and placed a dead fly at his feet.

dip," Blinky commanded. So Miss Silver-eye dipped her beak into the lucky-dip.

"What's in it?" everyone demanded.

"A feather!" said Miss Silver-eye delightedly. "Just what I want for my nest."

"Next please!" shouted Blinky.

Up came Mrs Lizard.

"Where's your present?" Blinky asked.

"Here it is," she said, and placed a dead fly at his feet. Crawling into the bin she came out with a parcel between her teeth.

"Open it!" they all cried, craning their necks to see what treasure it held.

"Poof! It's only a stone," said Mrs Lizard disgustedly. "I think the dip's a take-down." And tossing her head in the air she wriggled away.

There seemed to be an air of dissatisfaction at once among the customers who waited their turn as each had come with a present that had taken quite a deal of thinking about, to say nothing of the hunting for it.

"No remarks are allowed in future," said Blinky. "Take the good with the bad. Now who is next?"

"Me!" called out a tiny voice.

"I can't see you. Stand in front please," Blinky shouted in his bassiest voice.

"I'm here!" came the reply. Looking down Blinky saw Master Trapdoor Spider at his feet.

"Where's your present?" he asked.

"I haven't brought one," Master Trapdoor said boldly. "But if you don't let me have a dip I'll poison you."

"A nasty fellow! Let him have his dip," whispered Mrs Possum.

"I'll get your prize out for you," said Blinky, in a generous voice, and Master Trapdoor's eyes glistened with excitement.

"Help! help!" he screamed,
"I'm falling."

Blinky Bill Grows Up

Blinky pulled out a parcel, unwrapped the leaf and a huge frog jumped out.

In a twinkling he had gobbled up Master Trapdoor.

"That's what comes through being rude!" said Blinky, as he eyed the rest of the customers sternly.

Several very quietly crawled or flew away, as they evidently did not want the same thing to happen to them.

"Come on, who's next?" Blinky called.

"I am!" cried Madam Hare.

"Where's your present?" Blinky asked.

"Here it is, and a very valuable one too!" Madam Hare replied, as she placed a whisker at his feet.

"Looks as though it's been used," muttered Blinky. "Take your dip quickly please." He had good cause to remember Madam Hare, and thought it best to be polite.

With a bound Madam Hare sprang right on top of the dip. Blinky bit his lip and clenched his paws, he was feeling so savage.

Madam Hare gave a kick with her hind legs and sent dozens of parcels flying out of the dip.

"Hey! Stop that!" cried Blinky angrily. But Madam Hare only gave another kick. Out came more parcels.

"Stop it! Stop it at once!" cried Blinky, and pounced on Madam Hare, biting her ear.

She turned suddenly and sprang out of the bin with two parcels in her mouth.

"Catch her! Catch her!" Blinky called, as he raced away after the thief.

Madam Hare was too quick for him. Away she bounded, over the stalls, knocking things down as she went and not caring a button for the shouts and screams behind her. Into the bush she raced and didn't stop until she came to her home. There she untied the parcels, and savagely kicked them about when she saw what they

112

contained. One was a bundle of straw and the other the leaf of a stinging-nettle.

"The robbers!" she cried, as she kicked them again and again.

Losing no time, Blinky raced back to the lucky-dip, just in time to find all the customers opening the parcels that Madam Hare had kicked out.

"Put them down! Put them down!" he roared. The customers scampered away, each carrying a prize. As Blinky stood and gazed at the empty lucky-dip, feeling very sorry about it all, and still very angry, his friends the butcher-birds hopped round.

"Was it a success?" they inquired.

Blinky said nothing.

"Where are all the presents?" they asked.

"Go away, or I'll *eat* you both," Blinky growled.

"He's in a bad temper!" whispered the butcher-birds, and flew off while it was safe.

Curling himself up in a corner Blinky decided to have a sleep, as chasing Madam Hare and fighting Mrs Flying Fox had made him very tired.

Nodding his little head, and curling his toes up he was soon dreaming again of Mrs Koala and Mrs Grunty. He did not wake until daylight, and looking around he was surprised to find all the bush folk had vanished. The presents and goods had all gone too, and only an old owl gazed at him from a nearby tree.

"It's time you made a start for home," said the owl.

"I'm not going home," replied Blinky.

"Wise little bears won't stay here too long," said the owl.

"Why?" asked Blinky.

"This is Mr Smifkins's favourite shooting-place," replied the old owl. "He has a gun and a big dog, and when they come along and find you here you'll be rabbit pie in two twos."

"Where does Mr Smifkins live?" Blinky inquired.

"Down behind the moon! Whoo! Whoo!" answered the owl.

"Whoo! Whoo!" echoed Blinky. "I'm not afraid of Mr Smifkins. I'm going to see where he lives."

"Whoo! Whoo!" cried the owl.

"You'll be rabbit pie in two twos." said the old owl.

"I beg your pardon?" said Blinky.

"Whoo! Whoo!" the old owl called again, his great round eyes gazing at Blinky.

"Will you show me the way to Mr Smifkins's, *please*, Mr Owl?" Blinky pleaded.

"Follow me. Whoo! Whoo!" the owl answered and flew away to another tree.

Blinky trotted along, his funny little legs going wobbly, wobbly as he went.

The old owl waited patiently until his little friend was under the tree, then crying whoo, whoo, off he flew again to the next tree.

Here he waited for Blinky and flew to the ground to meet him.

"Little bear," he cried softly, "it is too light for me to see farther, we must sleep now until the sun goes down. I am as blind as a bat in the day time and here is a tree with nice young gum-leaves on it waiting for you to taste."

"I'm very hungry," said Blinky. "They never think to have food for bears at bazaars. Only nasty flies and frogs and mosquitoes."

"Well, come up into the branches and I will show you gum-leaves made specially for young bears," said the kind old owl.

Blinky climbed up the tree and sat next to his friend chewing young tender leaves until he could eat no more.

"Whoo! Whoo! It's time to sleep!" said the owl.

"I feel tired, too," replied Blinky. And so cuddled together, a strange-looking pair, they snoozed and waited until the moon arose.

"Little bear," he cried softly,
"it is too light for me to see
farther."

CHAPTER III

Mr. Smifkins' Farm

BLINKY was awakened by a soft "whoo, whoo". He sat up and blinked his eyes. There was the moon shining through the leaves like a big golden penny and Mr Owl's eyes looked almost as large as he gazed at Blinky.

"Time to get up," he said very quietly.

"Is Mr Smifkins's far away?" Blinky inquired.

"About six tree stops from here," Mr Owl replied. "We'd better make a start while the bush is cool."

Grunting with glee Blinky crawled down the tree and as he reached the ground the old owl flew on ahead. After they had reached six-stopping places Blinky looked up in the tree as Mr Owl hooted.

"This is as far as I come," he said.

"Where is the farm?" Blinky asked.

"Follow the track you are now on and in a very short time you will come to a fence. That is where the Smifkinses live."

"Thank you so much, Mr Owl, for showing me the way," Blinky called out.

"Whoo, whoo!" the old owl cried and on noiseless wings he was gone.

Blinky Bill Grows Up

"Seems to be very quiet and lonely just here," Blinky thought as he pattered along.

Presently he came to an opening in the tree and peering through he saw the fence just a few yards ahead. Farther on he could see a house with a light gleaming in the window and smoke rising from the chimney. Under the fence he crawled and through a potato patch, then very quietly he crept through the orchard. Here he sat and waited. Mr Smifkins's dog was barking and Blinky remembered what Mr Owl had said about that dog.

He waited until the light went out in the window and then crept nearer and nearer the house. On to the veranda he climbed and softly tiptoed round to the back door. Everything was locked up there, so he decided to explore the side of the house.

Peeping round the corner he saw a bed on the veranda and thought he'd have a look to see what was in it. So softly as a cat he went and sniffed the end of the blanket. Some very funny sounds came from under that blanket.

Blinky held his breath with fright.

"What a dreadful noise!" he thought. "I must see where it is coming from."

Climbing up on the bed he crawled along the side, and—oh dear, what a funny sight he saw!

Mr Smifkins was fast asleep making such queer noises with his mouth open; and over his head was a long white net.

Blinky gazed and gazed at him. Never had he seen anything so funny. Why, he even had whiskers just like Mr Wombat, only much thicker, and they drooped all over his chin, while Mr Wombat's stuck out straight and stiff.

"I must take some of those whiskers to show Mr Wombat," Blinky whispered to himself. Wouldn't Mrs Grunty like some to pad her gum-leaf cushion with! and then his mother could make use of them for sewing on buttons.

Mr. Smifkins took
one leap off the verandah,
the net all over him.

Snore, snore. Mr Smifkins had no idea he had a visitor.

Lifting the net very cautiously, Blinky put out his paw and made a sharp tug at the whiskers.

"Good heavens!" Mr Smifkins jumped six feet in the air.

Blinky put out his paw and made a sharp tug at the whiskers.

"Gee whizzikins! What the dickens was that?" he cried.

As he shouted he made a leap out of bed quite forgetting the mosquito-net over his head. Down it came, right over him, tangling up his legs and arms. He seemed to have six pairs of legs and dozens of arms.

Blinky made a dive under the bed, terrified beyond words, and lay there panting with fright.

"Fancy whiskers doing that!" he murmured.

Mr Smifkins's Farm

The whole bed was shaking in an alarming manner, and such terrible words and growls came from Mr Smifkins.

"To billy-o with his net!" he roared; while rips and kicks rent the air.

Just as the commotion was at its worst Mr Smifkins's dog came round the corner, snarling and growling. Blinky did not want to see what was going to happen. He raced from under the bed and down off the veranda and right into the legs of Mrs Smifkins.

"Burglars!" she screamed at the top of her voice, and kept on screaming.

Hearing this, Mr Smifkins took one leap off the veranda, the net all over him, and as he rushed along he waved his arms, frantically trying to get rid of it.

Poor Mrs Smifkins took one look and raced for her life round the house.

"Ghosts! Ghosts!" she yelled, as she tore round to the back door, with Mr Smifkins in hot pursuit. "Help! Help! Burglars! Ghosts!" she kept calling at the top of her voice, and ran right into old Neddy the draught-horse, who was snoozing under the kitchen window. He looked up, surprised to hear such dreadful screams on such a quiet night, and caught one glimpse of Mr Smifkins coming round the corner.

Hoosh! Up went his hind legs and with a frightened neigh he raced off for the paddock, crashing over the lettuce bed, through the tomato frames, and away into the night.

Mrs Smifkins reached the back door in a flash. Bang! and she was inside, still screaming "Ghosts!"

All this time Mr Smifkins was using those strange words at the top of his voice. He roared like a bull and made mad lunges at things that got in his way. Just as he rushed past the old appletree the net caught in the branches and thank goodness it stayed there. Mr Smifkins's dog added to the uproar with his yelps and

121

barks and tried very hard to bite his master's legs as the chase was in progress.

Panting and very, very cross, Mr Smifkins banged on the back door as his wife had locked him out.

"Don't be a fool!" he roared. But Mrs Smifkins refused to open the door.

She *knew* it was a ghost she had seen.

Suddenly Mr Smifkins thought of the cause of all this trouble. What on earth could have pulled his whiskers? So once again he set off to investigate.

Blinky was very thankful that Mr Smifkins's dog chased his master, as it gave him a chance to hide.

After colliding with Mrs Smifkins he was nearly collapsing with fright. Over the garden he rushed and through a gate that had foolishly been left open. Here was shelter at last he thought, as he saw a shed in front of him. Stumbling and rushing on he darted through a hole in the wall, and—landed right in the middle of the fowl-house where all the silly old hens and roosters were asleep. They cackled and crowed with fright; fell off their perches, and floundered around all over the fowl-house in the dark. You never heard such a row!

Somewhere Blinky was in the middle of it. Feathers flew, and the old hens became hysterical. To make matters worse Mr Smifkins and his dog were coming.

"I'll have you, whatever you are!" he called at the top of his voice.

"A fox. I'll bet my hat it is!" he cried as he came nearer and nearer. Blinky was lucky in being able to see in the dark and through the feathers and straw that flew about he spied a box in the corner.

With a bound he was in, and, ugh! something soft cracked under him. He did not know he was in a nest and had sat on Mrs Speckles's best egg. He lay there huddled up, straw and

Mr Smifkins's Farm

feathers all over him, one eye peeping round the corner watching for Mr Smifkins. It was a terrible moment and his breath seemed to leave him altogether.

"What the dickens did I do with my matches?" Mr Smifkins growled, as he crawled into the fowl-house. His entrance caused more cackling and the poor old hens flapped about madly. They were not used to midnight visitors. But Mr Smifkins took no heed of the cackling and squawking, he was determined to find the animal that had caused all this disturbance. Worst of all he called his dog in.

"Here Bluey! Skeech him out of it," he ordered at the top of his voice.

Bluey was a cattle-dog and it did not take him many moments to nose his way to the nest.

Blinky scratched his nose as hard as he could and kicked with all his might. Bluey yelped with pain and fright and darted round to the back of the box.

"Here, let me there!" called Mr Smifkins, who had found his matches by now and was holding the light in his hands. Carefully peering into the box he saw Blinky, shuddering with fright, one paw raised, ready to scratch.

"Well, I'll be blowed!" Mr Smifkins cried in astonishment. "A koala—of all things. You young beggar. Come out of it my lad, and let me have a look at you."

But Blinky had no intention of coming out. He growled louder and louder.

Mr Smifkins bent his head lower to have an extra good look at the mischief maker. At the same moment, Blinky kicked out a bundle of straw, feathers, and a broken egg, right into Mr Smifkins's face. The match went out and—oh! Mr Smifkins lost his temper.

"You young devil!" he roared. "You bad young egg-stealer! You'll come along with me now, and I'll teach you how to behave

123

like a gentleman. Sneaking round a fellow's bed in the dark—frightening the wits out of his wife and hens, and driving old Neddy into twenty fits all at once. Come out of it or I'll rake you out!"

Blinky only huddled up all the closer in the nest and growled his loudest.

"So you won't come out!" shouted Mr Smifkins, seizing the rake he kept to clean the fowl-house with. "Out you come, and no nonsense," he cried as he poked the end of the rake in the box. Blinky bit it and scratched with rage. Mr Smifkins poked harder and poked Blinky right in the tummy.

This was too much for him. With a scurry and flurry he bounded out of the box. But Mr Smifkins was waiting and grabbed him by a hind leg as he tried to dart past.

"I've got you! I've got you!" he yelled. "You bad young turnip!"

Blinky was too angry to be frightened any longer. He turned like lightning and bit Mr Smifkins on the arm, at the same time clawing and scratching for all he was worth.

"A nice kettle of fish, you are!" Mr Smifkins cried. "Just wait a moment my boy, and we'll soon settle this argument."

With one hand firmly holding Blinky's hind leg he managed with the other to take off his pyjama trousers. Wrapping them tightly round Blinky, he crawled out of the fowl-house with a struggling, kicking bundle under his arm.

He did look funny, as he walked away, his shirt-tails flapping behind him and his pyjama coat torn in patches.

Blinky kicked and kicked; but it was useless. He was held a prisoner. Goodness knows what would happen now. Perhaps he would be made into rabbit pie as wise old Mr Owl said.

Mr Smifkins stumped home with a very determined step, saying the most frightful things all the time. He hammered on the back door.

Mr Smifkins's Farm

"Who's there?" Mrs Smifkins called.

"Open the door at once!" her husband replied. "I've caught the burglar!"

"Has he any guns on him?" she asked in a frightened voice.

"No! but he's got claws like a tiger," Mr Smifkins replied.

"We can't keep a tiger here!" his wife screamed. "Shoot him! Kill him quickly."

"Open the door!" Mr Smifkins roared. "I'm catching cold in the legs."

Very slowly the door opened an inch or two and Mrs Smifkins peered out with one eye.

"Where's the tiger?" she asked trembling.

"Here he is!" said Mr Smifkins, pushing the door wide open with his foot and holding up the struggling bundle.

"Whatever is it?" Mrs Smifkins asked, her eyes wide with amazement.

"A young bear, and a very lively one, too!" her husband replied as he walked into the kitchen and carefully placed the bundle on the floor.

"Oh, how beautiful!" Mrs Smifkins cried. "I'll have him for a pet."

"Will you!" Blinky thought to himself as he struggled to get free.

"He's as fat as a young pig," Mr Smifkins remarked as he untied the pyjama trousers.

"Good heavens! He's in knickerbockers," Mrs Smifkins cried. "He must belong to some child."

At last Blinky was free. He looked a sorry sight. Torn bockers, fur all rumpled, and straw and egg sticking all over him.

"I'll give the poor little thing a bath!" said kind Mrs Smifkins.

"Indeed you won't," thought Blinky, as he darted away under the table.

125

Blinky Bill Grows Up

"I don't think it would be wise to bath him tonight," Mr Smifkins advised. "Wait till the morning and we'll have a good clean up then."

"Where will he sleep?" Mrs Smifkins then asked. "Will I take him in my bed? Or perhaps he'd be happier in yours, as he knows you better."

"To billy-o with the bed!" said Mr Smifkins. "Look what he's done to mine already."

"Well, I'll find a nice little box and he can stay here by the stove. That'll keep him warm and comfy," said Mrs Smifkins.

"That's a good idea," said Mr Smifkins.

So a box was placed by the stove with an old jacket in it to keep Blinky warm. But, he had been watching preparations carefully, and had made up his mind that no box would be his bed, as the last box caused him to be caught. He looked all round the kitchen trying to find some way of escape, but there seemed to be none. The window was closed and the door also.

"Come to your bed, little bear," called Mrs Smifkins kindly.

Blinky only grunted savagely and glared at her.

"Leave the little chap alone, he'll find his way into the box when we put the light out." So Mr Smifkins and his wife said good night to Blinky, turned out the lamp, closed the door again and were gone.

"Thank goodness!" sighed Blinky. "Now I can explore." He waited till his little heart stopped pounding so loudly, then softly crept from under the table. There was the box, all cosy and warm. Blinky took one look at it, growled, and walked around the kitchen to see if there was a way of escape.

"Yes!" he thought, as he came to a door not quite shut, "here's where I escape."

Pushing his little fat body through the opening he was disappointed to find himself in another room, much smaller, with rows and rows of shelves running all round it.

126

Mr Smifkins's Farm

"Looks like a shop!" he said to himself. "I'll find out what's in here."

Climbing on a chair he stood on tiptoe and had a good look all round.

There were dozens of jars of jam and preserves, boxes with lids on, bags filled with things, and piles of apples and oranges.

He sniffed an orange, and felt it with his paw. "Don't like the smell of it," he thought, then finding he could squeeze himself on to the shelf, he had a look at the bottles of jam.

Plum, apricot, orange, peach, loganberry, pineapple, and melon. Each bottle was labelled. But Blinky did not stop to read the name—he did not know the meaning anyhow. So the quickest way, he thought, to find out the contents was to taste. The plum jam was the nearest. Breaking the paper top with his claws he dipped his paw in and scooped up the lovely red jam. He tasted it, licked his lips and decided to try the next bottle. Loganberry it was labelled; scratching away the top, in went his paw and out came the sticky jam. It dropped all over the shelf and down Blinky's front. But it was good! So the next bottle must be tasted. Every pot of jam was sampled, and that naughty bear's paws and face were covered with a mixture unlike anything ever seen before. All his pretty fur on his chest and tummy dripped jam. Every bottle was covered with the sticky stuff and the shelf too. As he carefully walked in and out of the things on the shelf he left jammy foot-prints behind.

He quite forgot to look for an escape as he was having such a glorious time.

Suddenly he caught sight of a dish full of eggs. "They look funny things. I must see what they are," he murmured.

Patting one with his paw he found it cold and hard, and decided to taste it; but he could not catch it in his paw so put out his claws to get a firmer hold.

Crack! The egg broke and out came everything.

Blinky Bill Grows Up

"That's funny!" laughed Blinky, and gave another egg a smack with his paw. Crack! It went just like the other one.

"Goodness! What silly things!" And Blinky laughed. Then he stood on his hind legs and with his two front paws came down smack! smack! on all the eggs. Oh, what an awful mess there was! Eggs and jam were all over his paws; and such nasty things, too, for a little bear to have on his fur. He licked one paw after another to shake the sticky stuff off.

Poor Mrs Smifkins's best tea-cups, standing so neatly on the shelf, in a jiffy were spattered with eggs and jam.

Still exploring the wonderful shelf, he found a jug of milk. In went the paw and up to his mouth. "Um, um," Blinky grunted, as he licked his paw all over. The milk tasted good, so another dip in the jug and another lick followed. Finding it so nice, he stuck his head in the jug to have a good long drink. The milk was the best taste of all.

"Ker-chew! Ker-chew!" he sneezed as the milk ran up his nose.

"Ker-chew! Ker-chew!" Blinky sneezed as the milk came

up his nose, but he drank and drank until the jug was empty. Then, grunting with satisfaction, he sat down to see what next he could taste.

Some cakes under a wire cover looked very nice, and just as Blinky was crawling along the shelf to try one, he caught sight of a tiny mouse peeping out of his hole.

Blinky gave a grunt.

The mouse popped his head back in his hole. In a few minutes he had another look out.

Blinky gave another grunt. But the mouse became brave and gazed up at Blinky with bright little eyes.

"Good evening, Mr Bear," he said in a tiny squeaking voice.

"Good evening, Mr Mouse," Blinky replied. "What are you doing in here?"

"I've come to look for my supper."

"Do you like sticky things?"

"No, Mr Bear," the mouse answered. "I like cheese and crumbs."

"Cheese? What's that?"

"The best thing in the world to make your whiskers grow," the mouse replied. "And I smell some somewhere."

"Then come out of your hole and I'll help you to find it," Blinky said boldly.

"You won't eat me, will you?" the little mouse asked anxiously.

"No," said Blinky softly. "I've seen Mrs Kookaburra eat dozens of your relations, but I don't like tails!"

"I'll find you some cheese, then," said Mr Mouse. "And once you've tasted it, you'll eat nothing else."

Coming out of his hole Mr Mouse scurried here and there; into corners he popped, and bags and boxes he'd gnaw so quickly and silently that Blinky was astounded.

"Wait a minute, Mr Mouse," he whispered. "I'll come down and help you."

Very carefully he walked round the shelf again, all through the sticky muddle until he reached the chair. He climbed down, leaving jam everywhere. The pretty blue chair that Mrs Smifkins had just painted was decorated with paw marks and blobs.

"What a fat bear you are!" Mr Mouse remarked.

"I've just had a nice drink," Blinky replied. "But where's this cheese?"

"Let's look over in that corner behind the sugar-bin," Mr Mouse advised.

"You go first," Blinky whispered.

Mr Mouse scampered away and Blinky saw his tail disappear round the bin.

"Here it is! Come and smell," Mr Mouse called. Blinky crawled over to the corner, but he was far too big and fat to squeeze round behind the sugar-bin.

"Let's have a look," he said in a whisper.

"See, here it is, right in the corner!" Mr Mouse said, pointing to a funny looking object.

"It looks like wood to me," Blinky replied as he squeezed his nose and eye round the end of the bin.

"It looks different to what it usually is," said Mr Mouse. "But I can smell it, and the smell's the same."

"Stick your paw in and see," advised Blinky.

"All right," said Mr Mouse. "You keep an eye open for Mrs Smifkins."

"Hurry up, then," said Blinky. "She may be in any minute." Really and truly he had forgotten all about the Smifkinses, and now that Mr Mouse mentioned them, he felt rather nervous.

Mr Mouse crept closer to the strange object. He put out his whiskers and sniffed. Yes, it was cheese, and no mistake.

"Grab it," Blinky whispered.

Mr Smifkins's Farm

Mr Mouse became braver and made a dart at the cheese.

Snap!

"Goodness! What was that?" Blinky asked, frightened beyond everything. Mr Mouse made no reply.

"What was that noise?" Blinky asked again. But still Mr Mouse did not reply.

"Are you gobbling up all the cheese?" Blinky asked angrily. Still Mr Mouse did not reply.

Becoming alarmed at his friend's silence, Blinky pushed his other eye into the narrow space and— oh, how dreadful! He turned pale with fright and sprang out of the corner.

Poor Mr Mouse was lying on the floor, his head caught in the trap and his body as flat as a pancake. Even his tail looked dead, Blinky thought. It lay so still and straight.

"Well, if that's cheese, I don't want any," he muttered to himself. "And I'm getting out of this Smifkins place. It is too dangerous."

"Well if that's cheese, I don't want any." he muttered to himself.

Trembling with fright and still quite pale, he pattered around the pantry, and imagine his joy when he saw a tiny window open not far above the shelf. He wasted no time in climbing up again,

131

and in his excitement knocked down Mrs Smifkins's very best fruit dish.

"Poof!" he said as he took a hurried glance at the broken dish. "Serves her right for killing Mr Mouse." Up to the window-ledge he climbed. It was a very small window, just large enough as it happened for him to squeeze through, and best of all, outside stood a big gum-tree, with one branch right up against the window. Blinky was in that tree in no time. But when he had time to think about matters, he thought it wisest to go right away from the Smifkinses' house; so softly he climbed down out of the tree. Over the orchard he went, and back into the bush again.

Oh, dear! it was beautiful to see all the gum-trees again. And he felt very, very happy as he heard the different birds calling to one another just as day broke. Finding a comfortable tree, one that was very tall and straight, he climbed to the topmost branch and there, cuddled up in a corner, closed his tired little eyes and went to sleep.

CHAPTER IV

Blinky Meets Willie Wagtail

TUG, tug, tug. "Whatever is that?" Blinky thought as he opened his eyes and looked around, still feeling rather sleepy. Something had pulled his ear.

Before he had time to make quite sure that he was not dreaming, another tug fully awakened him.

"Could it be Mr Smifkins again," he wondered, and carefully put up his paw to feel his ear.

Imagine his surprise when he felt a little bird, and screwing up his eyes he tried to see what cheeky fellow was trying to nest there.

All he could see was a very pretty tail that kept bobbing about, first in one direction and then in another.

"Ah! I know who you are!" Blinky said very cheerily. "You're Willie Wagtail."

"Quite true," came the reply. "I'm sorry I woke you, Mr Koala, but I'm in such a hurry to finish my nest. My wife is growing quite impatient because she wants to lay her eggs and the nest is not quite ready. Do you mind if I gather a few more hairs from your ears? They are so silky and pretty, and besides, I think the colour will look very well with the grass I have gathered."

"Go ahead," Blinky answered. "Only don't pull too many at once."

"Thank you very much," Willie replied. "You know it is very difficult to gather the necessary materials for our nest right here in the middle of the bush."

"How is that?" Blinky inquired, as the tug, tug at his ears proceeded.

"There are no cattle or sheep," Willie replied.

"What use are they to you?" said Blinky curiously.

"Why, we gather the hair from the cows' and horses' backs, and the wool from the sheep," Willie Wagtail explained. "It makes a nest so cosy when lined with wool, and of course the hair binds the grass together."

"Don't pull so hard!" Blinky cried impatiently. "And for goodness' sake keep that tail of yours still."

"Sorry," said Willie in an apologetic voice. "I forgot for the moment that I was plucking a bear's ears and not a cow's back. Their hair is much harder to pull. Do you know, I actually pulled hair from the back of Mr Smifkins's cat once."

"You were brave."

"Yes, it was rather a daring thing to do," Willie replied. "But the cat did not seem to mind."

"Did you ever try pulling Mr Smifkins's whiskers?" Blinky asked with a twinkle in his eye.

"Goodness gracious, no! I wouldn't be so bold!" Willie replied.

"Well, I did," said naughty Blinky, "and he did get cross. In fact, he went quite mad for a time."

"You must be a brave bear," said Willie. And he gave an extra sharp tug at Blinky's ear.

"That's enough!" Blinky cried. "You'll leave me bald soon; and I've been very kind to give you so many."

"You have, indeed," Willie said politely. "You've no idea how

Blinky Meets Willie Wagtail

pleased Mrs Wagtail will be with these hairs. They are quite a novelty."

"How often does your wife lay eggs?" Blinky inquired. "Because if you are short at any time I know where you can get heaps and heaps."

"She lays them twice a year," Willie replied. "But I never know the day when she will stop, so I'd be

'That's strange!' said Willie Wagtail.
'I wonder if my wife has been 'laying away'.'

pleased to know where I could find some—just in case of emergency."

"Well, you fly into Mrs Smifkins's pantry," advised Blinky, "and you'll see dozens and dozens of them."

"That's strange," said Willie Wagtail. "I wonder if my wife has been 'laying away'?"

"These are huge eggs, some white and some brown," explained Blinky, who began to realize he may have said something that was not quite right.

"Oh, then they are none of ours," said Willie. "You mean hen eggs, I think."

Blinky Bill Grows Up

"I believe you're right," said Blinky, "because now I come to think of it, I sat on one in a nest in the fowl-house."

"Oh! Whatever did Mr Smifkins say?" Willie asked in a shocked tone.

"Nothing, nothing at all!" Blinky carelessly murmured. "By the way, Willie, what do you do with all your children? You must have hundreds of them by now."

"Possibly," said Willie, very seriously. "But as soon as they are old enough to feed and take care of themselves, we shoo them off. One can't feed dozens of birds all the time, you know!"

"Well, my mother has only me for a child, and she says: 'Thank goodness there are no more.' That is, of course, when she is angry with me. But at other times she says: 'I don't know what I'd do without my son. I wish I had more.'" Blinky's eyes had a far-away look in them as he talked to Willie.

"That's just like all mothers," said Willie Wagtail, knowingly. "But I'll have to be going, or I'll get into trouble."

"Take care of those hairs," Blinky called as Willie flew off.

"Of course I shall," called back Willie, and Blinky watched him as he darted this way and that until he was out of sight.

"A nice little fellow," said Blinky softly, still watching the trees through which his friend had flown.

"I beg your pardon. Were you speaking to me?" said a tiny voice.

Blinky turned round in surprise. He thought he was alone.

"Oh, it's you, Miss Possum! How are you?" he said bravely. He was not going to let anyone see he had been startled.

"Very well, thank you," Miss Possum replied. "You're a long way from home, aren't you?" she asked.

"Oh, no, not so very far," said naughty Blinky. "Anyway, a change of trees is good for a chap."

"Quite so," agreed Miss Possum, "providing you're in the right one."

"Don't pull so hard!"
Blinky cried impatiently.

"Is this a private tree?" Blinky inquired.

"Not exactly," Miss Possum replied. "But we don't allow all the ragtag to come here."

"Who are the ragtag?" Blinky asked.

"Well, there's Mrs Snake, and old Granny Goanna, and a few more grumbly things. We don't want them in our tree. They're always crotchety and creeping around, peering round corners when we least expect them; and their eyes seem to be everywhere. If we make the least noise, they complain and hiss."

"Why don't you push them out?" Blinky asked.

"We did," said Miss Possum proudly. "And what do you think we found when they had gone?"

"Don't know," Blinky said carelessly.

"They left a note to say that they would come back some day and steal our babies." And Miss Possum's eyes nearly dropped out with fright.

"The old thieves," Blinky exclaimed. "Old Granny Goanna would eat a possum as soon as look at it, and as for Mrs Snake, she tried to kill me when I was a baby."

"How dreadful!" cried Miss Possum. "What do you think we could do to frighten them away?"

Blinky thought very hard for a minute, his nose wrinkled and his eyes blinking rapidly.

"I know!" he cried. "We'll dig a big hole at the bottom of the tree and when the rain comes it will fill, and then, when they come to steal the babies, they'll fall in and be drowned."

"But Mrs Snake and Granny Goanna can swim," exclaimed Miss Possum disappointedly.

"Well, that won't do," said Blinky. "I'll have to think of something else.

"We could carry stones up the tree and when they come along, pelt them with big ones and kill them."

Blinky Meets Willie Wagtail

"I can't carry stones and climb as well," Miss Possum replied.

"Oh, well," Blinky said impatiently, "I'll have to go and see Mr Owl. Perhaps he could think of something to do."

"I'll come with you if you'd like me to," Miss Possum said quietly.

"No thanks!" Blinky replied. "I'll manage by myself, and I'll be back before long."

Down the tree he climbed and scrambled through the bush, gazing up at every tall gum-tree in search of Mr Owl. Presently he heard away in the distance a soft "Whoo, whoo."

"That's him!" thought Blinky and hurried along as fast as he could. Nearer and nearer came the call of Mr Owl, and in a very short time Blinky saw him sitting away up in a very high tree. He trotted along to the tree, and then began to climb. Half-way up, just as he reached the lowest branch, Mr Owl flew down to meet him.

"Hulloa, little friend," he said. "I see you've returned safely from Mr Smifkins."

"Yes," replied Blinky, "but I've come to ask you a very serious question."

"What can it be?" the old owl asked.

"Miss Possum is very frightened," Blinky explained. "She says that Mrs Snake and old Granny Goanna are going to steal the babies, and we don't know what to do. Could you advise us?"

"Whoo! whoo!" Mr Owl said, as his eyes opened wider than ever. "They're a wicked old pair. Just you wait a moment while I go away to think."

Dear old Mr Owl flew into a branch higher up. Here he sat very, very still, gazing at nothing really. His eyes never blinked, and not a feather on his body stirred. Presently he shook his head and called "whoo! whoo!" then down he flew to where Blinky was waiting.

"Have you thought of something?" Blinky asked excitedly.

"Yes, little bear," replied Mr Owl. "But tell me first, do you know where Percy Bull Ant lives?"

"Yes, I know," replied Blinky.

"Well, go to him and tell him everything," Mr Owl said softly. "You can say I sent you, and give him my respects at the same time. Tell him I thought the matter over, and decided that an army of his relations, if hidden in suitable places, could suddenly march out and attack Mrs Snake and Granny Goanna, as they come to steal the babies."

"That's a fine idea," cried Blinky. "I don't know why I didn't think of it. Good-bye, Mr Owl, and thank you ever so much."

"Whoo! whoo!" said Mr Owl, and flew off immediately.

Blinky hurried through the bush in the direction of Percy Bull Ant's home. All along the way he passed the homes of Percy's relations, and as hundreds lived in one nest he could see a very large army mustered when they all marched to fight the old robbers. Not a bull ant was to be seen above ground, they were all so busy in their homes, nursing the babies, storing the food, and cleaning out the parlour.

At last Blinky reached Percy's home. It was not much to look at. A litter of tiny sticks and twigs, small pieces of charcoal, loose sand and clay, all heaped in a mound; and everything about it looked very dry and ugly. It certainly looked quite harmless, just as other mounds did; but as Blinky gave a poke at it with his paw, it instantly bristled with life. Angry ants rushed out from nowhere, big red fellows, bristling with indignation, to see who had had the impudence to disturb their peace.

"Ah! Percy Bull Ant," said Blinky as he cautiously moved

backwards a little. "I've come with a message for you from Mr Owl, and he sends his respects."

An ant larger than the rest advanced to Blinky and eyed him curiously, still waving a leg in a dangerous manner, and a nasty fighting look about his whole body. Blinky did not feel too safe and moved another step backwards.

"Look here, Percy," he said very politely, "kindly put that leg of yours down, and don't look so bristly."

"You're Blinky Bill, aren't you, if I'm not mistaken?" said Percy Bull Ant.

"Yes, I am," replied Blinky. "And for goodness' sake send all your brothers back in their nest. I feel quite nervous. They seem to have such a lot of legs."

"Oh, they're harmless," said Percy in an off-hand manner. "All the same, I'll do as you wish."

"Back to your work, all of you!" ordered Percy, and instantly they disappeared back to nowhere. "Now, my lad, tell me what Mr Owl said." And Percy carelessly picked up a stick and started chewing the end of it, his head on one side and his wicked big eyes pausing to gaze at Blinky in a cold rude manner.

"Please, Percy," Blinky began, "Miss Possum is very frightened. Mrs Snake and Granny Goanna are coming to steal all the babies that live in her tree. She's nearly dead with fright, and fainted twice while I was speaking to her."

"Dear, dear," said Percy Bull Ant.

"Yes, Percy, it's very serious, and Mr Owl thought the best thing to do would be for you to gather all your relations together and fight the old robbers when they came for the babies."

"Um," said Percy, as he threw down the stick he had been chewing, "so that's their caper, is it? Well, I'll hold a meeting and let you know what we decide to do about it. Hold on a minute, I'll not be long." And Percy disappeared into nowhere.

Blinky Bill Grows Up

Blinky waited patiently, keeping his eyes glued on the ant-nest. He did not trust any of them.

In a very short time Percy appeared again and slowly advanced to Blinky with a decided tread. His head was downcast, and anyone at a glance could see he was deep in thought. He kicked a grain of sand out of his pathway, and nearly fell over a tiny ball of clay.

"Ants' pants!" he shouted. "I nearly broke my big toe."

"I'm sorry," said Blinky in a whisper, as he did not feel a little bit safe. Percy Bull Ant was such a queer fellow. Good-natured one moment, and bad tempered the next; in fact, he was what is known as temperamental.

"Oh, quite all right, old fellow," said Percy. "Some careless ant has left things about where they've no business to be. Now about this matter of the babies. I've had a talk to all the young bloods down there, and they're keen for a fight. At the moment they are sharpening their nippers and filling up with poison at the bowser. How would a couple of thousand warriors do?"

"Leave it to me!" said Percy winking an eye.

Blinky Meets Willie Wagtail

"Splendid!" cried Blinky, dancing around with glee. "How pleased Miss Possum will be! And I hope you kill Mrs Snake and old Granny Goanna."

"Leave it to me," said Percy, winking an eye.

"When will you come?" Blinky inquired.

"In a few moments," Percy replied. "You'd better lead the way, or get back as quickly as you can. When the boys are on the fighting track they're pretty nasty." Blinky did not wait to hear more. He hurried as fast as he could. The more distance between Percy's boys and himself the better for any bear, he thought. He puffed as he ran, and felt terribly hot, but came to the tree where Miss Possum waited in a very excited state.

"I'm nearly dead with fright," she called from the topmost branch. "I'm sure Mrs Snake is not far away. I can almost smell her."

"Stuff and nonsense!" Blinky exclaimed as he excitedly climbed the tree. "I've good news for you," he said as he plumped himself down beside her.

"What is it? Do tell me," she cried excitedly as she clapped her paws together.

"Well," said Blinky, with a brave air, "Percy Bull Ant is bringing along two thousand soldiers. They'll be here any minute now and then Mrs Snake and Granny Goanna will be feeling pretty sick I think. They're coming armed to the teeth, with a fresh supply of poison and extra sharp nippers."

"You're wonderful!" said Miss Possum, blushing, and Blinky just managed in time to avoid being hugged.

"Gosh!" he exclaimed. "Don't you ever dare to do that again. I'll tell Percy if you do, and he'll set all his boys on to you."

"Oh, don't, don't, *please!*" cried Miss Possum. "I was so excited for the moment, that I quite forgot you were a bear, and grown up, too."

143

"It was bold of you!" said Blinky sternly. "And, anyhow, I hate girls."

"Oh, how dreadful," sighed Miss Possum. "I *am* sorry."

"Here they come! Here come the soldiers!" shouted Blinky, as he danced up and down and nearly knocked Miss Possum out of the tree.

Blinky was right. Percy Bull Ant marched at the head of a vast army, bent on business.

"Left, right, left, right," Percy called. There seemed to be hundreds of thousands of bull ants as they advanced along the pathway. Everything scurried out of their way. Lizards rushed helter-skelter and many dropped their tails with fright. Some of the soldiers stopped to taste the tails; but, Percy, catching sight of them, ordered in a stern voice:

"No eating at present. Drop the loot and attend to business." The ants cast wistful eyes at the tails they had to leave behind.

"Such waste!" they murmured to one another.

When they came to the foot of the tree where Blinky and Miss Possum were sitting, Percy gave his order in a ringing voice and he looked every inch a soldier, as he stood as stiff as a poker.

"Halt!" he called. Immediately the long line came to a stand-still.

"Form fours!" he ordered, and the soldiers obeyed in a twinkling.

"Numbers 674 and 675 stop kicking, and stand to attention. Now, boys," Percy called, "listen to me, and carefully follow my instructions. There's to be no fighting among yourselves. Keep your nippers sharp, and don't waste your poison, as you'll need it later on. When I give the order, advance four at a time and climb half-way up this tree. Each four must take its place until the trunk of the tree is a living mass of soldiers. When Mrs Snake and Granny Goanna come along wait for my order to advance. Keep per-

"Look here Percy," he said very politely,
"put that leg of yours down, and don't look
so bristly.

fectly still; don't blink an eye; then, when I call out 'Charge!' fight and poison with all your might."

"Good, captain!" came the chorus.

"For the present, stand at ease," Percy called.

Every ant lounged in the most amusing way. Some twisted hind legs round one another; others leaned on his neighbour's shoulder, and many were tempted to use their nippers.

"Attention," called Percy. Instantly heels clicked, and there stood the bristling army ready for attack. "Advance," he ordered in an anty voice. "Left, right, left, right—keep in step—left, right." Up the tree they swarmed; nearer and nearer to Blinky and Miss Possum they came.

"Let's climb higher," Blinky whispered. "They look so dreadful." So Miss Possum immediately took his advice and a higher branch was sought.

Percy waited at the foot of the tree, watching and ordering the army into position, until the last ant was off the ground. The tree was a living mass of bull ants, right up to the first branch.

"Silence!" roared Percy as he gazed at the soldiers; then creeping very quietly away into the bushes, he lay in wait for the robbers.

He had not to wait long. Presently a hissing and slithering announced the coming of Mrs Snake and her companion. Percy kept very, very still and listened intently.

"You steal Mrs Ringtail's baby and I'll steal Mrs Siever's," whispered old Granny Goanna.

"What a fine supper they'll make," hissed Mrs Snake. "That'll teach them a lesson for chasing us out of the tree."

Softly they crept nearer and nearer, and Percy Bull Ant quivered with rage. He tiptoed back to the tree and called in a very quiet voice: "They're coming, boys; prepare to kill and poison."

Blinky Meets Willie Wagtail

Not an ant stirred. The tree looked lifeless, and Percy hid behind a stone at the foot.

Hiss! Hiss! Along came the old robbers; stealthily they crept through the bushes.

"The tenth joint in my tail is rather stiff," grumbled Mrs Snake. "It makes things very awkward for me."

"My nails are not as sharp as they were," replied Granny Goanna, "but I've a few good teeth left."

Nearer the tree they came, and both paused to whisper.

"Seems to me," said Granny Goanna, "that the tree looks redder than usual. Do you think we've made a mistake?"

"No, no," replied Mrs Snake. "This is the right tree. Don't I know it well!"

"Well, my eyesight must be failing," sighed Granny Goanna, "because I'll bet my last scale that the tree looks very red."

"Nonsense!" said Mrs Snake impatiently. "You've no doubt got dust in your eyes."

"Maybe, maybe," sighed Granny Goanna, as she floundered along.

"Now, then, boys, be ready for your order," called Percy in a whisper.

Right along to the bottom of the tree came the two old robbers. Old Granny was actually licking her lips, as she thought of the supper in store. She slobbered at the very idea of a baby possum.

"Come along, dear," she called to Mrs Snake. "Everything is quiet and safe."

"You go first," whispered Mrs Snake, "and I'll follow."

Granny Goanna placed her two front legs on the tree and prepared to climb. Mrs Snake waved her wicked head to and fro and gave Granny a nudge which had the desired effect, for she made a plunge and lifted her hind legs from the ground. Mrs Snake gave a wriggle and started up behind her.

Blinky Bill Grows Up

Percy Bull Ant sprang out from his hiding-place and called in a terrible voice:

"Charge!"

Like lightning, the whole tree became alive. The soldiers sprang at the enemy. In a second they were swarming all over Granny Goanna and Mrs Snake.

"Oh, my tail!" screamed Mrs Snake as she tried to wriggle away, lashing her body in the air in agony.

"For heaven's sake save me, save me!" moaned Granny Goanna, as she hissed until all her hisses had gone.

"Go for them, boys!" shouted Percy. "Kill them as quickly as you can."

No order was necessary, as the ants covered the robbers from head to tail. They bit with all their power. Several were killed as Mrs Snake's tail and Granny Goanna's lashed them against the tree; but the numbers seemed never to end.

"Oh! Oh! I'm dying!" groaned Mrs Snake, and she fell with a thud to the ground. In another second down plopped Granny Goanna, as dead as a door-nail.

"Eat them up!" ordered Percy. At once the feast started, and hungry soldiers bit and ate all through the night until only skeletons of the two wicked old things were left.

"It's time we went down and had a look," said Blinky to Miss Possum, just as daylight was dawning. So, scrambling down excitedly, they were just in time to see Percy marshalling his soldiers in readiness to depart.

"How is that for good work?" said Percy Bull Ant proudly, as he pointed to the skeletons.

"Wonderful!" cried Miss Possum and Blinky together. "Your soldiers are very brave."

"They're a husky lot," said Percy, blowing out his chest. "Would you care to have a look at our homes? They're very interesting, although you may not be received with open arms."

"It's time we went down and had a look," said Blinky to Miss 'Possum.

Blinky Bill Grows Up

"Thank you very much," replied Blinky nervously, "but I really must hurry home now. I've been away for a long time and I'm sure I can hear my mother calling me this very minute." And he began shuffling about very uncomfortably.

"Well, good-bye," called Percy, as he gave the order to march, much to the relief of Blinky and Miss Possum.

"Gosh!" sighed Blinky. "That was a narrow squeak!"

"I think you're awfully clever," said Miss Possum. "Perhaps you'd like to come back and meet my mother. She'd be so pleased to thank you for saving the babies."

"Sorry, I can't," said Blinky, looking very important. "I've such a lot of people to see before I go home. Good-bye." And hurriedly looking around him, he darted into the bush.

"Stupid creature!" he muttered to himself. "All possums are silly, specially girls."

"Hey! Where are you going?" Oh, dear, whatever was that? The bush seemed to be full of voices when one least expected them.

"Where are you?" Blinky called. "I can't see you."

"Just here," came the reply.

Then something pricked Blinky's paw and gave him such a fright that he fell head over heels in the dust.

"Good gracious! What a stupid fellow you are!" said the voice.

Thoroughly annoyed, Blinky picked himself up and gazed about.

"Why, it's Mr Hedgehog!" he cried gladly. "You did give me a fright. I thought for a moment one of Percy Bull Ant's soldiers had bitten me."

Mr Hedgehog raised his bristles in surprise.

"Indeed!" he said. "As if I'd hurt you on purpose. Where are you going, by the way?"

"Home," said Blinky meekly.

Blinky Meets Willie Wagtail

"Did you run away?" Mr Hedgehog inquired.

"Oh, no, I just wanted to see a friend," Blinky replied coolly.

"Come and see my home. It's so snug and cosy," said Mr Hedgehog, "and I'm sure you must be tired. You could have a sleep and then, when the moon rises, go on your way."

"I'd really like to, Mr Hedgehog, if it's not very far away, 'cause I'm dreadfully tired," Blinky replied.

"It's just over here," said Mr Hedgehog, "in amongst that bracken fern."

"Thank you! I'll come," said Blinky, as Mr Hedgehog led the way.

"Mr Hedgehog is such a long word to say. Couldn't I call you something else?" Blinky inquired.

"I'm generally called Spikey round here," Mr Hedgehog replied. "Mrs Snake is called 'Snakey'; Miss Goanna, 'Ganna'; Mr Wombat, 'Womby'; and Miss Wallaby, 'Walley'. So what does it matter?"

"Did you know Mrs Snake and Granny Goanna were killed?" Blinky said in a whisper.

"Good heavens! Is that true?" Spikey could hardly believe his ears. "Who did it?"

"Why, Percy Bull Ant and his soldiers!" Blinky replied.

"Well, that's great news," said Spikey. "If I'd only known about it in time, what a feast of ants I'd have had!"

"You don't eat ants, do you?" Blinky asked, his eyes nearly popping out of his head.

"I should just say I do. Why, they're the finest meal I know of— except perhaps a few fat worms."

"Ugh! Don't you eat gum-tips?"

"What's the good of those things to me?" Spikey laughed scornfully.

"But I can tell you like them. You smell like a gum-tree."

"And you smell like a thousand ants!" said Blinky rudely.

"Get out!" Spikey replied. "Why I haven't had more than six dozen to-day."

"Well, they must have been the smelly kind, 'cause you *do* smell of ants," Blinky answered sharply.

"Look at my house, and don't be so grumpy. Isn't it a beautiful place?" And Spikey raised all his quills with pride.

"You don't eat ants do you?"
Blinky asked, his eyes nearly
popping out of his head.

Blinky bent down to peep inside, just as Spikey raised his quills, and gave a loud cry of pain.

"Oh, that's my nose!" he screamed. "Can't you see I've got a nose?"

"No one could miss it for one minute," Spikey said, very annoyed. "It's nearly your whole face."

Blinky felt very angry and raised his paw to hit Spikey; but the quills bristled more than before.

"Follow me and don't start any capers, because I feel rather bilious to-night", Spikey said in an irritable way.

Blinky Bill Grows Up

"Can't you put those things down?" he asked in a very rude manner.

"Yes, when you ask me nicely I will," Spikey replied.

"Oh, well, *please* put those things away," Blinky said. But he still felt very annoyed. His nose was actually bleeding where the spike had pierced it.

"Use your handkerchief," Spikey advised.

Blinky grabbed the torn leg of his knickerbockers and wiped his poor little nose.

"Now come inside and rest," said Spikey as he flattened all his bristles.

"You look very nice now," Blinky remarked as he crawled inside the house.

"Isn't it cosy!" Spikey said proudly, as he curled himself up in a ball.

"Yes, it's very pretty and warm," Blinky replied as he looked around.

The house was just a snug hole under the bracken fern. A few twigs and dried grass helped to make it cosy, and no one could believe that a little home was hidden away under the ferns so safely.

The sun made everything warm, and a drowsy little bear fell asleep, in a nest not meant for koalas.

CHAPTER V

The Lyre-Bird's Home

"IT'S time to get up!"

Blinky rubbed his eyes. Where was he? Oh, yes, of course. There was Spikey standing a few feet away eyeing him very seriously.

"Don't you feel hungry?" he asked.

"Yes, I do. And I'm going to look for some supper," Blinky replied. "These nests are all very well for folk like you, but I like my own home best. I've only to wake up and climb a few branches and my supper is all there."

"Well, I'm going ant-hunting now, so I'll bid you good night," and Spikey raised all his quills and proceeded to walk away.

"Hey! Wait a moment," Blinkey called. "I want you to show me the way home."

"I'm going the other way," Spikey answered.

"Which way?" Blinky inquired.

"Down by the Lyre-bird's home," Spikey replied.

"Could I come, too?" Blinky asked in his most polite tone.

"S'pose you can," Spikey replied. It was certainly not a very pressing invitation, but Blinky was a bear who poked himself everywhere, whether welcome or not. He was out to see the world, and if he waited for invitations--well, he'd see very little.

"Follow me. But don't start any capers, because I feel rather bilious tonight," Spikey said in an irritable way. "I think I'll have to give up eating sugar ants. This is the second time they've upset me lately, and my head's splitting."

"I'm very sorry," Blinky answered. "Is there anything I can do for you? Mrs Grunty always has bad headaches, specially when she's been extra nasty."

"What does she do for them?" Spikey inquired as he slowly crawled along, dragging one leg after the other in a very painful manner.

"Oh, she just wants us all to fuss around her, and pretend we're awfully sorry. But I'm terribly glad and wish she'd have two headaches all at once," Blinky retorted.

"You're not very kind," Spikey mumbled.

"Well, you shouldn't eat ants. It's a wonder you don't get tummy ache, too!" said naughty Blinky. "But I s'pose it couldn't get in your tummy through all those spikes."

"That's enough!" Spikey roared in anger, and his quills stood straight up and quivered with rage.

"Dear me, I'm sorry," said Blinky, quite frightened. "But those spikes sticking out of you from everywhere, must be the cause of your headaches. What if someone stroked you the wrong way?"

"Hump!" growled Spikey. "They'd better not try."

"Is it very far away to the Lyre-bird's home?" Blinky asked.

"No," his friend replied. "I don't travel far from my home, just keep on behind me and you'll be surprised how soon we'll be there."

The little animals pattered along, brushing the ferns and grass aside as they went. The moon showed the way, shining through the trees and only the soft pad, pad of Blinky could be heard.

The Lyre-bird's Home

Suddenly quite close at hand a kookaburra laughed.

"Jacko's very merry tonight!" Blinky remarked.

"That's not Jacko," Spikey replied. "That's Mrs Lyre-bird. She's so clever at mimicking all the bush birds that sometimes she deceives me for a minute."

"She must be clever," Blinky replied. "I could bet that was Jacko laughing."

"She's mighty clever," Spikey replied. "I've heard her mimic the butcher-birds so that you couldn't tell the difference; and she simply loves to call like the magpie and old Mr Owl. There isn't a noise in the bush that she can't imitate. Why! One night when I was prowling round, looking for a few ants I got a terrible fright. I made sure Mr Smifkins's dog was chasing me. The yelping and barking drew closer and closer as I neared the Lyre-bird's home, and I hurried along, to see if they would shelter me. Imagine my surprise when I found Mrs Lyre-bird imitating the Smifkinses' dog. I was very annoyed at first, as I was all out of breath, and hot, and my bristles were cold with fright. But it was a relief all the same to find I had been mistaken."

"Did you tell Mrs Lyre-bird how she had frightened you?" Blinky asked sympathetically.

"Yes, and she only laughed. She said she'd frightened many bush folk that way; and just to show me how really clever she was she made a noise like Mr Smifkins chopping wood. Then, seeing me more surprised, she pretended to strike matches. I had to laugh. It sounded so funny."

"Listen! What's that?" Blinky stopped still, and listened very closely.

"That's a train coming up the hill," Spikey replied.

"There are no trains here," Blinky answered.

"Chuff, chuff, chuff, chuff," came the noise again.

157

Blinky Bill Grows Up

"Well, they must have put a train here in the night," Spikey laughed, as they trotted along.

Nearer and nearer came the chuff, chuff until Blinky became quite frightened. He'd never seen or heard a train in his life and he wondered if it would eat him. He grew quite pale, and held on to his knickerbockers very tightly.

"Ha, ha!" laughed Spikey. "She's tricked you, too!"

"Is that Mrs Lyre-bird?" Blinky was astounded. But before he could make any further remark, he saw with his own eyes that Spikey was right.

At the feet of some tall trees a wonderful sight was seen. Just close your eyes for a minute and try to imagine you're in Blinky's place.

Great gum-trees standing erect, with the moon peeping through the leaves, out of a blue, blue sky. The grass and bracken a soft brown, fading away to grey, and right in front of you, only a few yards distant four grown-up lyre-birds and six little ones.

A dancing lesson was in progress and the ground was cleared for a little space, to give the dancers room to perform. That is what Blinky saw, as he gazed at the enchanting scene.

"Shh!" whispered Spikey. "Keep very quiet, and you'll see wonderful things."

The mothers and fathers were dancing in the daintiest way, stepping ever so lightly, and then running backwards and forwards, pirouetting, bowing, and hopping, while the little ones looked on, watching every movement, and occasionally giving a little squeak of delight.

"Come, children," called Mrs Lyre-bird. "It is time you learned to dance."

The little ones twittered with delight, as they took their places in the centre of the ring.

"One, two, three; hop, skip, and a jump," called one of their

The mothers and fathers were
dancing in the daintiest way.

mothers, and the children very clumsily tried to imitate their parents.

They toppled over one another, fell on the ground and squawked with delight when one managed to pirouette for a moment.

The parents were very patient and showed them over and over again how to perform.

At last one little chap did a surprisingly clever dance and the mothers and fathers became very excited, as they danced up and down, encouraging the dancer, and calling to him all kinds of nice things. As time went on the children became quite clever and the dancing lesson ended with very happy results.

Nearby was the playground. Here a wonderful collection of toys—in the shape of pretty leaves, pebbles, and bright feathers—were spread on the ground. The children and the parents played all kinds of games, until Blinky disturbed their peace and fun by stumbling over a stone.

"Hey! It's only me," he called as the birds ran for safety. But all his pleadings and promises to be friendly were useless. Being very timid, they vanished into the bushes and had no intention of coming out again.

"They're very scared!" Blinky remarked, as he turned to Spikey. But Spikey had vanished too.

"Gosh! The place must be haunted," Blinky muttered to himself, as he nervously glanced around. "A fellow's all by himself."

"Well, I'll go home," he decided. And he suddenly thought what a long time it was since he had left his mother and Mrs Grunty.

He looked at his bockers, and tried to pat them, or what remained of them, into shape. They were just hanging by threads, and a very sorry spectacle he looked.

"I s'pose old Mother Grunty will say all sorts of things when she sees me," he growled. "I'm not going to stand it any longer. If she growls very hard at me, I'll run away again—and I'll get married next time. Then they'll be sorry, and want me home again." And Blinky gave a savage kick at the grass.

"Spikes and scissors! Look where you're going with your big feet!" a little voice cried.

"What's up now?" Blinky said, as he came to a standstill. "As if there's not enough growling without you starting, too!"

"Well, look what you've done to my web, and I've been hours and hours weaving it. Now it's all spoilt, and I'll never catch my supper, and I'm starving."

"Are you another ant-eater?" Blinky asked rudely.

"No, I'm not!" snapped the spider. "I eat gnats and mosquitoes."

"Gnats! I've never heard of them before," Blinky said. "Do they taste good?"

"Not as good as you'll taste if you don't get your big feet out of my way," the spider growled as he glared at Blinky.

"Oh! I see you've a red spot on your back, so I think I'll be going."

Blinky very quietly stepped aside and continued on his way. The moon was kind and showed him the pathway quite clearly and he thought by travelling all night he would reach home by daylight. But he had not considered what may be round the corner.

On he went, one minute feeling very brave as he thought of what he'd do to Mrs Grunty if she grunted, and the next, feeling rather frightened as he imagined her cross face round the gum-tree.

Pit-a-pat! Pit-a-pat! Someone was coming through the bush, and someone in a great hurry, too.

"Oh, dear! I'll be late, I'll be late," said a voice that came nearer and nearer.

Blinky Bill Grows Up

"What for?" Blinky called out from behind a tree where he had hidden.

"For the meeting," came the reply. "But what's it got to do with you? Who are you?"

Blinky cautiously peeped round the tree and there stood Belinda Fox of all people, dressed in her best coat of brown, with a very fine tail.

"You're up to mischief, I'll bet!" Blinky said as he came from his hiding-place.

"Me!" said Belinda Fox in surprise. "Why, I've not tasted a fowl for ages and ages."

"Where's the meeting?" Blinky asked.

"Down at the flat, under the trees," Belinda answered. "And I'll be later than ever if I stop and talk to you."

"What's on at the meeting?" Blinky called as Belinda started to walk away. "Stop a moment and tell me."

"It's those rabbits," Belinda complained. "They're holding a meeting—a race-meeting, I mean—and I'm just about tired of their noise. So I'm going to act as umpire, and the very first one I catch, I'll eat, toes and all."

"Good gracious!" Blinky exclaimed. "You're feeling very annoyed."

"Annoyed is no name for it!" Belinda answered sharply. "And what's more, I'm hungry."

"Well, what about some juicy gum-tips? They're scrumptious!"

"Huh!" Belinda grumbled. "Gum-tips, indeed! A juicy young rab is what I'm after. So good night to you, Mr Koala. I'm in a hurry."

"Yes," said Blinky to himself, "I'm in a hurry, too. I'll take a short cut down to the flat and tell the rabbits all about it. Belinda Fox will have no young rab for supper if I can help it."

Dashing into the bush he scampered along at a great rate.

Off raced
Belinda
Fox

Down the track, through the saplings, and over the hill, until the flat came in view. There the bunnies were—mothers and fathers and their babies, grandmothers and grandfathers and bunny uncles and aunts. Such a crowd of them! And they scampered backwards and forwards, frightfully excited, their little white tails bobbing about ever so prettily and their long ears twitching with the thought of all the fun.

"Oh, dear, I hope I'm not too late!" Blinky thought, as he rushed down to the flat.

A line of baby bunnies were standing in a row, waiting for the signal to start the race.

Mr Grandfather Rabbit stood at the farther end of the flat against a blackberry-bush. He waited with one paw raised, ready to wave a "four o'clock" as the signal to start. The young rabs were skylarking and delaying matters considerably, for just as

"Oh dear, I hope I'm not too late,"

everything seemed ready for the word "Go!" some young scamp rushed away before his time and then the whole line had to wait again until all was ready.

Blinky dashed across the flat and right into the middle of the spectators. He was breathless.

The Lyre-bird's Home

"Stop! Stop!" he cried. "Don't let the babies go!"

At once there was great excitement. Rabbits scuffled and hopped around him, their eyes popping with curiosity.

"What's the matter?" they cried. "What have you come for?"

"For goodness' sake don't let the babies race," Blinky gasped. "Belinda Fox is coming along, and she's going to catch the first one and eat him."

"Shiver my whiskers!" a father rabbit called out in alarm. "That Belinda Fox is just a bit too smart. She's been poking her nose round here too much lately."

"Well, hurry up and do something," Blinky cried. "She'll be here any minute."

"Just a moment, dearie," piped up old Great Granny Rabbit, "I've an idea, a splendid idea."

"What is it, granny?" all the rabbits asked.

"I've a surprise for Miss Belinda Fox. Just you wait here

165

while I get it. I won't be a moment," and she hobbled away to her burrow.

The rabbits crowded round the entrance waiting to see what great granny's idea could be.

"I suppose it's one of those stale old turnips she's been collecting for weeks," said one bold young rab.

"Or perhaps an old tuft of grass," another chimed in.

The rabbits danced with excitement as they waited and one of them thumped impatiently on the door-way with his hind leg.

"Don't do that, you silly old pop-eye," said a big father sternly. "She'll think it's the alarm signal and never come out."

But great granny rabbit was not a scrap alarmed and presently she appeared tugging and pulling at something almost as big as herself. The others rushed to her assistance and imagine their surprise when they pulled out a dead rabbit, very fat, so fat indeed that he looked as though he'd had twenty suppers.

"Gee whiskers!" they exclaimed. "Where did you get this old fellow? What's he for?"

"Ah ha!" great granny smiled; "he's very very old; but he'll make a fine supper for Belinda Fox. I've had him longer than any of you young fellows can remember, and I've kept him for just such an occasion as this."

"He's very fat!" Blinky said, as he patted him with his paw. "And—oh! he's prickly!"

"He's prickly right enough," great granny chuckled. "Haven't I stuffed him with Scotch thistles and nettles? Just you wait and see the surprised look on Belinda's face when she takes the first bite."

"Oh, lovely, lovely! That's a wonderful supper for Belinda!" said the rabbits, laughing.

"Give me a hand to push him along!" great granny called.

She was nearly knocked over in the rush, as all the rabbits scrambled and pushed, and tugged the old thing full of prickles.

"If he belonged to me I'd warm his pants
for him, my word I would."

Blinky Bill Grows Up

Away down to the flat they rolled it, and over to where the bunny still stood with his paw raised ready to give the signal.

"Prop him up here!" great granny called as she pointed to the blackberry-bush, "and then Belinda Fox can have a good look at him before she dines."

The rabbits all helped, and stood old Prickles up on his hind legs. They placed one of his ears over the back of his head and the other over one eye. Then they stuffed a few blades of grass in his mouth to make him look just as though he were eating his supper. They pushed him a little farther into the blackberry-bush so that he seemed to be peeping out. Then, quite satisfied with all they had done, they scampered back to the starting place. Just as they lined up, ready once more for the race, Miss Belinda Fox strutted into view. Down she came lipperty-lop, lipperty-lop, until she reached the bunnies.

"Good evening, young rabs," she said politely, with a wicked smile on her face. "I see you're having a race, and a fine night you have for it."

"Good evening, Miss Belinda," the rabbits replied. "We're so glad to see you."

"I'm sure you are," Belinda replied, with a sly look at the babies. "I came along to see if I could be umpire."

"So Blinky was telling us," said an old rabbit, scratching his ear, and looking very unconcerned. "Well, I think it's a fine idea, and shows a very kind nature. We've just been having an argument as to who should act as umpire, and now the question is settled. We'll gladly accept your services."

"Just tell me what to do, and I'll be only too pleased to help," Belinda replied with eyes glistening. Such a fine plump lot of babies she'd never seen before. What a feast she was going to have!

"Their tails and all I'll gobble," she thought to herself as she patted one gently on the nose.

The Lyre-bird's Home

"I'll line up the babies," Blinky said, as he trembled with excitement. "And you, Belinda Fox, walk down to the other end of the flat; and when we're ready, give the signal to start."

"What's the signal?" Belinda asked slobbering all down her front, and showing her cruel teeth while eyeing the babies all the time.

"Oh, just wag your tail, that'll do," Blinky replied. Off raced Belinda Fox,

"Their tails and all I'll gobble." she thought to herself.

down to the end of the flat. She was so thrilled that she didn't bother to look around, but came to a halt just in front of the black-berry-bush.

"Get ready," Blinky called to the babies. "But when you're half-way down the flat, run very slowly, and if Belinda has not seen old Prickles by then, turn round and race back to your burrows as quickly as you can."

"Hurry up. Can't you move things along?" Belinda called impatiently, as she waited, panting and moving about restlessly. She turned suddenly to look behind as something made a scratching noise. Now the cunning rabs had ordered one of their number to squat behind old Prickles and at the right moment to scratch

169

the ground, so that Belinda would turn round to see for herself what a fine fat rabbit awaited her. Needless to say, the scratcher was well hidden from view and ready to make his escape at a moment's notice.

Scratch, scratch, scratch, came the noise.

"Gobble me up!" Belinda exclaimed in rapture, "if that's not a fine supper right under my very nose, and much fatter than the babies all put together! The silly old grass-eater must be blind."

Pretending she did not see Prickles, she hastily turned round and faced the crowd at the far end, but she kept old Prickles in view out of the corner of her eye.

Such a fine supper was not going to escape her, she thought and dribbled most terribly.

"The silly old flop ears," she remarked aloud, "fancy thinking he could hide from me."

"Are you ready?" Blinky called at the top of his voice, beckoning to Belinda.

"Yes. Let them go!" And she gave her tail a very frisky wag.

"Ready!... Set!... GO!" called Blinky in a loud voice.

Away raced the bunnies, their tails bobbing up and down as they went helter-skelter down the flat.

At the same moment Belinda Fox made a spring in the black-berry-bush, and with a snap, grabbed Prickles in her teeth. As it happened she grabbed him right round the tummy in the most prickly part. She gave a leap in the air and a scream of agony, as she shook her head from side to side. She could not cry as her mouth was full of prickles. They stuck between her teeth and pierced her tongue, and as she swallowed with rage they stuck in her throat. With a yell of anger she made another bite at old Prickles and shook him violently, so violently that he came in halves. Then realizing that a trick had been played on her, she raced round and round, biting at the air and snapping at the remains of Prickles. She coughed and spluttered, and tried to tear the prickles out of her mouth, but it was useless, they pricked like a thousand needles. Exhausted at last, she fell in a heap, right in the middle of the blackberry-bush and lay there gasping for air.

The baby rabbits seeing what had happened when half-way down the flat, turned and raced back to their burrows, chuckling with glee, and dancing around on their hind legs.

"She's caught this time!" Blinky laughed. "Let's go down and have a look at her."

Even old great granny joined in the rush. Her left hind foot was swollen with rheumatism, caused through living in a very dark and damp burrow, but she forgot all about it for the moment and trotted along on her three legs with a queer hop now and again. Her old whiskers (the few she had left) twitched with enjoyment and her eyes looked brighter. She grinned and showed her poor old teeth, worn to the gums with many years of hard work on tough grasses and plants.

"Come on, great granny!" a baby bunny called. "Shake a leg, or you'll miss the fun."

"I'm shaking the three of them as fast as I can," she chuckled, and gave an extra spurt just to show the cheeky young rabs what she *could* do.

Belinda Fox heard the rabbits coming and took a look to make sure. Oh, how mad she was! She kicked the blackberry-bush with all her legs at once and only added more prickles to her skin.

The rabbits stood round in a circle laughing at the top of their voices, poking fun, and calling her names.

"And now, Miss Belinda Fox," old great granny cackled, "how do you like rabbit for supper?"

Belinda gave a leap and tried to grab great granny, but she

fell back in the blackberry-bush with a cry of pain and closed her eyes.

Blinky felt sorry for Belinda, because it was not really her fault that she liked rabbit for supper. "Perhaps," he thought, "if I'd been a fox I'd like rabbit, too." So, walking quietly up to Belinda, who looked as though she were dead, he said in very kind tones:

"If I help to pick the prickles out of you, will you promise to *never never* eat bunnies again?"

Belinda opened one eye and looked at him sorrowfully. She could not speak, so nodded her head weakly.

"How do I know you'll keep your promise?" Blinky asked. But Belinda could not answer; she only nodded again.

"Cross your paws," Blinky commanded. "Then I'll know you mean it."

Belinda raised her front paws very slowly and crossed them.

"Now, I'll pick all the prickles out, and you'll be able to run home." And Blinky cautiously stepped up to Belinda and sat down beside her.

The rabbits were amazed to see Belinda Fox so sorry and offered to help with the prickles. But Blinky ordered them home, saying:

"Go while the going's good."

And the rabbits wisely took his advice.

All night long, until daylight, Blinky picked the prickles out. There was such a pile of them; but as Belinda's mouth and throat were clear after Blinky had spent two whole hours unpricking, she felt better and sat up and helped to pick the nasty things from her paws and tail.

"How do you feel now?" Blinky asked when all but a few were out.

"Much better, Mr Koala," Belinda answered. "Now I think I'll go home. And I'll never come down this way again."

The Lyre-bird's Home

And Belinda Fox ever after kept well away from the flat. Even when she was terribly hungry, she would not for a moment look at a rabbit. If one happened to cross her pathway as she rambled through the bush, she immediately sat on her haunches, crossed her front paws, and looked the other way.

Blinky's life was certainly full of adventure. But once more he set out to find his way home, feeling very happy that he had done a good deed, and saved the baby bunnies from a horrible death.

CHAPTER VI

Blinky Returns Home

"WHAT'S that noise?" said Mrs Grunty, as she peered through the branches.

"Must be a possum," Mrs Koala replied as she also gazed through the branches.

"That's no possum," Mrs Grunty answered in a decided tone. "I wouldn't mind betting my spectacles it's that son of yours returning."

"Oh, how wonderful!" Mrs Koala cried, "Do you really think the dear little chap has come home?"

"Dear little chap," sniffed Mrs Grunty with a stern look on her face. "I'd like to see Snubby running away from home! He wouldn't do it the second time. And I'd also like to know what you intend to do with that son of yours?"

"I suppose I'll have to spank him," and Mrs Koala sighed very deeply.

"Suppose, indeed!" Mrs Grunty scoffed. "Why, if he belonged to me I'm warm his pants for him. My word I would!" And she folded her paws over her tummy in a very determined way, and glared through the branches again.

174

Blinky decided there and then that
he'd fight.

Blinky Bill Grows Up

"Is anyone there?" she snapped and nearly fell headlong out of the tree as she bent over to look.

"Just keep cool. This is my business," Mrs Koala said firmly, as she broke a twig off the tree.

"It's my business, too," Mrs Grunty growled. "I won't have that young runaway playing with Snubby. Goodness knows what ideas he'll put in his head."

"There isn't room in his head for many ideas!" Mrs Koala said snappily as she began to climb down the tree.

"Dear, dear," Mrs Grunty sighed. "More trouble. That boy of hers will be the death of her yet."

Mrs Koala quietly climbed down from one branch to the other.

"Blinky!" she called in a whisper. "Is that you?"

"Yes, mother," came a meek little voice.

"Come up here at once!" Mrs Koala ordered.

"I'm not coming if Mrs Grunty's there," naughty Blinky answered.

"Do as I tell you this minute," his mother commanded.

"Shan't," Blinky answered in a very trembly voice.

"Well, I'll soon see about that!" And Mrs Koala climbed right down the tree to the ground where Blinky stood. What a sight met her eyes! A grubby little bear, bockers torn to ribbons and dirty; dirty paws and face.

"Good heavens!" Mrs Koala cried. "Where have you been? Just look at you. Dirt from head to foot. It's no use, its no use!" poor mother bear cried. "I *can't* keep you clean."

"It's only dirt," Blinky whimpered, as he looked at his mother very sorrowfully.

"Where have you been all this time?" Mrs Koala asked angrily. "I've been worried almost to death, and my hair's turned grey with fright."

"I didn't want to go to Mrs Magpie's school, and I hate Mrs

Blinky Returns Home

Grunty. She's always growling," Blinky said, and a tear ran down his face.

Mrs Koala put her paws behind her back and gently dropped her stick on the ground.

"She is an old growler. You're right, Blinky. I think we'll both go away from her," and Mrs Koala patted Blinky's head.

"Oh, do let's go!" Blinky implored, "and I'll never run away again."

"Very well, dear," Mrs Koala said kindly. "We'll go tonight."

"Oh, good!" Blinky cried as he hugged his mother.

"It's only dirt," Blinky whimpered, as he looked at his mother very sorrowfully.

"Wait here until I go up and collect a few leaves, as we'll probably need them on the way," Mrs Koala said kindly.

"Say good-bye to Mrs Grunty for me, and give her a scratch," naughty Blinky called out as his mother climbed up the tree again.

"Don't be cheeky, Blinky," Mrs Koala replied. "Mrs Grunty can't help growling."

"She's got an extra big growler inside her," Blinky mumbled. He waited patiently until his mother returned. Her apron was full of juicy gum-tips and she seemed very pleased at the prospect of leaving.

"Where are we going?" Blinky inquired.

Blinky Bill Grows Up

"I don't know," his mother replied. "You should know a good place for us to make a new home after all your travels."

"I know of lots!" Blinky cried joyfully, and danced up and down.

Just as they were ready to start a big gum-nut came hurtling down and hit Blinky right on his nose. He looked up at the tree in surprise. Surely Snubby wouldn't do a thing like that. He was such a good little bear.

"It's that horrid Mrs Grunty," he said at the top of his voice, as he caught sight of her hiding among the leaves, and looking down at him. She was shaking her paw savagely.

"Hope you fall out of the tree," Blinky called to her.

"It'll be a bad day for you if I do," she called back.

"Good-bye, old Grunty legs!" he answered, and scrambled after his mother, who had started on the pathway into the bush.

"It's good to have you back again," dear old Mrs Koala said. "I'm sure we'll be happy now."

"As happy as spiders," Blinky replied. "I know a beautiful big gum-tree, away from Mrs Grunty."

The two bears trotted on and on, the stars shining seemed to wink and laugh at them, and a breeze dancing through the bush played with them as she blew leaves in their faces.

"Shh!" Mrs Koala whispered. "I can hear voices, I'm sure."

"It's only Mr Owl."

"No, no! There are men coming," Mrs Koala whispered again. "Where shall we hide?"

"Behind this bush," Blinky replied. "Quickly, mother, and don't breathe."

The two bears crawled under a wattle-tree and waited with thumping hearts to see what would happen.

"Here they come!" Blinky whispered. "Don't move an eyelash." He was right. Two men with guns and sacks came tramping through the bush, crushing the leaves underfoot and whistling loudly.

"It's a funny thing we haven't seen a possum yet," one remarked.

"Bears are what I'm after," the other replied.

"Oh, is that all!" the first one answered. "Well, you'll have a long tramp after them. There are none round here."

Blinky and his mother looked at one another terrified. "What if they find us?" Blinky whispered.

"We're safe, if you keep very still." And Mrs Koala patted Blinky in a comforting way.

"How about boiling the billy?" one man suggested as they stopped right opposite the wattle-tree where the two bears were hiding.

"A good idea," his friend replied. "I feel like a cup of tea. Here's a good tree to rest under." And pointing to the wattle, he flung his sacks down only a few inches from Blinky and his mother.

"You'd better have a look round for snakes, before you sit there," the first man advised.

Mrs Koala gave Blinky's arm a squeeze. They were trembling with fright.

The man who had thrown his sacks down started to kick away the leaves and twigs. Nearer and nearer his boots came to the little bears, until he kicked Blinky on the back.

"Hulloa! What have I struck?" he called out. "Something soft, and not a snake."

"A possum, you may be sure," his friend replied as he dashed over to have a look.

Pushing aside the low branches of the wattle, they discovered Blinky and his mother, huddled up together and growling savagely.

"Well, I'll be blowed!" said one of the men. "If it isn't Mrs Koala and her son! What luck!"

Blinky Bill Grows Up

"Get the sack and be very gentle with them," his friend replied. "They're grand little fellows and I wouldn't hurt a hair on their heads."

"Very healthy looking bears, especially the young chap," the other man remarked.

"You grab one and I'll get the other, then we'll put them in the sacks," the first man said.

"Easier said than done, I think," his friend remarked as he approached Blinky and Mrs Koala. They growled louder than ever, and snarled at the man.

"Come here, old chap," the man said kindly as he reached towards Blinky; but Blinky decided there and then that he'd fight before he'd be popped in a sack.

"So you want a scrap, do you?" the man asked, as he tried to pat Blinky.

With a growl Blinky darted out his paw and scratched the man's arm.

"You young beggar!" the man cried. "It's time your toenails were cut." And as quick as lightning he grabbed Blinky by the back of the neck.

"Caught!" the man called excitedly. "Now for the mother."

When Mrs Koala saw Blinky caught she wisely decided to give no trouble, but to go with her son, wherever they were taken to. She allowed the other man to catch her and stroke her pretty ears. In fact, she rather liked the feel of those hands. They were very gentle and the man spoke kind words. Surely no harm would come to them from these men.

But Mr Blinky thought otherwise. He was mad. Fancy being caught just as he was out on another adventure! And he had such a wonderful lot of things to show his mother.

"This young fellow's like a jack-in-the-box and as savage as a lion," the man remarked who held him.

"Pop him into the sack," his friend replied, "but be very careful not to hurt him. His mother's behaving like a little lady."

180

Blinky Returns Home

Blinky was put in the sack, feet first.

"Tie the bag round his neck, and let the little fellow see his mother," the first man said, so a string was tied round the bag, and Blinky looked very funny as he was propped up against the tree, with just his head showing. His ears looked larger than ever and his eyes glistened with anger. He kicked and kicked the sack and altogether behaved shockingly.

The men laughed loudly as they watched his antics.

"The young nipper's in a bad temper," one remarked. "I'll sit beside him with his mother on my lap. That might quieten him." He did so, and Mrs Koala put out a paw and patted Blinky's nose. It was hot and dry. "Dear me, Blinky," she said. "Don't get so angry. You're making yourself quite ill."

"They'll kill us," Blinky cried.

"No, I'm sure they are kind men. I heard them say something about a zoo just now," his mother replied.

"Well, I don't want to go to a zoo," he wailed.

"Oh, we'd have great fun!" Mrs Koala said. "We would meet other bears and see all kinds of strange things."

"It sounds like an adventure, and I suppose we'd be taken great care of, and if you're with me, mother, I don't think I'd mind so much," Blinky replied quite cheerfully.

"That's the boy!" Mrs Koala said. "Now, if you stop that kicking and growling and behave very nicely, perhaps the men will take you out of that sack."

Blinky did as his mother advised, and sat there as quiet as it was possible for him to sit. Presently, after the men had finished their tea, one turned to look at Blinky.

"The little fellow's quite tame now," he remarked. "I guess he's tired after all that kicking."

"Poor little chap!" the other said kindly. "How about letting him out for a while?"

"Do you think it wise?" his friend asked. "I wouldn't lose him for the world."

"He won't wander away while his mother's here," the other replied. "Let him out and see what he'll do." So Blinky was taken out of the sack and held in kind arms up to his mother.

"Don't kick or scratch," Mrs Koala whispered, "or they'll pop you back in the sack again."

But Blinky was cunning enough to know that, and instead kept very still until at last the man placed him on the ground. He cuddled up to his mother and felt ever so much happier.

"Well, it's time we made tracks home again," one of the men remarked, as he stamped out the smouldering fire. "Pop the two of them in the sacks and we'll ride very carefully."

A long journey followed through the bush; to Blinky it seemed days and days. The gum-trees were gradually left behind, and in their place green fields and houses came into view. The earth had not the sweet smell of the bushland, the air seemed dusty, and the songs of the birds disappeared altogether.

Both bears were held very gently and patted and talked to in a caressing way by the men, so all fear of harm had left them. Indeed, they were enjoying this new adventure, especially dear Mrs Koala, who had never been from home before. She could hardly believe her eyes when she saw the first train pass by in the distance, and wonder after wonder caused her and Blinky to utter queer little grunts as they came nearer to the township. The next day, the men took the bears on the train and it was very amusing to Blinky to have such a fuss made of him. It was better than any adventure he'd ever had before. Mrs Koala enjoyed it, too, and in her mind wondered however she had lived so long with crabby Mrs Grunty. After the train journey they were carried on board a boat and taken across the water.

"Good gracious!" Mrs Koala exclaimed, as she gazed on Sydney harbour. "They seem to have a great deal of rain here. I've never seen such a lot of water over the ground before. The rabbits will be in a bad way."

Blinky was too surprised to reply. He tried to look at everything at once—boats, people, flags, wharves, and very tall buildings. It was really marvellous. He was too surprised to even grunt. The men still carried them in their arms, and patted them as before.

The boat drew alongside a jetty and the men carried the bears ashore. Through a big gate they went and along paths bordered with beautiful flowers, and oh, joy! gum-trees grew all around.

Mrs Koala and Blinky were enraptured as they saw the trees of the bushland, and every moment they became happier as an old friend was seen.

"Why, there's Mrs Wallaby, I do believe!" Mrs Koala cried in excitement. "And, oh, dear, what a great number of children she has now! When I first knew her she had only one; now she has dozens."

"Good heavens!" she cried in alarm as they passed along the path. "Just look at Mrs Snake. How fat she's grown since last

Blinky Bill Grows Up

I saw her! And I'm sure as can be *she* hadn't all those children then. Oh, there's her husband, I suppose. See, Blinky, that big snake lying asleep in the corner."

"That's not our Mrs Snake," Blinky replied with a worldly air. "She's dead and eaten by the bull ants."

"Dear me," Mrs Koala sighed. "I've heard so little living away in the bush. There's no doubt about it we koalas have seen very little."

"I hear Jacko!" Blinky cried with excitement. "He's here, too!"

Sure enough—the kookaburras were giving the little bears a grand bush welcome to their new home.

"Good afternoon," Mrs Koala called. "You've also added to your family, Mr Kookaburra, since I saw you last."

Another hearty laugh greeted Mrs Koala's words.

"Great gum-trees! What on earth is that?" said Mrs Koala, pointing to a giraffe.

"Well, well, I've never seen a tree like that before. What a funny looking branch that is growing out of the stump. It's spotted like the gum, but the spots are larger. Good gracious, Blinky, it's moving! Look at the branches walking along the ground. And, oh, the spotted branch has eyes and ears on the top!"

"Silly!" Blinky retorted. "That's not a tree. That's an animal, mother."

"And is that huge thing over there an animal?" Mrs Koala asked as she pointed to an elephant. "I've never seen an animal with a nose like that! Just look at it—all crumpled and so very, very, long. I'm sure it's not an animal."

"Look! Look!" Blinky cried excitedly. "He's picking up something with his nose! And now he's curled it into his mouth!"

"That's *not* a nose," Mrs Koala said decidedly. "It's some kind of fishing-line he's stuck on his face. Whoever saw anyone pick up things with their nose?"

Blinky Returns Home

Blinky and his mother had no further time for argument as the men carried them into a building, where they were at once surrounded by several more men who admired them, patted them, and offered some delicious fresh gum-tips for refreshments.

"Remember your manners, Blinky, and don't eat so quickly," Mrs Koala whispered, as she nibbled her leaves.

"They are so good, mother, and it's such a long time since we've had our own gum-tips. I hope we'll get plenty more." And Blinky crammed his mouth with leaves until a smart smack on the nose from Mrs Koala made him remember his manners.

"Aren't they the quaintest little bears," someone said as Blinky and his mother continued their meal. "And what a delight for the children!"

They have indeed been a delight and joy to thousands of children —and grown-ups as well—in Taronga Park. Such cuddly, trusting, amusing little bears. How many of you children who visit the zoo long to steal Blinky just for your very own? No wonder, especially when he reaches out a furry paw to shake hands with you. But while you are longing to cuddle and steal him, remember how sad he would be if parted from his mother. He would die in a very short time, as his natural food is most necessary, that is— his special gum-tips; and although Blinky has been through so many bold adventures, he must have his bushland surroundings to make his life happy.

As I walked past the koalas one day recently when paying a visit to the zoo, I asked Mrs Koala how she liked her new home. Before she could reply naughty Blinky pushed his way in front of her, held out a paw for me to shake, and said in a very cheeky voice:

"It's just the juicy gum-tip!"

So there I left the two little koalas with other friends from the bush feeling very happy and looking quite contented.

"Goodbye, my mother wants to see me privately."

Blinky Bill and Nutsy

Blinky introduces his new friends, Nutsy and Splodge.

CONTENTS

CONTENTS

AN INTRODUCTION

DO you remember that bad lad called Blinky Bill? Yes? I thought you would. Well, just listen to the news I have to tell you. He has escaped from the zoo! Yes, escaped! He is back in the bush again. More exciting still, his mother is there too, and a little girl koala called Nutsy, who Blinky says is his girl friend. You can imagine how bold he is when he talks like that. I really think he has become fifty times worse since he lived at the zoo. I suppose it is the environment. All those cheeky monkeys, next door to him, and all kinds of little boys passing cheekier remarks as they discussed the animals in the zoo. No wonder the poor child has grown so bold. And less wonder that Mrs Koala has two deep wrinkles on her forehead, and an even more surprised look than usual on her face. She told me in confidence that she's surprised at *nothing* nowadays. So you can imagine what sort of a time *she's* been having. Splodge, a gentleman of the bush, a kangaroo also in captivity at the zoo, proved himself a loyal friend by helping the koalas to escape—while he also did the vanishing trick. Peanuts, were the cause of it all. When I tell you how it all happened I know you'll clap your hands and say "Good old Splodge". He told me the news himself. So I know it's perfectly true.

D.W.

Chapter 1.
THE ESCAPE.

"**B**OLD little wretches!"
Splodge the largest kangaroo
in the zoo lay on his side, eyes
tightly shut, teeth grinding with anger, and his tummy fairly boiling
with indignation.

"I wish I could spit like the llamas next door." . . . Bang!
Another peanut hit him right on the nose. "That makes the tenth!"
Splodge mumbled opening one eye just the tiniest bit to have a look
at his tormentors. "Wait till the next arrives! I'll give that kid
with the freckles on his face the biggest fright he's ever had in
his life. As for that old woman with the umbrella—she'll jump
sky-high. I had to move from my favourite corner because she in-
sisted on poking me with her gamp just to see me jump. *Now*, I'll
see who jumps the highest." Closing his eye again he waited tensely
for the moment of battle, listening with ears pricked to the conversation of the freckled boy and his companion.

"You watch me plant one on his tummy!" freckle-face laughed
as he took aim.

"And you watch me pepper his nose," his companion shouted
as he dived into the bag of peanuts for ammunition.

"What funny boys you are!" the old lady giggled watching
the performance with great amusement.

"Here she goes!" freckle-face shouted as he threw a peanut
straight at Splodge's tummy.

Blinky Bill and Nutsy

Whack! It hit and bounced right off again. Instantly a wild fury came hurtling through the air, over the fence, and plop!— right on top of the old lady, knocking her down amid shrieks and high-pitched screams of terror. She hadn't a chance to jump. In a flash Splodge went bounding down the path. The boys, too overcome with surprise and scarcely realizing what had happened, just stood and stared in amazement. The whole zoo became electrified. Lions roared, monkeys screeched, parrots chattered, the macaws cawed, the kookaburras laughed, and amidst all the noise and confusion keepers came racing down the path to find out what it was all about. Splodge, being a cunning kangaroo, knew this was the opportunity to hide. He made straight for the fence where the undergrowth lay thickest, and, as dusk was falling, it was quite an easy matter to take cover.

Thump! Thump! Thump! He bounded in great leaps, getting nearer and nearer his objective. Round the koala's compound he came like lightning, just catching a glimpse of the little bears out of the corner of his eye.

"Hi! You! Where are you off to? Kicking up the dust like an elephant in a fit!" This cheeky voice came from a koala. You can guess who.

Splodge hesitated a second, then started to hop away again.

"Hi! Hi! Can't you spare a moment? I won't eat you!" the cheeky voice called again. "Come back! I've got something most important to ask you."

Splodge put his back pedal on, and came to a standstill, nervously glancing all round him.

"For goodness' sake keep quiet," he hissed. "Can't you see I'm escaping?"

"Where to?" the cheeky bear asked excitedly, climbing nearer the wire fence that divided him from Splodge.

"That's my business," Splodge replied coldly.

The Escape

"Anyhow, what do you mean by stopping me? You can see I'm in a desperate hurry. Why—I don't even know your name, let alone recognize you. For all I know you might be a spy."

"I'm not! I'm Blinky Bill, Mrs Koala's only son. And what's more I'm going to escape too—seeing that a great big animal like you can do it."

"*Do* be quiet! Hold your tongue!" Splodge growled. "You'll have the keepers down here in a minute if you make such a noise. Can't you whisper?"

"Of course I can, only don't go—please don't go," Blinky pleaded. "Can't you help me to escape too?"

"*And* me!" a voice whispered so softly that it could hardly be heard.

"Oh dear! Why did I stop?" Splodge growled. "Can't a fellow escape from zoos and peanuts without having to take the raggle-taggle with him?"

"Raggle-taggle! Indeed! Do you know I'm Mrs Koala, and come from the same bush as you?" She squeezed her nose against the wire enclosure and looked angrily at Splodge.

"I'm not at all interested," he replied. "And I've no more time to waste. If you had a tail you might have escaped long ago."

"The monkeys have tails and *they* don't escape," Blinky replied quickly. "It must be your brains that helped you. You must be a very clever animal, in fact the cleverest animal in the zoo, because you're the only one that's escaped."

"Piffle!" Splodge said with a sly look at Blinky. "It's peanuts and umbrellas that did it; but I'm not denying that I didn't use what brains I have. . . . Now you've mentioned the matter, I really believe it was my brains."

Splodge licked a paw to hide his feelings.

" 'Course it's your brains!" Blinky replied immediately. "And, if they were extra special brains they'd get to work and think out a way of helping mother and me to escape. But of course, they couldn't do that. They're only kangaroo brains after all."

"Ump!" Splodge grunted. "Well, just to show you what excellent brains I have, I'll find a hiding-place until dark, then, when I'm alone I'll think out a way for you to escape; then I'll come back and tell you—only, mind, it's to be kept a strict secret. If you dare to breathe a word to any one about it I'll leave you to your fate and jump the fence to freedom without even so much as looking your way."

That was the most dreadful thing Splodge could think of at the moment to enforce quietness on his young friend.

"I won't breathe until you come back," Blinky replied, his eyes wide open in excitement.

"In that case you'll die," Mrs Koala interrupted rather tersely. "And we don't want dead bodies around here. At least, I don't!" She snapped her little jaws together and folded her paws across her tummy, just to show the whole world what she really thought of the position.

"Don't get off your bike: I'll pick up your pump!" Blinky retorted cheekily. "We'll never escape if you are going to be haughty."

"Bike!" Mrs Koala said coldly, raising her eyebrows. "Where did you hear that word? Another dreadful expression you've picked up since we've been at the zoo, and for all I know it might be a naughty word." Mrs Koala began to cry.

"Fancy my son calling me a-a-bike!" she sobbed.

"Nonsense!" Splodge interrupted quickly. "He didn't say any such thing. I'd give half my tail at the present moment if I could get hold of a bike."

"Hurry!" Blinky whispered. "Hurry, for goodness' sake. Here comes a keeper."

"I hope he hasn't heard us," Mrs Koala

whispered with fright. "Dear, dear, how dreadful! Hide yourself, Mr Kangaroo, as quickly as you can."

But Mr Kangaroo needed no advice. He was gone like a flash, and as silently as a mouse.

"Serves me right for stopping to gossip," he mumbled to himself. "Those keepers never can mind their own business. My goodness! Where's that fence? If I don't find it in a moment I'll be discovered."

Panting with excitement and fright he stopped for a second to look around. With a peculiar little grunt of satisfaction he noticed the fence showing above the undergrowth only a few yards away. Working his way through lantana bushes he sought the thickest cover, then flopped down on the earth to await results. It was dark by now, so it just needed a little patience on his part to escape the searching keeper. Splodge heard him running down the pathway, then for a few breathless minutes saw him peering into the lantana bushes, carefully pulling aside a few branches and stooping to gaze underneath.

"A pretty sharp fellow!" he grumbled to himself. "Getting away like that, right under my very nose. He can stay there till daylight, because I'm not hunting around in these snake-holes for all the kangaroos in Australia."

"Good shot!" Splodge whispered. "That just suits me nicely."

The keeper gave the lantana bushes a savage kick with his boot to show the contempt he had for that rubbish, then quickly disappeared the way he had come.

"There he goes!" whispered Blinky to his mother as the keeper hurried past the bears' compound, "and he hasn't caught Mr Kangaroo."

"I'd have been surprised if he had!" Mrs Koala exclaimed with satisfaction. "That proves what I've always said to you in the past. A bush animal is a very clever being once he gets among the cover. Keep

quiet, don't clatter about like humans do, and you'll elude them nearly every time."

"What's all the fuss about? You two seem to have a great deal to say to one another." A most inquisitive looking old lady bear eyed Mrs Koala with suspicion. "You're not plotting are you?"

"No! We're just minding our own business," (Mrs Koala glared at the intruder as she snapped out her reply), "and I'd give all I possess for sixpenneth of privacy."

"And I'd give the same," her neighbour remarked angrily. "Ever since you came here with that son of yours, we older bears have had no peace. Why only this morning I was preparing to have my doze and had picked a beautiful branch in the sunlight, when that impudent cub came along and broke a twig right under where I was going to sit. A good thing for him I happened to hear it, otherwise I'd have fallen to the ground and injured myself."

The indignant bear waddled off, ruffled with annoyance.

"Did *you* do that?" Mrs Koala gritted her teeth as she looked at Blinky with a stony stare.

"Yes I did!" he replied. "She's always giving me a nasty nip whenever I go near her, and bumping me if I pass her on the tree. I wanted her to come a cropper."

"*A cropper!*" Mrs Koala repeated the

words slowly, "and what's a c-r-o-p-p-e-r? It is any relation to a hopper?"

"Yes, only it's upside down," Blinky replied quickly. "Instead of jumping up, you turn a somersault and come down with a bump!"

Mrs Koala grabbed her son by the scruff of his neck and shook her paw angrily in his face.

"Don't you *ever* let me see or hear of you making croppers. You bad cub! You dreadful child! I'd no idea what terrible things croppers were."

She gave Blinky a good shaking, making his teeth chatter until he hit back with a naughty kick from a hind leg.

"What did I tell you? Didn't I say he's the worst bear in the zoo!" This remark came from the old bear who had been the cause of the argument. Mrs Koala very wisely said nothing in reply; but grabbing her son by an ear toddled off to the farthest corner of the compound. There she sat deep in thought, one arm round Blinky who, feeling thoroughly ashamed of himself, patted her nose every now and again, just to show how sorry he really was. By now, all the other bears were enjoying supper, nibbling at the gum-leaves and grunting with satisfaction, so that when a large, dark form silently hopped up to the wire fence, no one saw him except the two little bears who were waiting so anxiously for his appearance.

"There he is!" Blinky whispered excitedly, poking his mother in the ribs.

"Sh-h!" she replied. "Keep very quiet. He has seen us."

"Do as I tell you and ask no questions. Don't say a word," Splodge whispered through the wire. "Stay where you are, and when I jump the fence scramble on to my back as quickly as possible. There are spies all around us, I'm sure."

Mrs Koala and Blinky watched with their hearts pounding as though they would burst.

"Get ready! I'm coming!" Splodge whispered, and at the same moment sprang right over the fence of the compound and landed in the middle of the enclosure. He did it very silently and cleverly; but the other koalas in the trees nearly fell from the branches with surprise. Blinky and Mrs Koala made a wild scramble up Splodge's back, gripping his ears and fur, determined not to fall off and waste time.

"Hang on!" Splodge called out, "and look out for a bump."

"Hi! Hi!" Blinky cried as he felt himself being hurled through the air. Then, plonk! down on the ground Splodge landed, his little friends still gripping his fur for dear life. Away he bounded, down the path, and into the lantana bushes again.

"Poosh!" he grunted. "That's over. Now for the big fence and away to freedom."

Back in the compound twenty or more little koalas sat blinking at one another in sheer astonishment. They had nothing to say, as everything happened like a whirlwind and left them stunned with surprise. Even the old lady bear could not believe her eyes, and just sat and stared and stared.

Splodge lost no time in looking about for a suitable place from which to make his big spring over the zoo fence. Blinky too, was busy helping to find a suitable place for escape. He scrambled about on his funny little legs, poking here and there and stumbling over the undergrowth in his hurry. He never was happy on the ground. The tall gumtrees were his element; he climbed those as easily as winking. Suddenly he stopped, clawed a paling in the fence, then forced a paw behind it.

The Escape

"What luck!" he whispered to himself. "It's loose, and Mr Kangaroo can easily rip it down." He hurried to Splodge.

"Quickly! Come here! I've found a way of escape," Blinky said.

He showed Splodge the loose paling, and in a twinkling Splodge had his powerful claws at work, ripping away that paling and the next, until a gap was made that with a tight squeeze he could crawl through.

"So much for fences!" he exclaimed with a grin, while his pretty brown eyes danced with joy.

Mrs Koala and Blinky scrambled through with the greatest of ease.

"Free! Free!" Splodge cried happily. "No more beastly peanuts and umbrellas; but the hills and the trees to roam in for the rest of my life."

"Yes, that's all very well," Mrs Koala replied quietly; "but we've got to get there yet."

"And we can't fly," Blinky interjected.

"We'll do the next best thing to flying. Hop on my back as quickly as you like, and I'll do the rest," Splodge laughed.

"I knew you had brains, Mr Kangaroo," Blinky puffed as he scrambled up his friend's back.

"My name's Splodge!" that gentleman replied with a pleased look on his face.

"What a nice name," Mrs Koala panted as she finally squatted well up on her friend's shoulders.

"Well! I didn't think I'd have company on my journey," Splodge remarked as he made a bound.

"Have you a speedometer?" Mrs Koala asked as they flew along at an incredible speed.

"Not what you'd strictly call one," Splodge replied. "But my tail tells me what speed I'm travelling at. Just now, it is over sixty miles an hour: it becomes slightly cold when I exceed that limit."

"Oh gracious!" Mrs Koala cried. "Please don't go sixty miles an hour. I think speeding's terribly dangerous, especially when you're riding pillion and no brakes."

With a frightful jerk Splodge stopped dead. Mrs Koala screamed, while Blinky laughed.

"How's that for brakes?" Splodge inquired slowly, turning his head to take a look at his passengers.

"Bosker!" Blinky cried, while poor Mrs Koala only gripped tighter than ever the clump of fur that saved her from a nasty spill. She gulped slowly and turned very pale, but said nothing.

"Well, off we go again!" Splodge called. "Grip tightly, because I'm going to make this trip a record. We must reach the bush by daylight unless we want to be recaptured."

It was not an easy matter to go bounding through suburban streets with blinding motor-car lights dazzling his sight, and evading curious policemen at street corners. But no motor-car travelled as quickly as Splodge. If he'd had a tail number-plate no policeman could have seen it in time, as Splodge simply flashed along the roads. Twenty, thirty, forty, fifty miles were behind them in no time. As the night drew on tall gum-trees, wattles and scrub took the place of paved roads and houses. Deeper and deeper into the bush he pressed, slackening his speed only when necessary to avoid a dead tree that straddled his pathway. These he took with long graceful bounds, always to Blinky's delight and Mrs Koala's terror. They saw the trains in the distance rushing along like huge glow-worms, and heard the shrill shriek of their whistles. But all had only one thought in their minds, and that was to get as far into the bushland as possible.

"This is where we branch off!" Splodge cried, slackening his speed. He turned his head from side to side, paused for an instant, stuck his nose out as far as possible, then took a long deep sniff. "We're near the mountains," he said cheerily. "I can smell the mist and creeks."

Mrs Koala began to whimper.

"Take us far, far away in them," she pleaded. "Take us back

"Have you a speedometer?" Mrs Koala asked.

to our old home. Take us away from men and zoos, and where I can make Blinky a good boy again."

"And please Mr Splodge take me where there are slippery gum-trees, the ones all smooth with no branches sticking out for a long way up, so's I can have slides down them in the moonlight."

"Don't do any such thing!" Mrs Koala ordered, changing at once from her sweet kind mood into an angry mother bear. "The very idea! And in your good knickerbockers too! Remember, my lad, I'll have no monkey tricks when we get home. Obedience is what I'll have—or look out!"

"Don't argue on my back!" Splodge exclaimed. "It makes me feel most uncomfortable when you two wriggle and twist about like a couple of snakes."

Harmony reigned again, and no further arguments took place. Splodge, travelling ever ahead into the mountains, only stopped occasionally to drink at clear running streams. Sometimes he dipped his nose in the water without drinking, just to feel the delight of the clear cold stream, just to make sure once more that he was back in the bush. Daylight was heralded by the laugh of the kookaburras and the glorious notes of the magpies. All bird-land awoke with song in its heart. The inhabitants of hundreds of trees and bushes set about the day's task of looking for food, and what a joyous undertaking it was, judging by their song.

"There goes old Wombo!" Blinky cried clapping his paws with glee. "Hullo! Old Wombo, we're back!"

"So I see. So I see." Mr Wombat stood by the side of the track he'd made through the bush on his many excursions when looking for roots and other delicacies to stock his larder with. "My cupboard's empty or I'd ask you to breakfast with me," he said sadly. "I'm getting old and can't go far afield for my tucker nowadays; but I'm glad to see you back. Your home is just as you left it a year ago. Sometimes when I've seen strangers about I've ordered them on to other parts, always hoping you'd come back some day."

"Hullo! Old Wombo, we're back!"

Blinky Bill and Nutsy

"That *is* kind of you, Mr Wombat." Mrs Koala's eyes filled with tears. How dear everything was in the bush, and how wonderful to be home again. "We'll be giving a tree-warming as soon as I have time to settle down, and you must come along, Mr Wombat."

"Gosh! don't miss that!" Blinky interrupted. "I wish I'd brought you back some peanuts."

"They're my favourite dish," Mr Wombat said, licking his whiskers. "Pity you didn't think of it. I hear that a man's growing them over the next hill, and there's acres and acres of them dying to be picked—but my old legs won't carry me there. I smell them all right, and that makes me feel very sad."

"The look of 'em makes me sick!" Splodge said crossly. He'd listened with great patience to this conversation, but could stand it no longer.

"*I'll* get you some peanuts," Blinky said as he looked at Mr Wombat's quivering whiskers.

"Ah, you're a good lad, Blinky. I always did say you were not as bad as they made out."

Old Mr Wombat shuffled off along the track, poking his nose here and there, sniffing for something that may have escaped his notice when last he was that way.

"You'll *not* steal those peanuts!" Mrs Koala said under her breath, as she grabbed her son's ear. "Don't you dare to steal *one* of them."

"No, mother," Blinky said meekly. "It was only the look of old Wombo's whiskers that made me say I would. They twitched so quickly when I said I'd get peanuts."

"Don't look at them again—that's all," Mrs Koala replied shortly.

"Good gracious! Here's our home," she cried almost in the same breath. "Look at it! Look at it! Just the same dear old tree —and not a branch missing."

"What about Splodge? Where's he going to sleep?" Blinky

"Don't be cheeky, and don't ruffle me!"

asked anxiously as he slid off his back and ran to look up into Splodge's face. "Can't you climb our tree?" he asked.

"I'm afraid I can't. But I have cousins who could," Splodge replied. "I'd rather camp on the ground at the foot of the tree."

"You'll stay here and not hop away then?" Blinky asked.

"I'm staying here for the tree-warming—after that I can't promise." Splodge lay on his side idly flicking his tail. "What joy it is to be home again," his eyes said as they roved all over his surroundings. Meanwhile, Mrs Koala was making rather slow progress up the tree, followed by Blinky.

Blinky Bill and Nutsy

"Move on, mother! You're as slow as a snail," Blinky remarked as he climbed up behind his panting parent.

"Don't be cheeky, and don't ruffle me. I'm out of practice since being at the zoo," Mrs Koala replied. "And I believe I've put on weight as well."

"You're t-e-r-r-i-b-l-y fat from here," Blinky remarked.

"That'll do! Not another word!" his mother snapped, as she eventually came to rest on a branch high up from the ground. "We'll curl up for a nap here," she said, settling down in the comfy fork of the branch.

"But I don't want to go to sleep," Blinky protested.

"Oh! bother you—run away and let me have forty winks. My patience is frayed." Mrs Koala just nodded her sleepy old head and fell into slumberland, too happy to worry over her naughty son for once. Needless to say he took full advantage of this opportunity to explore his old home—with the most startling results.

"Oh! bother you—run away."

Chapter 2.
THE TREE WARMING.

AS Blinky Bill climbed higher up the tree his sharp little eyes noticed that gum-leaves had been picked and chewed very recently from the nearest limbs.

"That's funny!" he murmured to himself. "Someone's been here stealing our supper. If it's old Mrs Grunty I'll have something very nasty to say to her. The cheek of her! Our very own tree, and our very own leaves!" He became quite angry the more he discovered the loss of the leaves.

"It's time we had a policeman in this bush. For two pins I'd turn policeman myself. Now I come to think of it that's what I *will* do!" Suddenly a twig snapped. Blinky looked up like a flash; but there was no one to be seen.

"Come out of it, you stealer!" he shouted. Silence as deep as the sea greeted his command.

"Come out of it or I'll eat you to death!" he shouted at the top of his voice.

COME TO THE
TREE WARM-
ING

Blinky Bill and Nutsy

"Oh! don't do that! *Please* don't do that! I didn't mean to steal leaves. I just wanted to taste them," a frightened little voice replied.

"Are you a girl?" Blinky roared, angrier than ever. " 'Cause if you are you'll be dead in a minute. I *hate* girls."

"I'm not a girl. It's only my dress that makes me look like one," the little voice replied.

"Show yourself at once! Do you think a fellow can hunt round this tree for hours looking for robbers?" Blinky shouted.

"Here I am—*please* don't eat me," and the sweetest little girl koala poked her head around the tree not two yards away from where Blinky stood.

"Hum-n!" he grunted. "You're a girl. I can tell by the silly way you're looking at me; besides, you're too clean for a proper boy."

"I'm a boy!" the little bear said defiantly, stamping a tiny foot.

"Do-you-wash-behind-your-EARS?" Blinky asked in a slow cold voice, trying to freeze his little visitor with a glare that would have made any bear shudder.

"Of course I do!" the little koala replied indignantly.

"Then that settles it! You're a girl. No proper boy washes behind his ears. Come out here while I take you in charge! Don't you know I'm a policeman and this is *my* tree?" Blinky advanced towards the little bear who stood too frightened to move an inch.

"Don't kill me, will you?" she pleaded.

"I'll see about that later on. What's your name?" Blinky shouted, at the same time grabbing the little bear by the ear.

"My name's Nutsy," she cried, tears trickling down her funny little nose. "I'm an orphan."

"An *orphan!* What's that?" Blinky demanded.

"I've no mother or father," Nutsy wailed, "and no brothers or sisters. There's only me."

"Well—you'll have to be locked up just the same, because the

"Do you wash behind your ears?" Blinky asked.

law says 'all animals, specially orphans, mustn't steal'." Blinky gave her ear a pull.

"Stop it or I'll bite you!" Nutsy exclaimed, shrieking at the top of her voice.

Mrs Koala awoke, rubbed her eyes and listened. "What is that bad boy up to now?" she sighed. "Blinky! Come down here immediately." She called her son with a decidedly angry voice.

"I can't!" he replied, shouting. "I've found an orphan and she won't come."

"An orphan!" Mrs Koala repeated loudly. "How did an orphan get in our tree? That's that old Mrs Grunty! She's been stealing our leaves, and cooking them—of all things. Well, she won't get her orphan back. I'll keep it for the tree-warming. It'll be very useful to make a cup of tea in. Bring it down to me, Blinky. Has it any holes in it? Are they stuffed up with rag? Because if there are holes and rag I won't use it."

"It's an *orphan*—not a saucepan," Blinky replied, shouting loudly.

"What's the difference?" Mrs Koala called.

"It hasn't a mother or father," Blinky shouted.

"No orphans have," Mrs Koala replied. "Has it a handle?"

"No! It's got ears and eyes and it bites," Blinky answered.

"Good gracious! Hold it until I come up and have a look," Mrs Koala cried excitedly, scrambling up the tree as fast as her old legs would go. "Dear, dear," she panted.

212

The Tree Warming

"What a strange thing an orphan is. I've never seen one before."

Grunting and puffing she reached the bough where Blinky and Nutsy stood. Taking one look at Nutsy she raised her paws in surprise and delight.

"*That* an orphan! What nonsense! Why, it's a little girl. The dear little thing! Come here darling while I have a look at you. And tell old Mrs Koala you name."

"She can't. She's under arrest," Blinky roared.

"Whatever for?" Mrs Koala inquired. "And who's going to arrest her?"

"*I* am!" Blinky replied, throwing out his chest. "She's been stealing our leaves, so I've turned into a policeman and I'm going to lock her up."

"I'll box your ears if you do any such thing," Mrs Koala said stoutly. "And don't talk rubbish to me. A policeman indeed! You're my son. If there's any locking up to be done, I'll do it and you'll be the first to taste it if you're not careful."

"Gosh! Aren't mothers awful?" Blinky sighed. "Can't even be a policeman but what she spoils it. Go on, sweet little darling; go to the kind lady." These last words he addressed to Nutsy, giving her a sly pinch as he pushed her forward. "I'll make her sorry for being a girl," Blinky muttered under his breath.

"Well, if this isn't a surprise!" Mrs Koala said, smiling all over her face, and gently taking Nutsy's paw. "Won't Mrs Grunty be jealous? And I've always wanted a little girl."

"Don't tell stories, mother!" Blinky said angrily. "You've always said you're glad I'm a boy, and you wouldn't have *ten* girls if they were given you."

"How stupid of me! I must have had a bad headache when I said that," Mrs Koala replied. "Here—Blinky, help me to get this little girl down the tree."

"I don't want him—he pinches."

Blinky Bill and Nutsy

Nutsy drew nearer Mrs Koala. "And anyway I can climb up and down by myself."

"That's wonderful!" Mrs Koala replied. "We'll all go down and have some supper."

"I can't come!" Blinky said, staring at Nutsy with looks of contempt.

"Why not?" Mrs Koala asked.

"I'm on my beat!" Blinky answered.

"Come down here and have your supper or I'll be on the beat!" Mrs Koala ordered sternly. "And put this policeman business out of your head at once. The idea of living in a tree with a policeman!" Mrs Koala mumbled away to herself. She was very annoyed.

Once down on the cosy corner of the gum-tree that she liked so much her ruffled temper subsided. She asked Nutsy where she came from and how she came to be in the tree. "You must have a mother and father somewhere, child," she said, patting Nutsy's soft ears.

"No! I just woke up one day and found myself in this tree," Nutsy replied. And no further questions of Mrs Koala's produced a different answer.

"I can't come!"

214

"*That* an orphan! What nonsense! Why, it's a little girl."

"Oh well, from now on, you'll live with Blinky and me. I'll be delighted to have a little daughter, as I've been feeling lately I'd like to twist a little girl's curls up every night in gum-leaves. I can't do that with a boy—specially Blinky. There's no knowing what he'd do next if I started." Mrs Koala heaved a big sigh of contentment.

Together the three bears ate their supper, chattering and grunting with the pure joy of living. Out of the corner of her eye Mrs Koala noticed Blinky pass Nutsy several young juicy leaves—not once, but on several occasions. Smiling to herself she wisely said nothing.

"We'd better write out an invitation to the tree-warming," Mrs Koala said when they had finished their meal.

"Don't ask Mrs Grunty," Blinky said instantly. "She'll spoil everything."

"We can't ignore her like that. It would be so rude," Mrs Koala replied. "But we needn't make a fuss of her."

"Well, don't kiss her when she comes," Blinky said, looking very glum. "When you kissed her, before we went to the zoo, I always used to notice she thought that was the sign to gobble up all the best leaves and give you bad advice about me."

"I never thought of that, let alone noticed it," Mrs Koala replied. "She always had such a lot to say that my head would become a whirlwind in no time —being a simple body. However, let's get that invitation printed."

"I'll do it!" Blinky exclaimed, "and we'll stick it on the bottom of the tree."

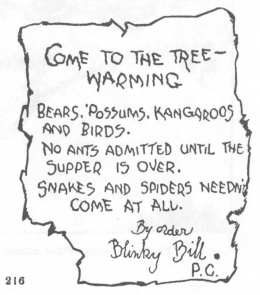

COME TO THE TREE-
WARMING

BEARS, 'POSSUMS, KANGAROOS
AND BIRDS.

NO ANTS ADMITTED UNTIL THE
SUPPER IS OVER.

SNAKES AND SPIDERS NEEDN'T
COME AT ALL.

By order
Blinky Bill.
P.C.

The Tree Warming

Later in the evening three little bears stuck a notice up on the tree.

"What's the P.C. for?" Splodge inquired as he gazed at the notice.

"Possum's Companion," Blinky replied loudly. Then drawing Splodge aside whispered in his ear: "It means Police Constable. But don't you say a word to mother. She won't let me be a butcher man or anything I want to be."

"Well, I'm glad we're to have a P.C. because some of the kangaroos round here want sending about their business. Hanging about gum-trees all night long and frightening respectable lady wallabies out of their skins. It's a scandal!" Splodge thumped his tail on the ground. "For a few bushels of peas, I'd become a policeman myself!"

"No you won't!" Blinky said crossly. "There's only work for one policeman here, and I thought of it first, so it's mine."

"Oh, I don't want the job really," Splodge said, chewing a straw thoughtfully. "You'll have your work cut out if you have to run Mrs Snake in, or a couple of dozen of those Bull-jo ants when they become obnoxious. And there's also the bees. I remember seeing a whole colony drunk one day. Been stealing the sugar from Farmer Scratchet's home brew. How would you like to arrest *them* for disorderly conduct?"

That certainly made Blinky think.

"Well, I'll make you my assistant if you like," Blinky said condescendingly.

"That'll do me!" Splodge replied, "as long as I can do a bit of kicking when it's required. Now, I can sign letters after my name. Mr Splodge—Police Assistant. That's fine!"

"It's far too long," Blinky interrupted. "You'll sign yourself like this"—picking up a twig he scratched on the tree:

SPLODGE, ASS.

Splodge examined it closely.

"You don't mean to be rude or clever do you?" he asked uncomfortably.

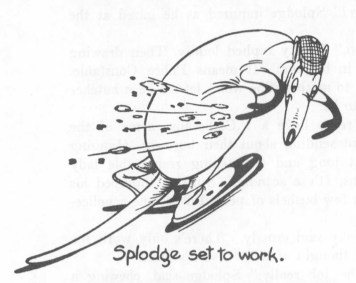

Splodge set to work.

"Of course not!" Blinky replied. "Can't you see that's short for assistant?"

"Oh! very well," Splodge answered, still looking doubtfully at the signature. "Perhaps I'm over self-conscious."

"Stop talking so much and come and help me to prepare the tree-warming," Mrs Koala interrupted. "Talk about women gossiping——"

"Tut! Tut!" Splodge replied. "Tell me what to do and I'll get to work."

"There's a patch to be cleared round the foot of the tree to start with," Mrs Koala remarked, "and the supper to collect."

"I'll get the gum-nuts!" Nutsy said, half-way up the tree.

"Blinky—you gather some of the best leaves off the tree—only don't take the *very* best—and I'll see what I can collect."

Mrs Koala padded away through the bushes. Splodge set to work with a will. He scratched all the dead leaves and rubbish away from the foot of the tree, and scraped the lichen off a large flat rock with his sharp nails, preparing it for the table. He carried small bunches of wild berries in his mouth, laying them across the table. Nutsy threw from the branches overhead, dozens of gum-nuts, and Blinky sent down a shower of leaves. Certainly not the *very* best, as some had clearly been well nibbled beforehand. Mrs Koala returned, delighted with her find: an armful of watercress.

Blinky and Nutsy scuttled down the tree to see the treasure.

"You don't mean to be rude or clever do you?" Splodge asked uncomfortably.

"Don't touch it!" Mrs Koala commanded. "It will probably kill you if you eat it. You know, as I've often told you, only special gum-leaves are for koalas. This is for Splodge."

"Thanks awfully!" Splodge said. "Do you mind if I have a taste now?" He licked his lips at the very thought of that delicious meal.

"Well—well—I'd rather you waited for the party," Mrs Koala replied. "We want to make the food look as much as possible."

"Quite so. Quite so," Splodge replied, licking his lips all the more.

"What do you think? I met Mrs Froggles down at the creek. She had her family of taddies with her, and fine lads they are too!" Mrs Koala carefully spread her watercress on the ground, giving Splodge a doubtful look at the same time.

"You didn't ask Mrs Froggles and the tads to the party, did you, mother?" Blinky inquired.

"Yes. The dear thing's coming. And how excited she was at the thought of it," Mrs Koala replied.

"Oh bother! Now I'll have to catch spiders and flies," Blinky growled, "and I s'pose the tads only eat mossies."

"No. She's going to bring her own flies," Mrs Koala explained. "I told her we usually threw any flies or spiders away that we found on the tree."

"Here's a special gum-nut for you, Mrs Koala," Nutsy said as she handed out an extra large nut from her pocket.

"Such unselfishness I've never seen before," Mrs Koala said as she took the nut.

"That's what I hate about girls," Blinky whispered to Splodge. "Always trying to be pets!"

"Men haven't time to bother about that," Splodge replied— "specially policemen. By the way, Blinky, where's your baton?"

"That's what I hate about girls."

The Tree Warming

"Should I have one? And what is a baton?" Blinky asked.

"It's a piece of wood, that dangles from your belt. All real policemen carry one. It's for banging people on the head who don't behave." Splodge explained.

"Gee! I'll have to have one," Blinky replied thoughtfully.

"Leave it to your assistant. He'll see to that!" Splodge announced, bounding away into the bush.

"He's a real fellar!" Blinky said to himself.

"Come children, we'll wait up in the tree until the guests arrive," Mrs Koala said as she placed the last gum-leaf on the table. So up the tree they all climbed, and sat waiting anxiously for the first visitor to appear. Who should it be but old Wombo!

"Good night Wombo!" Blinky called out. "Read the notice."

Mr Wombat being near-sighted had to screw his old eyes right up against the notice to read.

"Are there any peanuts?" he asked immediately.

"No! But there are gum-nuts!" Nutsy called out.

"And watercress!" Blinky shouted.

"*Watercress!*" Old Wombo sprang at the table.

"Leave it alone! Leave it alone!" Mrs Koala screamed. "It's not supper time yet." But old Wombo already had a mouthful of the luscious green.

"Put it back!" Blinky shouted. Mrs Koala was already half-way down the tree to rescue her precious dainty. "How rude of you!" she said angrily. "Eating up our party before the guests arrive."

"I thought I was to have supper," old Wombo said in a surprised voice. "And it was so nice."

"Oh well—as you're very old I'll overlook it this time," Mrs Koala said kindly. "But *please* don't eat any more."

"Funny sort of a party," old Wombo growled to himself as he sat on the ground to wait.

The next visitor to appear was Mrs Wallaby. She carried a baby in her pouch.

Blinky Bill and Nutsy

"I'm glad to hear you're back, Mrs Koala," she said with a sweet smile.

"We're giving a tree-warming," Mrs Koala replied. "Do stay and have some supper."

By this time the news of the great event had been flashed through the bush, and animals and birds arrived in dozens—Mr and Mrs Possum, several families of wallabies, the kangaroos of course, flying foxes, rabbits, weasels, mice and bush rats, kookaburras and willy wagtails. Away in a tree all by himself sat Mr Owl, looking at everything and every one in silence.

"I didn't expect so many friends," Mrs Koala said nervously. "I'm afraid we won't have enough to eat, and I've no grubs for the birds."

"We'll all bring our own!" several birds called, and flew off to gather their supper.

"*I'm going to eat that watercress,*" old Wombo growled to himself.

Meanwhile Splodge had returned and fastened a knotty stick to Blinky's belt. "Just to keep order in case it's needed," he explained

When the supper commenced, Nutsy helped Mrs Koala by handing round the nuts. The guests were at their gayest, calling and squeaking at the fun of it all. In the excitement of chatter and hopping, no one noticed old Wombo silently gobbling all the watercress round at the back of the tree. He munched with delight; then, when he had finished, took a last look at the visitors, turned, and slowly ambled home

"Look at the ants!" someone cried. Immediately there was confusion. "Where? Where?" they shouted. Blinky grabbed his baton and rushed in the direction where all the guests pointed.

Dozens and dozens, in fact hundreds of ants stood on tiptoe, surveying the scene. Their antennae waved with excitement as they thought of the grubs

The Tree Warming

and flies that could easily be theirs when they decided to advance.

"Hey! you fellows!" Blinky called out, swinging his baton, "Get back to your dug-outs."

The ants took no notice whatever.

"Don't-you-know-we've-an-ant-eater-with-us?" he asked deliberately, "and he'll eat you all in one swallow." As he delivered this dreadful news he banged his baton down on the ground with a—crash!

Quicker than that every ant had vanished.

"That scared them!" Blinky chuckled and walked back to the party, feeling very proud of himself; but no sooner was he there than a piteous cry went up.

"Quickly! Quickly! He's choking!" Poor Mrs Froggles was beside herself with fright. She hopped all over the place, on the table, over the guests' heads, and right into Mrs Kangaroo's pouch. All in mistake of course.

"Get out! Get out!" Mrs Kangaroo screamed, as she took a leap over Mr Pelican's head. Out flopped Mrs Froggles, her eyes, that usually popped, now seemed to be almost out of her head.

"Save him! Save him!" she croaked louder than ever.

"What's the matter?" every one asked in chorus.

"My poor child—my eldest taddy—he's choking. A grub's stuck in his throat," Mrs Froggles croaked between hops.

Nutsy rushed to the rescue. Grabbing Freddie Taddy who was black in the face, she turned him upside down and shook him violently.

"Hey! you fellows!"

Blinky Bill and Nutsy

"You greedy little wriggler!" she scolded, shaking all the harder.

"Thump him on the back!" someone called.

Nutsy did so, and out popped a grub almost as large as Freddie Taddy himself, while he lay on the ground gasping for breath.

"Throw some water over him," Mrs Magpie advised. But there was no water near.

"I'll make him come to life in a second," a nasty crawly voice remarked, "or it's supper for me, and no mistake."

With a horrified cry every one ran, for there lay Mr Carpet Snake eyeing poor little Freddie with a cruel look in his eyes. How *he* came to the party unnoticed no one ever knew.

Mrs Froggles gave one ear-splitting croak and fainted.

"Get your baton out!" Splodge called to Blinky. Scarcely were the words out, when Blinky rushed to the rescue. Waving his baton over his head and calling out at the top of his voice, he made a vicious blow at Mr Carpet Snake. He missed. A groan went up from the excited spectators and all kinds of advice was shouted at him.

Mr Snake reared his head and prepared to spring. Mrs Koala and Nutsy screamed. Blinky was ready to strike again, when something came flashing through the air, struck Mr Carpet Snake on the head, and there stood Splodge.

"That was a good kick!" he calmly remarked, as he looked at the body of the dead snake.

Every one rushed to congratulate him, patted him on the back and nose, until Splodge reminded them that poor little Freddie Taddy was still on the ground. He was saved and, after some gentle stroking, soon recovered. Mrs Froggles decided to go home at once, as sixty children were too many to watch at one time. So calling her taddies to her side, she ordered them to hop on her back and away she went, croaking loudly.

The party ended by those who were able to climb or fly inspecting the old gum-tree and wishing its occupants the best of luck.

"You greedy little wriggler!" she scolded, shaking all the harder.

Blinky Bill and Nutsy

When all was silent, and three little bears lay cuddled together in sweet sleep, an army of ants dined on Mr Carpet Snake. Such a supper they'd not had for a long time. And, after it, a constant stream of black and brown bodies carried little pieces of Mr Snake down to their home underneath the ground.

All day long the three bears slept. Mrs Koala snored a great deal; once she even woke herself up with the noise. Turning to look at Blinky whom she was sure had made the noise, she sighed and murmured:

"Poor little chap—he has adenoids very badly. I'll have to see Dr Owl about it." Then, snuggling down again, she fell asleep once more.

At dusk, when the bears were awake, and busily collecting their supper, Mrs Grunty came along. She was alone, having left Snubby, her son, at home; for "Goodness knows what mischief that bad boy Blinky will put in his mind after being in the zoo," she said.

"*Nice* goings on in the tree last night!" she exclaimed, before she'd even said "How do you do," or any other polite greeting to her friend who had been absent for so long.

"Oh, how are you? I'm very pleased to see you again, Mrs Grunty," Mrs Koala said sweetly.

"*Nice* goings on!" Mrs Grunty repeated. "We'll have our bush talked about next. In fact, I wouldn't be surprised to hear you were letting the gum-tree out in flats."

"Nice goings on!"

"You seem all worked up," Mrs Koala replied coldly. "Can't a widow bear give a tree-warming if she wants to?"

"Such city notions!" Mrs Grunty scoffed. "And I was not invited."

"*Every one* was invited," Mrs Koala replied. "Didn't you read the notice?"

The Tree Warming

"*Me* read the notice!" Mrs Grunty sniffed. "As if I'd have time to go round the bush reading notices. I was far too busy turning the heel of Snubby's new winter socks."

"Dear, dear, I'm sorry," Mrs Koala said meekly. "I know how busy children keep one."

"Especially one like you've got," Mrs Grunty snapped.

"She'll be sorry for saying that!" Blinky exclaimed from behind the tree where he and Nutsy were hiding. "She's always poking about and saying 'noxious, nauseous, nasty things. And as for her Snubby—he's a *twink!*"

"What's that?" Nutsy whispered.

"Something awful and dreadful," Blinky replied, while Nutsy looked at him in wonder.

"How shocking!" she said in a whisper.

"Yes! and I'll be just as pleased, Mrs Koala, if you tell that Blinky of yours to keep away from our tree." Mrs Grunty flung these words at her friend as she prepared to depart.

"Pass me that stick!" Blinky ordered Nutsy.

"Good night, madam!" Mrs Grunty said, just as Blinky poked the stick right in front of her feet. She tripped, stumbled and fell, wildly clutching at a branch to save her fall, then turning a somersault landed on the limb of the tree immediately below.

"She's come a cropper!" Blinky shouted at the top of his voice, while Mrs Grunty roared

she tripped, stumbled AND FELL.

with temper. To make matters fifty times worse, Nutsy threw down
a pawful of gum-nuts right on top of Mrs Grunty.

"I'll see the policeman about this! I hear we've got a policeman in the bush now! I'll have you punished. I'll have you *exported!*"
Mrs Grunty shouted as she regained her feet and climbed down
the tree.

"Who threw those nuts?" Mrs Koala demanded. "And who made
the cropper?" She waggled her paw at the two culprits.

"*I* made the cropper," Blinky said nudging Nutsy.

"And *I* threw the nuts," his little companion whispered, looking
very ashamed of herself.

"A nice hotch-potch!" Mrs Koala growled. "All the same I'm
glad—perhaps she'll mind her own business after this."

"I'm sure she will," Nutsy said meekly, very relieved to find
Mrs Koala's temper had subsided so quickly.

Mrs Grunty growled all the way home.

"There'll be no peace now!" she said aloud. "I've a good mind
to move. If I stay here my Snubby's bound to get into trouble with
that lad. My word! he's an outlaw."

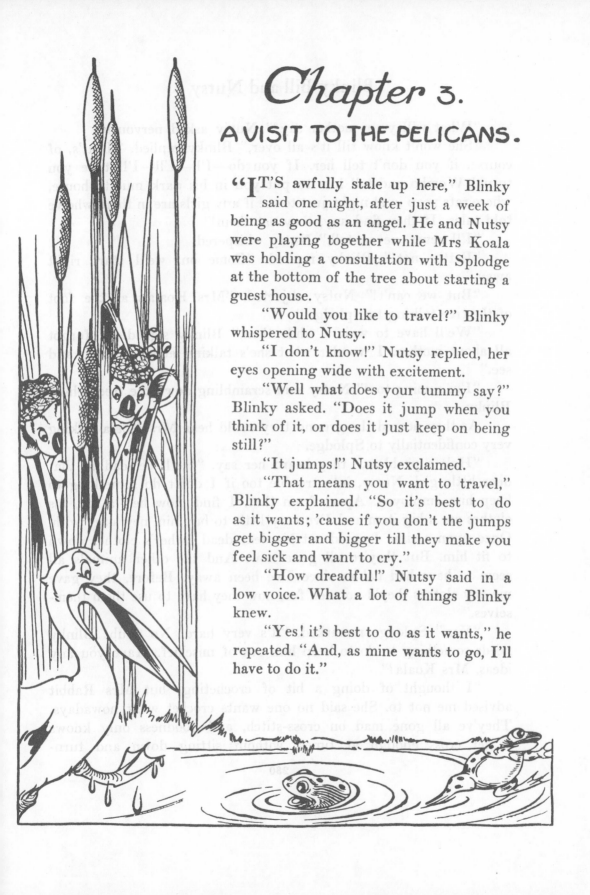

Chapter 3.

A VISIT TO THE PELICANS.

"IT'S awfully stale up here," Blinky said one night, after just a week of being as good as an angel. He and Nutsy were playing together while Mrs Koala was holding a consultation with Splodge at the bottom of the tree about starting a guest house.

"Would you like to travel?" Blinky whispered to Nutsy.

"I don't know!" Nutsy replied, her eyes opening wide with excitement.

"Well what does your tummy say?" Blinky asked. "Does it jump when you think of it, or does it just keep on being still?"

"It jumps!" Nutsy exclaimed.

"That means you want to travel," Blinky explained. "So it's best to do as it wants; 'cause if you don't the jumps get bigger and bigger till they make you feel sick and want to cry."

"How dreadful!" Nutsy said in a low voice. What a lot of things Blinky knew.

"Yes! it's best to do as it wants," he repeated. "And, as mine wants to go, I'll have to do it."

Blinky Bill and Nutsy

"What will your mother say?" Nutsy asked nervously.

"She won't know till it's all over," Blinky replied. "That's, of course, if you don't tell her. If you do—I'll—I'll—I'll take you to old Wombo and tell him to put you in his dark muddy house, where rats peep in at night just to see if any girls are in there who've told tales. If they find any, they eat them!"

"I'll never, never, tell," Nutsy whispered.

"Better not!" Blinky replied. "Come on, we'll start right away."

"But we can't!" Nutsy objected. "Mrs Koala's at the foot of the tree talking to Splodge."

"We'll have to wait a while then," Blinky sighed. "I forgot all about mother. I wonder what she's talking about. I'll go and see."

"I'm coming too!" Nutsy said scrambling down the tree behind Blinky.

As they neared the ground they could hear Mrs Koala talking very confidentially to Splodge.

"He's a problem," they heard her say. "He'll be leading that dear little girl, Nutsy, into trouble too if I don't do something to keep him employed. Apart from that, I find, now he's a lad, his clothes are a big item and I've very little to buy him new ones with. Once upon a time I could cut his dear dead father's clothes down to fit him. But they're all gone now. And the other animals all seem to have had babies since I've been away. Before, they gave me any clothes they'd no need for, now they have to use them themselves."

"Yes," Splodge remarked, "it's very hard. No doubt Blinky needs something to do to keep him out of mischief. Have you any ideas, Mrs Koala?"

"I thought of doing a bit of crocheting; but Mrs Rabbit advised me not to. She said no one wants crochet work nowadays. They've all gone mad on cross-stitch, and goodness only knows I get cross enough at times, without sitting down and turning it into doilies and mats," Mrs Koala said with a deep sigh.

"Quite right!" Blinky murmured to Nutsy.

"I'm ambitious, you know, Mr Splodge," Mrs Koala continued. "Since my visit to the zoo and seeing with my own eyes the quantity of food the animals over there, *stuffed*, positively *stuffed* into themselves, especially the elephants and kangaroos——"

"Pardon!" Splodge exclaimed placing his paw behind one ear as if to hear better.

"Oh! I didn't mean to be rude," Mrs Koala explained, "or personal. I always noticed *you* never gobbled. In fact *I* thought what a gentleman you were, compared to the rest."

"Quite so. Quite so," Splodge returned. "But what's that got to do with your ideas, Mrs Koala?"

"Simply this—as I was saying, when I saw those animals eating so much, I thought some day if ever I escaped from the zoo I'd start a guest house! Now what do you think of that?" Mrs Koala beamed all over her face.

"Capital idea!" Splodge announced. "Of course you'll want a manger."

Splodge flung out his paws in a hopeless gesture.

A Visit to the Pelicans

"What for?" Mrs Koala exclaimed.

"Well, for instance, say Mr Fox came along and wanted board and residence for the night, and then tried to steal silently away without paying—and he's a sly fellow, mark my words, a sly, cunning fellow—what would you do then, Mrs Koala?"

Splodge flung out his paws in a hopeless gesture.

"It *would* be awkward. I never thought of that happening," Mrs Koala replied.

"And then there are the possums. I've great regard for them, and I'm not suggesting for one moment they'd do such a thing. But what if one got to your potato bin—and, mind you, I wouldn't trust them for a second where potatoes are concerned—what would you do then?"

Again Splodge flung out his paws, and stared with a sorrowful look on his face, while poor Mrs Koala felt her hopes suddenly dashed to the ground.

"Then again," Splodge continued, "there are the rabbits to think of. You know me well enough, Mrs Koala, to realize I'd think badly of no one; but 'pon my soul those rabbits need watching with ten pairs of eyes. Just imagine—you having gone to all the trouble of making a delicious watercress salad"—(here Splodge licked his lips)—"*Just imagine* your feelings if, when you went to put it on the table, you found it had gone, that some sly, quiet-stepping animal had actually pinched it while your back was turned. What would you do then?"

"It couldn't hurt a salad very much if it *was* pinched," Mrs Koala replied. "Only a few leaves bruised."

"I should have said *purloined*," Splodge returned. "In other words, *stolen*; but I'm not saying the rabbits would do such a dastardly thing, I'm only s'posing."

"I wish you would not use such big words," Mrs Koala said in a meek voice. "I'm only a plain body and it takes very little to start my headaches."

"Sorry, I didn't mean to bamboozle you," Splodge said kindly. "But what would you do if such things happened? And they are likely to happen to any widow."

"How dreadful!" Mrs Koala managed to say. Really, she was almost speechless.

"But there's no need to worry!" Splodge laughed, hopping around in great bounds, until Mrs Koala muttered to herself, "He's daft!"

"No need to worry a teeny, weeny bit!" Splodge laughed again. "A manager will see to all that. He'll see that no one steals things."

"Will he really?" Mrs Koala exclaimed with joy. But her face fell almost immediately. "Where can I find a manager?" she asked looking all round. "Do you think old Mr Wombat would do?"

"He!" Splodge yelled and hopped with surprise. "Old Wombo a manager! Why, you'd have nothing left in your larder after one night. Nothing!"

" Why, here! right here! "

"Well what *am* I to do? Where can I find a manager?" Poor Mrs Koala was nearly in tears.

"Why, here!" Splodge shouted, patting himself on the chest.

"Oh! *You* will be so kind as to be the manager?" Mrs Koala asked joyfully.

"'Course I will," Splodge replied. "With my experience and worldly knowledge I'll see that even a mouse gets away with nothing. Tush! Just let me catch them trying."

"That's a load off my mind," Mrs Koala sighed.

"We'll shake paws on the agreement," Splodge replied holding out a paw to Mrs Koala who solemnly took it, and both shook with a grunt.

"That's done it!" Blinky whispered to Nutsy. "A guest house of all things! Rabbits and rats in the best beds, and snails and spiders using the bathroom. I'm off! And I'm going in a minute too."

"I don't think I'd like living in a guest house either," Nutsy remarked.

"'Course you wouldn't!" Blinky exclaimed. "You'd be made a waitress. And you'd have to carry plates of soup up and down the tree all day long, and peel potatoes and onions till your eyes drowned."

"And what would you do?" Nutsy asked, not very impressed with this horrible picture.

"Me? Oh, I suppose I'd just ring the dinner-bell and sit down to eat with the guests and laugh and tell them my 'speriences," Blinky said with a bored look on his face.

"Indeed you wouldn't!" Nutsy replied indignantly. "You'd have to clean Mr Centipede's boots every morning, and help your mother to make stews and stews, and you'd have to eat *porridge*, lumps and all!"

"'Ndeed I won't—and wouldn't —and *shan't!*" Blinky replied, and started to scramble through the thick bracken fern that grew at the

"You'd be made a waitress."

foot of the tree. Nutsy hurried after him calling out in a whisper:
"Wait on! Wait on! I'm coming."

Mrs Koala and her manager were too busy to notice what was happening just round the gum-tree.

Blinky pushed straight ahead, while Nutsy stumbled and struggled to catch up with him.

"Where are we going?" Nutsy panted as she came up to his side.

"*I'm* going to see the pelicans," Blinky announced.

"*I'm* coming too," Nutsy replied.

"Gosh! Can't you see you're in the way?" Blinky asked crossly. "Can't a fellow go pelicanning by himself?"

"I might be useful," Nutsy replied. "Anyhow I'm coming." She tossed her little head in the air and pushing past Blinky took the lead.

"Stand back! Halt! In the name of the policeman!" Blinky shouted, scarlet with rage. (How dare a girl be so rude to him!)

"I won't stand back; and I won't halt; and you're not a policeman!" Nutsy called back, still scrambling ahead.

"You're arrested!" Blinky shouted. "Stop!"

"Here! Here! What's all the noise about?" A stern voice demanded, frightening the two little koalas almost out of their skins. There, right in front of them, stood Wally Wombat junior. He was old Wombo's great great grandson, and very like his great great grandfather he was. Had the same small eyes, wide brow, and that arrogant air of his ancestor.

236

A Visit to the Pelicans

"Oh, it's you, Wallo!" Blinky gasped with relief. "My word, you *did* give me a fright."

"And who told you to call me Wallo?" Mr Wombat junior asked, looking very displeased. "I'm *Walter* Wombat—Wally to only my oldest acquaintances. Remember that!"

"He's snaky!" Nutsy whispered to Blinky. "Be polite or he might kill us."

"Where are you going?" Mr Walter Wombat asked.

"To see my great great grandmother," Blinky replied, never blinking an eyelid.

"Is she ill?" Walter inquired.

"Terribly ill. If we don't get there very soon she'll be dead."

"Oh well, under those circumstances I'll let you pass," Walter declared. "Only remember, next time you meet me, salute and say: 'Good morning, Your Eminence. How goes it?' Then pass on."

"Certainly, Wallo."

"What's that?" Mr Walter Wombat roared.

"I didn't say a word," Blinky replied, shaking with fear.

"Keep on that way, my young man, and some day you'll be as great a fellow as I am." Mr Walter Wombat gave his walking-stick a swish and passed on.

"How would you like to have to carry his shaving-water to *him* every morning at the guest house?" Nutsy asked mockingly.

"I'd put gum in it so's it would gum up all his whispers," Blinky replied coldly.

Nutsy remained silent after this remark, and found herself once more padding behind Blinky. He had taken the opportunity to get in the lead again, and things went along much more smoothly. Presently, to Blinky's surprise, he found himself walking along paw-in-paw with Nutsy as the journey progressed.

"How far is it to the pelicans' place?" Nutsy inquired.

237

Blinky Bill and Nutsy

"A long way off. Over two hills and then down along the swamp until we come to the lake," Blinky answered.

"How do you know?" Nutsy asked.

"I saw it when we were coming back from the zoo," Blinky replied, "and I counted all the hills home from that place.

"What's that noise?" he asked suddenly. "Listen! Someone is coming."

"Hide," Nutsy whispered.

Together they scuttled under the bushes and crouched silently peeping through the leaves.

"Dear, dear! This is dreadful—terrible—shocking," the voice was saying, as its owner pit-a-pattered nearer and nearer.

"I wonder what's the matter?" Nutsy asked in a whisper.

"Keep quiet," Blinky said, giving her a pinch.

"She'll die, I'm sure, if I don't get help," the voice was saying, "and I'll never have such a kind friend again." Here the poor animal started to sob.

Blinky and Nutsy, peering from their hiding-place, saw Mrs Field Mouse wiping her eyes with the corner of her apron. Over her arm she carried a basket almost as large as herself, and in it was a bottle almost as large as the basket.

Blinky gave a cough.

Mrs Field Mouse sprang in the air. "Good gracious!" she cried. "Are there robbers or cats about?"

"It's only us, Mrs Field Mouse. Don't be afraid," Nutsy called, scrambling through the bushes to her side. "What is the matter? You seem to be in trouble."

"Oh, my dear, such a dreadful thing has happened! I don't know what to do," Mrs Field Mouse sobbed. "My very, very best friend is terribly sick, and I've run and run for miles to get a bottle of eucalyptus oil from Dr Owl. And now I don't know how I'm going to rub it on her chest. What *will* I do?" She sniffed back her tears and wiped her whiskers with a tiny paw.

"Why! We'll come and help you. Won't we, Blinky?" Nutsy

"And who told you to call me Wallo?" Mr Wombat junior asked. "I'm
Walter Wombat."

turned to her companion who looked sorrowfully at the poor distressed little mouse.

"Only too pleased," Blinky replied. "Let me carry your basket, Mrs Field Mouse."

"How lucky I am to meet you," Mrs Field Mouse said as she dabbed her eyes.

"Is your friend terribly, terribly sick?" Nutsy asked sympathetically as they started to walk along.

"She's got whooping-cough most dreadfully," Mrs Field Mouse replied. "All last night I sat beside her; listening to her whoops. And the sneezing—it was dreadful too. So this morning I set out to see Dr Owl and tell him all about it. I've been away all day, and I've run for miles. Oh dear! I hope we're in time to save her."

"What did Dr Owl say?" Nutsy asked.

"He told me to put the patient in a mustard bath and poultice her chest and back," Mrs Field Mouse replied; "but I said I couldn't do it, as I'm not a nurse, so he gave me this bottle of oil, and told me to rub her chest with it."

"That'll make her better," Nutsy said. "And I'll do it for you and help you all I can. Where does she live?"

"At the bottom of my house," Mrs Field Mouse answered. "I have the attic and she has the ground floor. It's over on the other side of the hill. It's in one of Farmer Scratchet's wheat fields."

"Oh!" Blinky said with a knowing look at Nutsy. "Is it anywhere near his peanuts?"

"Not *exactly* near; but not very far away," his tiny friend replied—"but of course we don't go near his peanuts," she said hastily.

"Of course not!" Blinky said cheekily. "Does your friend like peanuts?"

"Is it anywhere near his peanuts?"

A Visit to the Pelicans

"No, they give her indigestion," the little mouse replied. "Besides, she likes wheat much better, so we always have supper together. Oh! I hope she doesn't die. I hope she doesn't die!" And poor little mousie started to cry all over again.

"Let's hurry!" Nutsy said. "We might get there in time to save her."

They ran and ran; then stopped for a few moments to get their breath; then ran on, until the top of the hill was reached. Down the other side they rushed, panting and puffing. Farmer Scratchet's house came into view, and to save time they scrambled under the fence instead of going through the new wire gate. Over the cabbage patch, and over the lettuce and asparagus beds, and through the potato field they rushed. Past the pigs' pen—giving Mrs Hog the most dreadful fright. She and the squealers were on a fossicking expedition, rooting up everything within sight.

"It's disgusting the way this farm's run!" she declared. "If Farmer Scratchet isn't discussing bacon in a most untactful manner, he's allowing dogs, cows, and all the rest of the good-for-nothing animals to tear and rush about this place, upsetting the nerves of the most important tenants. Come on, piglets, root in this corner." Squeals and a grand rush greeted her command; and to an onlooker one would have thought great earthworks were in progress.

"We're nearly there!" Mrs Field Mouse announced as they hurried through the wheat field. "Just another few yards to go," she panted.

She zigzagged through the tall grain stalks until a loud hacking cough was heard.

"She's still alive!" Mrs Field Mouse cried with joy. More coughing came, and sneezes by the yard.

"Good gracious!" Nutsy said in an alarmed voice. "Your friend has a terribly big cough and sneeze. She must have double whooping-cough."

"She has!" Mrs Field Mouse exclaimed. "But don't make too much noise; it may frighten her."

Now they were almost at the spot where the patient lay, hidden from sight.

"We're here," Mrs Field Mouse called encouragingly. "Don't give in! Keep up, 'cause I've got the medicine and friends." Another hacking cough came from the ground.

"It must be a terribly big mouse!" Nutsy whispered to Blinky, then—straight in front of them lay the whooping animal.

"Why it's a porcupine!" Blinky shouted. "That's not a mouse."

"Is that the name of her?" Mrs Field Mouse asked looking surprised. "I always call her 'friend' as I'd no idea who she was, except I knew she wasn't a cat."

"You've come at last; but I think you're too late," Mrs Porcupine gasped. "I can't even raise my quills now."

"You're not going to die," Mrs Field Mouse replied with a tear, the tiniest tear in the world, trickling down her nose.

"See! Dr Owl has sent this eucalyptus oil along and we're to rub your chest and back with it. That'll cure you in no time, and these friends are going to do it for you."

"How *can* we rub a porcupine's chest and back? Look at the spikes!" Nutsy whispered in dismay.

"Gosh!" Blinky half whistled, "we'd better pour it all over her and tell her to wriggle about on the ground." Then suddenly he thought of something. "Does it say *rub* her with it? All that writing on the bottle! Those are the directions. Let me see what it says."

Nutsy handed the bottle to Blinky while the others waited expectantly for his verdict.

"I'm *sure* Dr Owl said rub it on," Mrs Field Mouse remarked.

Blinky gazed at the label on the bottle. He didn't understand

"We're nearly there!" Mrs Field Mouse announced as they hurried through the wheat field.

a word of it; but his little brain was working quickly.

"Hu-u-m!" he declared with an important air. "I thought so!. It doesn't say anything at all about rubbing it on; it says, POUR THE OIL DOWN THE COUGHER'S THROAT!"

"Ah!" the others sighed with relief—that is, Nutsy and Mrs Field Mouse. The porcupine had other thoughts.

"You can't do that!" she whined. "I never drink."

"Well, you'll have to!" Blinky announced. "Unless, of course, you want to be a corpse."

"What's that?" Mrs Field Mouse asked anxiously.

"All stiff and cold, and no breath coming," Blinky explained.

The porcupine sighed, then commenced coughing again, rolling from side to side.

"Grab her spikes!" Blinky commanded, "while I pour it down her throat."

Instantly the porcupine raised her quills until they stood up like a pin-cushion.

"I thought you said they wouldn't work!" Blinky cried angrily. "She's only pretending."

"I'm sure she's not. I'm quite sure she's not," Mrs Field Mouse said crossly. "She nearly shook me out of bed the other day when she was whooping, and being upstairs you can imagine how the house shook and quivered."

The house of Mrs Field Mouse was a few wheat-stalks cleverly bent together, while her bed was nestled amongst the ears. That of the porcupine was directly on the ground underneath.

"Something must be done!" Nutsy said, looking with sorrow at the patient. "I know!" she cried excitedly, as she broke off a wheat-stalk, "we'll *paint* her throat."

A Visit to the Pelicans

"What colour?" Blinky asked immediately.

"No colours," Nutsy remarked. "We'll paint it with the oil."

"That's a blessing," the porcupine gasped, withdrawing her spikes.

Nutsy pushed the wheat-ear into the bottle, then stooped over the porcupine.

"Open your mouth *wide*," she said gently, "and don't gurgle when I poke it down."

Blinky and Mrs Field Mouse watched in silence, while the porcupine opened her mouth the tiniest bit.

"Open it wider!" Nutsy ordered.

The porcupine did as she was told and, losing not a second, Nutsy poked the wheat-ear right down her throat.

A dreadful spluttering and coughing was the outcome of the operation; in her fright the porcupine almost sprang in the air.

"She's taking convulsions!" Blinky shouted, scrambling for safety as the porcupine rolled and wobbled about in a most distressing manner, all her quills on end.

"How awful!" Mrs Field Mouse cried. "What will we do?"

But the porcupine gradually quietened. When the last quill lay flat on her back, she crawled under a tuft of dry grass; then, looking at Nutsy, she smiled weakly and whispered:

"I'm better—much better, and after a snooze I'll be *quite* better."

"How wonderful!" Mrs Field Mouse exclaimed running up a wheat-stalk with joy; then, taking a nibble of the ripe grain, ran down again.

"We'll go now!" Blinky said immediately. "Come on, Nutsy. We've to find the pelicans, and its getting late."

"I'm sure she's better," Nutsy said as she was bidding good-bye to Mrs Field Mouse. "If she coughs again poke the stalk down her throat."

So with the little mouse's thanks and tiny laughs ringing in their ears, the two bears pro-

ceeded on their way. Daylight found them on the outskirts of the lake, where hundreds and hundreds of pelicans were in residence. Unnoticed, they climbed a great gum-tree overlooking the birds' domain and, tired out with their journeying, fell asleep after a good meal of the finest leaves. Here, all through the warm day and late into the afternoon they slept. Just as the sun was sinking they woke and, presently, started to scramble down the tree again.

"I believe they're going to bed," Blinky remarked disgustedly. "What silly things! Why don't they play in the moonlight as we do?"

"Let's wake them up!" Nutsy said. "When they see who we are probably they'll have games with us."

"They might gobble us up in their big beaks," Blinky said doubtfully. "Golly! What *big* beaks they have. Look at them!"

"I'm sure they won't be angry if we speak to them politely," Nutsy remarked, "anyway I'm going to try. I'm not afraid."

"Neither am I!" Blinky exclaimed boldly. "You're only a girl and I'm ten times braver than you."

"Well—you go first then," Nutsy said slyly.

"No. Ladies always go first. Splodge told me that," Blinky replied, pushing Nutsy ahead as he spoke.

"Poof! You're afraid!" Nutsy said, with a note of contempt in her voice, as she bravely padded down to the water's edge.

246

"Open it wider!" Nutsy ordered.

Chapter 4

THE COUNCIL MEETING

"YOU shout at them," Nutsy ordered. "You've got the biggest voice."

"Gee up!" Blinky yelled. "Hip, hip, hooray!"

"That's done it!" Nutsy said, as dozens of pelicans ceased paddling about in the water and all, as if by command, faced the intruders with looks of great surprise.

"Caught anything?" Blinky shouted, waving a paw.

The pelicans just looked all the harder. They seemed rooted in the water.

"How's the fishing going?" Blinky asked at the top of his voice.

"You're too cheeky," Nutsy said, poking him in the side. "Ask them politely. No! Keep quiet and I'll ask."

"May we come and see you Mr and Mrs Pelicans?" Nutsy called as loudly as she could.

"Who are you?" came a guttural reply, as the largest pelican of all advanced to meet the bears.

"Only Nutsy and Blinky," the two koalas responded.

"I'm none the wiser," the big bird said shaking his head from side to side as he met the strangers.

The Council Meeting

"We're friends," Nutsy said meekly, holding her breath as she looked up at the huge bird with that very large bill.

"Do you mind telling me what's in your scooper?" Blinky asked as he eyed the great pouch attached to the pelican's bill.

"Nothing!" the pelican replied, and to show them how true it was he opened his mouth to its widest.

"Oh!" Nutsy gasped. "Gosh!" Blinky exclaimed.

With a snap the pelican closed his mouth, so quickly and decidedly that the two little bears jumped with fright.

"Don't open your gate again," Blinky said when he had at last recovered his self composure.

"Be quiet!" Nutsy hissed giving Blinky's foot a kick. "He could swallow us in one gulp."

"Now you see what the day's fishing has been like," the pelican remarked, "and we're holding a meeting to-night to discuss the whys and what-nots of it all."

"May we come?" Nutsy asked excitedly. "We'll be very quiet."

The pelican looked at her for a minute, tilting his head on one side, then on the other, eyeing her with curiosity.

"They're strictly private—our meetings," he said at last. "Only the aldermen are admitted. I'm the mayor, as no doubt you can see by my large paunch, and it all rests with me whether I say yes or no."

"How important," Nutsy said admiringly. "Couldn't you take us to the meeting as guests?"

"S'pose I could if it came to a scratch," the pelican replied, still looking very thoughtfully at the two little bears. "You'll have to be prepared for a rumpus," he said warningly. "And if there is one it's a case of every man for himself."

"What happens to all the womans?" Nutsy interjected.

"They're crushed to death," Blinky replied immediately.

"No such thing!" the pelican said with annoyance. "Women are not admitted to our council meetings, they're held in camera."

Blinky Bill and Nutsy

"Do-you-mean-to-tell-me-you-all-sit-in-a-camera?" Blinky asked in amazement.

"Yes! that's so," the pelican replied, puffing out the pouch in his bill.

"For goodness' sake don't open the gate again," Blinky said excitedly.

"Sh-h-h!" Nutsy scowled at him.

"And who takes the photos?" Blinky asked, returning to the former discussion.

"What photos?" the pelican asked.

"When you're all sitting in the camera," he replied.

"Well—upon my soul! You're goofy," the pelican retorted. "Don't you know what sitting in camera means? Well—really, I didn't think it possible." Here the pelican opened his mouth and gave a terrific yawn.

"Look out! You'll break the hinges," Blinky shouted as he quickly edged away.

The pelican ignored his remark completely. But coming right over to where Blinky was standing, half in and half out of a prickly bush, he snapped his bill at him and asked very crossly: "Didn't your mother send you to school?"

"Look out or you'll break the hinges."

"Oh!" Nutsy gasped. "Gosh!" Blinky exclaimed.

"No! I wouldn't go!" Blinky shouted, trying to cover up his nervousness by making as much noise as possible.

"*That* explains it!" the pelican said coldly. "*That's* why you don't know what 'sitting in camera' means."

"For goodness' sake tell me, and don't talk so much," Blinky retorted. He was clearly annoyed.

"It means sitting behind closed doors," the pelican replied.

"And what a smack you'd get if someone suddenly opened it," Blinky said with a sneer. "No closed doors for *me*."

"You're worse than I thought you were," the pelican said with disgust. "I've no more time to waste on such silly simpering people." Taking a huge watch from under his wing he shook it violently, then looked at its face.

"By Jove!" he exclaimed, "the meeting will have started if I don't get a hurry on."

"*Do* let us come!" Nutsy pleaded. "I'll see that Blinky behaves himself, Mr Pelican."

"Mr Mayor—if—you—*please!*" the pelican said looking sternly at the two bears.

"I beg your pardon. You see, you're the first mayor I've ever met in my life."

"That's quite understandable," the pelican replied. "Mayors are *very* rare."

So taking it for granted that they were to be admitted to the meeting, the koalas followed the pelican, round the edge of the lake to a secluded swamp fringed with tall reeds. Here thousands of pelicans had forgathered, and the snapping and scraping of beaks made a noise like a gale in the trees.

As the mayor appeared, all those hundreds and hundreds of pelicans opened their mouths to their full extent and snapped three times.

"If there's that thing the mayor called a rumpus, for goodness' sake keep away from their snappers,"

The Council Meeting

Blinky whispered to Nutsy. "We'd be cracked in halves like walnuts."

Twenty superior looking pelicans stood in a semicircle, to the centre of which the mayor advanced.

"Are the aldermen's wives at home?" the mayor solemnly asked before commencing business.

"Yes! Your Worship," came the chorus.

"Then we'll open the meeting," the mayor announced with great dignity.

Blinky heard a reed rustle close to where he and Nutsy were sitting on a water-worn stump of mangrove-tree. Quickly looking in that direction he saw many eyes peering through the reeds.

"They're the wives," he whispered to Nutsy. "Will I tell the mayor?"

" 'Course not!" Nutsy replied indignantly. "Mind your own business." Just at that moment the mayor rapped his large webbed foot on the stone that served as a table.

"Off we go!" he shouted. "Any complaints barring the usual one of pilfering fish?"

Such a clamour arose, so many bills snapped and opened, that it was impossible to hear an intelligible remark.

"Order! Order!" the mayor shouted, while the twenty aldermen began to mark time rapidly with their large webbed feet.

Squish, squash, squish, squash, they pancaked the mud.

"Stop that squelching!" the mayor shouted.

"They're the cause of all the trouble!" several angry pelicans screamed.

"Why? What? How?" the mayor asked above the noise.

"They're the cause of the famine," the others shouted. "Playing the organ all day long in the swamp; kneading the bread just where the mud's the thickest, until the fish all swim away, and no respectable pelican can wade in up to his knees without becoming covered in mud."

"What about our bills?" someone shouted above the uproar.

"Yes!" came a chorus of shouts. "What about our bills?"

"What about them?" the mayor shouted.

"Do you think we're all mud larks?" someone else asked. "Our pouches were made to catch fish in—not scoops for mud. Any one would think we were two-legged dredges."

"Sit down!" the mayor ordered, "or I'll close the meeting."

"And a jolly good job if you did," a pelican in the back row shouted.

"What about the frog banquet you and the aldermen had last night?" a tiny skinny moulting pelican piped.

"Your nose is too long!" the mayor shouted amid the uproar. "Aldermen, see that his nose is decapitated."

The aldermen hastily scribbled in large books that hung around their necks: "One nose—decapitate."

"Shame! Shame!" came a chorus of cries.

"Next complaint!" the mayor demanded, snapping his beak so that Nutsy and Blinky jumped with nervousness.

"He'll break his snapper, for sure," Blinky whispered.

"What about relief for the widows?" someone asked.

"Bother the widows!" the mayor mumbled under his breath. Aloud he asked: "Can any one suggest something?"

"*I* can!" came a squeaky voice from behind the reeds. "All you fat aldermen, the mayor included, go out and catch some fish for us poor widows."

The mayor puffed his pouch out with indignation. "The *very idea!*" he exclaimed. "I thought all the wives were at home," he shouted. "How did women get into this meeting?"

"They're the widows!" someone called, "and we're not responsible for *them.*"

"Make them go themselves," the aldermen shouted. "They're always stirring up trouble."

"That's a jolly good idea!" the mayor declared. Pointing to

the reeds he called out in a loud voice. "Widows—stand before me!"

With a rush the reeds parted in all directions, and out marched a hundred widows.

"Eavesdroppers!" the mayor hissed at them as they stood two deep in front of him.

"Traitors!" the aldermen whispered to one another. The widows ignored the remarks, and an old lady pelican stepped out from the rest. Advancing towards the mayor she astounded every one by rapping him sharply on the bill.

"Look here, my lad!" she exclaimed. "There's been enough of this nonsense. Frog banquets, eel snacks, and all the rest of it. Cut it out, or out *you'll* go!"

"What do you want?" the mayor asked looking very subdued.

"Equal rights!" the old lady shouted. "No puddling in squashy mud holes. No sitting in the background while you and the aldermen fish in the best and cleanest water. Give us permission to hold a fishing party—Now!"

"Here, hear!" the other ninety-nine widows screeched.

"And we want a *permanent* fishing-ground," the old lady pelican demanded. "None of your fished-out pools and corners with half a dozen tadpoles in them," she cried.

"Give them the weedy end of the lake," an alderman whispered to the mayor, who seemed to be speechless with anger and surprise. He nodded his head upon hearing this advice.

"Madam!" he said in an icy tone, "you and the rest of the widows can have the south end of the lake."

"It's full of weeds!" the old lady shouted.

"Take it or leave it!" the mayor thundered, now regaining his self-composure. "And in future," he added to the whole of the meeting, "you others keep away from that part of the lake. Those are the

widows' weeds. I'll have no arguments The matter's closed." And to emphasize his words—snap! went his beak.

And so, to this day that particular part of the lake is known as "The Widows' Weeds", and a jolly good fishing-ground it is too.

Seeing the determined look in the mayor's eyes the widows wisely said nothing more; but the old lady pelican, as she was retiring from the meeting, gave one of the aldermen a nasty dig in the side with her beak.

"Put that down in your book," she hissed. "South end of lake, reserved for widows only. And don't let me catch any of you aldermen snooping around."

"A nasty individual!" the mayor whispered to the nearest alderman.

The widows tramped as loudly as they could, leaving the meeting; snapping their beaks, tossing their heads, and causing as much commotion as possible.

"We've avoided a rumpus," the mayor said with relief. "And now gentlemen, we'll discuss the important business of aviation. There's been far too little gliding and soaring going on lately; we must keep our reputation of being the finest soarers in the bird kingdom."

"Let's follow the widows!" Blinky whispered to Nutsy. "I'm not interested in soaring and nose-diving. Are you?"

"I'd like to see them nose-dive with those big noses," Nutsy remarked regretfully as she followed Blinky through the reeds.

"We'll see the *real* nose-diving if we follow the widows," he said excitedly. "Keep in the shadows. Old mother widow will kill us if she sees us."

In and out of the reeds they stumbled and crawled, keeping at a safe distance from the widows. Suddenly, the procession halted.

"What's up now?" Blinky asked.

The Council Meeting

"Be quiet!" Nutsy whispered. "They're talking."

The little koalas crept closer, and peeping through the reeds saw to their surprise a large flat sandy clearing at the lake's edge. All the widows lined up with a great deal of chattering and pushing.

"Contact!" the old lady pelican shouted.

"My goodness! They're going to fly," Nutsy whispered.

"The cheek of them!" Blinky said crossly. "How are we going to follow them?"

Before they had time to discuss the matter, the old lady pelican shouted: "Soar!" and up the whole company of widows went.

"That's that!" Blinky said decidedly.

"Look at them!" Nutsy exclaimed. "Aren't they wonderful?"

The little bears were held spell-bound as they watched the great birds soar higher and higher, with the most effortless, noiseless and graceful action, then away—away to the south they flew in formation.

"Now we can't see the fishing party," Blinky wailed.

"Yes we can! Yes we can!" Nutsy cried dancing up and down. "Look! They've landed again."

And sure enough they had; but it was fully a mile away.

"Come on, let's hurry!" Blinky said, scrambling ahead. Round the lake they bustled and into the reeds again, always keeping the widows in sight. It was a long journey for little legs not used to the ground; but the excitement of what lay ahead kept their courage up, and after many rests and many exclamations of "Oh!" and "Bother!" when they stumbled, they at last came within a few yards of the Widows' Weeds. And weedy it was! Up to their knees amongst weeds of all descriptions, including beautiful yellow and pink water-lilies, the widows dabbled with their beaks.

Blinky Bill and Nutsy

Filling their pouches with all kinds of rubbish, they cleverly washed away the unwanted collection, then tipping their heads back swallowed the fish.

"Heck! I wish I had a fishing trap like that!" Blinky remarked, then laughed at the top of his voice.

"Look at them!" he said, pointing to two pelicans who were quarrelling over a catch.

One had her strong beak around the other's neck, just like a pair of scissors, trying to force back a fish that the second one was swallowing.

They tussled and wriggled, all the time the scissors held firmly round the victim's neck. But the owner of the fish was quite determined not to lose her catch. After fully five minutes of his wrestling she gave a quick jerk with her head, released the grip of the robber and swallowed her fish.

Frogs croaked in terror as they were gobbled up by the dozens. It was a great party for the widows. After the first excitement had died down, the fish became wise and swam farther into the lake. But the widows were prepared for this. Very quietly they waded out, forming a semicircle. The water was shallow, and great quantities of fish leaped in the air as they were pursued. Closing in, the widows began slowly to wade towards the shore, driving the fish before them. What a time they had! Each escaping fish was pounced upon and stored away in the pouch, until the pouch began to swell, then a quick jerk of the head, and many poor little fish went down a slippery dip into a dark tummy.

Now, as the fish were driven right up to the edge of the lake, a great noise arose. Wings flapped, beaks opened and shut like lightning and the widows dined as they'd never dined since their husbands died.

Nutsy and Blinky watched in silence. This was something they'd never seen before. For many hours they watched. Then,

The Council Meeting

"I'm going to try and catch a fish."

when the last widow had taken flight back to her home, two little koalas crept from their hiding-places.

"I'm going to try to catch a fish," Blinky announced.

"Me too!" Nutsy replied.

"Look out an eel doesn't bite you," Blinky said as he dipped one foot in the water, then the other.

But Nutsy was as brave as he. Carefully wading into the water, she showed Blinky that she was quite capable of looking after herself.

"Don't touch the frogs," Nutsy called, "only the biggest fish."

"Clear out of here and let me get some sleep," an irritable voice growled. "This poking about in the water all night long nearly drives me mad."

"Who's that?" Nutsy whispered.

Blinky stood still, water up to his tummy.

"Beg pardon!" he shouted. "What did you say?"

"Clear out! Clear out! and let me get some sleep," the voice came again.

"It's not *your* lake!" Blinky replied, "and we'll fish in it if we want to."

Almost at the same moment he gave a howl of pain and surprise; then flopped right on his back into the water.

"My toe! My toe!" he yelled. "Help me, Nutsy!"

Nutsy waded as quickly

"Who's that?"

as she could to where Blinky was floundering and yelling in the water. "Get up!" she cried with fright. "You'll drown."

"I can't," he shouted. "Help me! My toe's being bitten off."

"Here! Take my paw," Nutsy half sobbed with fright. "I'll pull you up."

Blinky grabbed with all his might, nearly pulling Nutsy down as well.

"My toe!" he kept crying. "My toe's gone."

"Put it up and let me see—quickly!" Nutsy said, trembling from head to foot.

With a great effort, still shouting with pain, Blinky lifted his foot from the water. Just as he raised it, a great ugly red crab fell with a splash, back into the water.

"Oh!" Nutsy gasped. "Oh!—Run for the shore or he'll bite you again."

"I will, and you too, if you don't clear out," came the angry voice from under the water.

Struggling and splashing the two little koalas raced for the brink of the lake.

"The brute!" Blinky cried. "The bad-tempered old thing!"

"No cheek!" came a deep command from the mud.

"Don't answer him. Run quickly," Nutsy said, still terrified.

But Blinky remained just long enough to hurl a large stone into the water, then scuttled away as quickly as he could.

"You're asking for trouble," Nutsy scolded. "Now we've all the way home to go, and you with a sore toe too!"

"It's not hurting! It never hurted!" Blinky remarked brazenly.

Nutsy was not surprised to hear this. She sighed, and gently taking Blinky's paw, they walked along, back past the pelicans' meeting-place, where all was quietness, and into the bush track again.

"Where are we going?" Blinky asked.

"My toe! My toe!" he yelled. "Help me, Nutsy!"

"Home, of course!" Nutsy replied.

"No I'm not!" Blinky announced, stopping in his tracks. "I'm going to see Mr Crocodile!"

"You're *what?*" Nutsy gasped.

"Going to see Mr Croc!" Blinky said, not daring to look at Nutsy.

"Do-you-know-what-he'll-do?" Nutsy asked with deliberation.

"Yes!" Blinky retorted cheekily. "He'll say 'Good day, Blinky! Would you like a ride on my back?'"

"*And would you go?*" Nutsy asked in amazement.

"Rather!" Blinky announced. "It would be most 'citing."

"You're coming home!" Nutsy said sternly. "And you're coming home with me." She grabbed him firmly by a paw and started to drag him along the track. He lay on the ground and kicked.

"You *bad, bad* boy!" Nutsy scolded. "Wait till Splodge hears of this!" She started to struggle with him again, dragging and pulling the kicking little imp along the track.

"Hey! What's this?" a gruff voice demanded. "What's all this dust kicking about?"

The Council Meeting

Out on to the track stepped Mr Walter Wombat again.

"He won't come home! He says he's going to see Mr Croc!" Nutsy cried. "And he'll be killed for sure."

"Going to see Mr Croc, is he?" Mr Walter Wombat remarked in a cold voice, grabbing Blinky by the ear. "You're going home my boy—that's where you're going," he said sternly.

"I was only pretending!" Blinky said sulkily. "Let go my ear or I'll bite you."

Mr Walter Wombat shook Blinky until his teeth chattered. "Get home at ONCE!" he roared, releasing his grip on the little scallawag.

Blinky scrambled away, far quicker than he thought it possible, Nutsy following.

"You big tell-tale," he said. "I *hate* girls!"

Growling and grumbling he trotted ahead, a very tired and irritable little bear. Dawn was fast approaching. A dim grey light appeared in the east and the trees gradually shed their dark shapes of the night. The birds awoke, calling and singing their morning greeting. Rabbits scurried from their burrows in search of breakfast.

"There's our tree!" Nutsy cried. "I'm so glad to be home again —and there's Splodge hopping about."

"I wonder where mother is?" Blinky remarked a little nervously.

"I s'pose she's up in the tree getting our breakfast ready, and crying and crying 'cause she thinks we're lost," Nutsy replied, looking very sad.

"*You* don't know my mother when she's angry," Blinky said with scorn. "She's most probably getting a big stick ready to whack us with."

"Will it hurt?" Nutsy whimpered.

"You bet!" Blinky replied, "specially if it's a new green stick."

"Oh! I've never been whacked before," Nutsy now began to cry in earnest.

"Fancy crying!" Blinky scoffed. "It's all over in a minute, and then my mother usually kisses me, and gives me the nicest gum-tips that she's collected specially for the occasion. Besides— she's not a bit grumpy for a long time afterwards. If I'm naughty right on top of the whacking she only says 'Don't do that, Blinky darling,' or '*Try* and be a good boy now.' So you see its worth the minute it hurts."

"But I don't want to be hurt," Nutsy howled.

"S'pose I'll have to let her into my secret," Blinky mumbled to himself, "and it's such a good secret too. Bother her!"

"Stop howling!" he commanded. "Come over here and help me to collect some leaves."

"What for?" Nutsy asked between sobs.

"For padding, of course!" Blinky remarked, looking with a very bored expression at his companion. "Hurry up, and don't look so vacant."

Scratching a pile of leaves together, Blinky then began to stuff pawfuls down Nutsy's little dress, then, when that had been completed to his satisfaction, he stuffed the back of his trousers with more leaves.

"Won't she notice how fat we look?" Nutsy asked doubtfully. "And I rustle terribly when I walk."

'Fancy crying!'

"She'll be too cross to notice anything 'cept we're back," Blinky replied. "Come on, let's get it over!"

"You're in for it!" Splodge remarked as he spied the two little bears.

"Is she very mad?" Blinky asked hurriedly.

"Ramping!" Splodge said waving

his paws about. "I've never seen your mother so snaky before. She says she's going to give you the biggest, soundest, hugest whacking you've ever had in your life."

"Gee!" Blinky whispered. "She *must* be mad."

Nutsy began to whimper again.

"Stop that noise!" Blinky gritted the words out between clenched teeth. "Don't you know you're *whack-proof?*"

"Get up the tree as quickly as possible," Splodge advised. "Every minute makes a difference."

Half-way up the tree Mrs Koala saw them.

"*My goodness!*" she said in a quivering voice. "Wait until you get up here!"

"We're both sorry!" Blinky shouted, "and I'll do all your messages for you if you want any."

"Come up here!" Mrs Koala commanded in cold tones. She reached down for Blinky's paw and landed him up on the branch beside her with a jerk. Then Nutsy followed. Both little bears began to talk rapidly and offer explanations.

"No excuses!"

Blinky Bill and Nutsy

"No excuses!" Mrs Koala said angrily, grasping a fresh green twig in one hand and Blinky by the scruff of the neck in the other.

"Get it over quickly!" he said, bending the well-padded region uppermost.

Whack! Whack! Whack! came Mrs Koala's stick. "That'll teach you to run away!" she said, panting from the exertion. "Go up to the highest branch and don't dare to move from there until I tell you."

"Yes, mother," Blinky meekly replied, rustling alarmingly as he crawled away.

"Are you going to whack me too?" Nutsy asked, looking at Mrs Koala with tears in her eyes.

"I won't this time," Mrs Koala replied, "as I'm sure Blinky put the idea into your head; but next time I'll do it, Blinky or no Blinky. Go over to that corner and stand with your nose in it until I get you to come away." Mrs Koala pointed to the cosiest corner of the old gum-tree—a corner well overhung with nice green leaves.

"The pet!" Blinky growled shrugging his shoulders as he climbed to his appointed place, then taking out the padding from his trousers, flung the leaves in a shower right on top of Nutsy.

"What's that?" Mrs Koala demanded, looking at the pile of leaves.

"Are you going to whack me too?"

"It's only the tree moulting," Blinky explained, screwing his nose up at Nutsy, who was watching him out of the corner of her eye, not knowing what was going to happen next.

"Pet!" he hissed at her. "I hope those leaves in your dress prick you most dreadfully."

266

The Council Meeting

Forgetting that Mrs Koala might be watching, Nutsy began to pull out the leaves.

Mrs Koala coldly watched the proceeding until it was over, then, stepping over to where Nutsy stood, asked in a slow deliberate voice, "What is the meaning of this?"

"That's the whack-proof!" Nutsy said trembling.

"The *what!*" Mrs Koala exclaimed, a glint of anger reappearing in her eyes.

"We've brought you back padding for the guests' beds!" Blinky called out from above, where he'd been watching everything in suspense.

"How thoughtful of you," Mrs Koala said, her anger changing immediately to joy. "Just what I needed, as Mrs Possum is coming to-morrow and she was most emphatic that I should prepare a soft bed for her."

"I can get you plenty more," Blinky shouted, "only of course, I'll have to come down and get them off the ground."

"And I could help him!" Nutsy said instantly.

"I don't want any help!" Blinky shouted.

"Well, I don't see why you both shouldn't help me," Mrs Koala replied. "After all, that's what children are for. Both of you go down and bring me up as many leaves as possible. Altogether, I've ten guests arriving to-morrow, and clean, soft beds are most necessary. My manager told me that!"

Mrs Koala spoke with a note of pride in her voice. The two little bears took no notice of this last part of her conversation, as they weren't a scrap interested in the guests' beds. All they wanted to do was to get down on the ground and collect leaves. It was much nicer than being confined to one spot.

Mrs Koala fussed and fussed about, poking and patting corners into cosy beds, while Splodge gave orders to Blinky and Nutsy who collected piles of leaves. Up and down the tree they climbed until Mrs Koala was satisfied that all lumps and bumps in the beds had been padded so well that all the guests would be most comfortable. Then a supper of leaves for themselves, eaten between calling out remarks to Splodge who sat at the foot of the tree, completed all arrangements.

Much to Blinky's and Nutsy's relief, Mrs Koala never mentioned the running-away again.

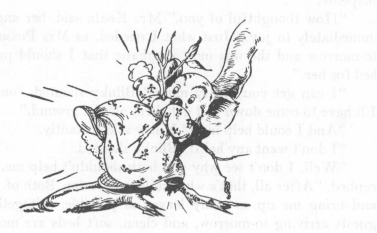

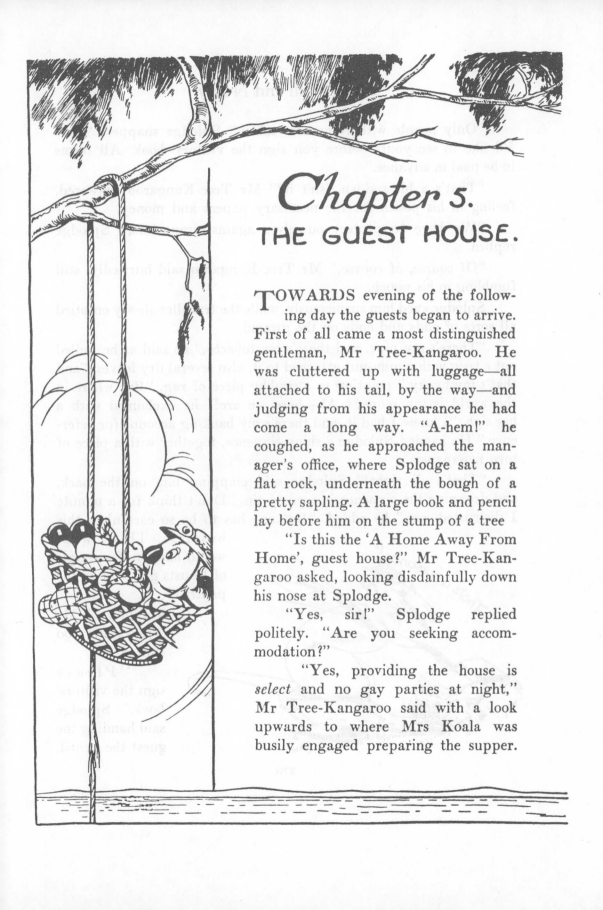

Chapter 5.
THE GUEST HOUSE.

TOWARDS evening of the following day the guests began to arrive.
First of all came a most distinguished
gentleman, Mr Tree-Kangaroo. He
was cluttered up with luggage—all
attached to his tail, by the way—and
judging from his appearance he had
come a long way. "A-hem!" he
coughed, as he approached the manager's office, where Splodge sat on a
flat rock, underneath the bough of a
pretty sapling. A large book and pencil
lay before him on the stump of a tree

"Is this the 'A Home Away From
Home', guest house?" Mr Tree-Kangaroo asked, looking disdainfully down
his nose at Splodge.

"Yes, sir!" Splodge replied
politely. "Are you seeking accommodation?"

"Yes, providing the house is
select and no gay parties at night,"
Mr Tree-Kangaroo said with a look
upwards to where Mrs Koala was
busily engaged preparing the supper.

"Only people with references taken," Splodge snapped. "And I'd like to see yours before you sign the visitors' book. All terms to be paid in advance."

"That's a bit sudden, isn't it?" Mr Tree-Kangaroo answered, feeling in his pouch for the necessary papers and money.

"We have to protect ourselves against impostors," Splodge replied.

"Of course, of course," Mr Tree-Kangaroo said hurriedly, still fumbling in his pouch.

Splodge eyed him suspiciously, while the traveller slowly emptied all sorts of odds and ends on the ground.

"There's my pipe, and there's my tobacco," he said as he pulled out a twig with a gum-nut attached to it, also several dry leaves, "and that's my hanky," pointing to a grubby piece of rag. "But where in the world is my money? Ah—here we are!" he exclaimed with a big sigh. "I knew I had it, and there's my banking account for reference." He handed Splodge a shiny sixpence, together with a piece of torn newspaper.

"That's all right!" Splodge said clapping him on the back, and dropping the sixpence in a rusty tin. "Don't think for a minute I distrusted you," he added. "But one has to be so careful in this business. Think what would happen if a couple of locusts got loose in the pantry!"

"Low fellows!" Mr Tree-Kangaroo sniffed.

"Please sign the visitors' book," Splodge said handing the guest the pencil,

"Ah—here we are!" he exclaimed with a big sigh.

"and do you mind not wetting it first—it's that bluey stuff. If you jab hard enough it will show up."

Mr Tree-Kangaroo jabbed right through the page.

"That's a nuisance!" Splodge remarked ripping out the under-neath page. "That's all loss!" And flipping the paper over his shoulder, he called to Blinky to help the guest carry his luggage up the tree.

"Oh!—by the way, do you want breakfast in bed?" Splodge asked.

"Is there any extra charge?" Mr Tree-Kangaroo asked.

"Not if you get up and carry it there yourself," Splodge answered.

"Is this a cash-and-carry business?" Mr Tree-Kangaroo demanded crossly.

"My apologies, sir!" Splodge said at once. "Perhaps I was over-eager to please you."

"And just a *little* too eager to please yourself," the guest remarked haughtily. "Boy!" he shouted. "Help me up with my luggage."

"He doesn't mean *me*, does he?" Blinky asked Splodge, pointing to the guest.

"Yes, yes," Splodge whispered hurriedly. "Help him up and be most polite. He's a bit ruffled already."

"So am *I!*" Blinky declared. Then walking over to the guest he announced in a loud voice: "I'm Blinky Bill, and that's what you've got to call me—not *Boy!*"

"A modern child I suppose," the guest remarked. "Never mind, we won't quarrel over names; give my tail a lift up, boy— and be mighty careful the way you handle it. I've had rheumatiz in the end of it very badly lately. That's why I've come here. A change of climate and a little warmth may work wonders."

"I'll teach him not to call me *Boy!*" Blinky mut-tered as Mr Tree-Kangaroo started up the tree.

The Guest House

"Lift it! Lift it!"

"Lift it! Lift it!" he shouted irritably as Blinky made no effort to help with his tail.

Rushing to his aid, Blinky grabbed the tip of the guest's tail and lifted with all his strength.

"That's the idea!" Mr Tree-Kangaroo grunted with satisfaction —then a howl of pain came from his lips, as Blinky bit savagely the very tip of the gentleman's tail. "That'll teach him!" he grunted to himself.

"It must be *acute* rheumatiz!" he said aloud, as Mr Tree-Kangaroo turned to inspect his tail.

"The worst twinge I've ever had!" he remarked. "Let's get up quickly. Another one of those and I'd *die!*"

"They must be pretty painful," Blinky replied, staggering under his load.

"Dreadful! Dreadful!" the guest puffed, mopping his head with his handkerchief.

Mrs Koala stood ready to receive her visitors, smiling and bowing graciously, while Nutsy stood behind her, peeping at the newcomer.

Blinky Bill and Nutsy

"Ah! Here we are at last!" Mr Tree-Kangaroo remarked as he shook paws with his hostess. "You really need a rope and basket to heave people up," he puffed.

"That's a fine idea!" Mrs Koala replied. "I'll mention it to my manager."

"I'll work it!" Blinky cried. "I'll haul them 'cause it's a man's job."

"You go and speak to the manager about it," Mrs Koala said to her son, "and ask him to make arrangements about fresh cabbages and potatoes, also carrots.

"I've been so busy making up beds that I've forgotten to order food," she explained to Mr Tree-Kangaroo.

"That doesn't sound like a home away from home," he replied coldly. "Haven't you anything for supper?"

"Oh, yes! I've provided for that," Mrs Koala said with a smile. "Let me show you to your room." Leading her guest to a very large comfortable bed, padded well with leaves, she pulled a few branches together to make it more private.

"This looks good!" her guest said turning back a few leaves and peering anxiously among them. "No spiders I hope!" he remarked off-handedly.

"Dear me, no!" Mrs Koala said with a shocked expression. "This is a *select* guest house."

Mr Tree-Kangaroo flung himself on the bed with a sigh of relief.

"Kindly take your boots off!" Mrs Koala said sternly. "This is a home away from home, and I'm sure you wouldn't do that in your own home."

"I quite forgot!" her guest apologized. Taking his boots off he flung them on the floor—as he thought; but they went sailing down through the branches to land right on top of the manager's head.

"Dog's body!" Splodge roared. "What was that?"

274

"Kindly take your boots off!" Mrs Koala said sternly.

"The guest's feet," Blinky remarked as he dodged the boots.

"Disgusting fellow!" Splodge expounded. "For two whiskers I'd throw him out."

"But you can't climb," Blinky said looking at his friend.

"I'll *shake* him out if he doesn't behave," Splodge replied. "Anyway, what are you here for? Can't you see I'm up to my tail in work."

Blinky gave his message to the surprised Splodge. "Now, where in the world am I to get all those things from?" he said scratching his head.

"I know!" Blinky exclaimed. "Over at Farmer Scratchet's. He's got dozens and dozens of cabbages and carrots, and piles and piles of potatoes."

"You mean we're to *steal* them!" Splodge asked.

"Not exactly," Blinky replied. "We'll only borrow them."

"Borrow cabbages! And how do you think we're going to return them when the guests have eaten them?" Splodge asked. "No! I'll have to ask Farmer Scratchet if he'll sell them to us."

Meanwhile three more guests had arrived all asking for accommodation.

Mr and Mrs Goanna, and their daughter, a fair-skinned, shy little thing, who darted around the back of the tree and hissed loudly when Splodge looked at her.

"We want a double bed and a single one!" Mrs Goanna said.

"You mean we're to steal them!"

"Run up and tell your mother to make up a double bed," Splodge ordered Blinky.

"She's not going to sleep near me!" Blinky said pointing at little Daisy Goanna. "She makes noises like ginger-beer bottles going off!"

"Are you referring to my Daisy?" Mrs Goanna asked with indignation.

276

The Guest House

"She's making awful noises," Blinky retorted, "just like escaping steam."

"Go up and deliver my message to your mother!" Splodge thundered, while he made efforts to calm Mrs Goanna.

"A *double bed!*" Mrs Koala exclaimed, upon hearing the message. "That's strange—well—I'll have to do it," and straightway she began piling the leaves from one bed on top of the other. "Fancy wanting a bed as high as that," she said when the work was completed.

"P'rhaps the guest's a bower bird," Nutsy suggested.

"Good heavens! Hide my blue slippers," Mrs Koala said excitedly. "They'll steal anything blue, those bower birds."

"When is the dinner-gong going?" came from Mr Tree-Kangaroo's direction.

"Any time now," Mrs Koala replied, still thumping and pushing the double bed into shape.

A great deal of hissing suddenly sounded at the foot of the tree, and Mrs Koala peering down nearly fell from the branch with astonishment.

"Good gracious! If it's not the Goanna family, all hissing like a lot of boiling kettles. Quick, Nutsy! Get the tea ready."

"Good heavens! hide my blue slippers!"

277

Blinky Bill and Nutsy

The Goanna family hissed extraordinarily as they climbed the tree. With studied care they advanced step by step, their great banded bodies bending from side to side, while their eyes were fixed on one spot—Mrs Koala's front door, or, in other words, the stout branch that served as a doorstep to the upper regions of the tree.

"Here we are!" Mr Goanna hissed as he wriggled on to the branch, followed by his wife and daughter. Mrs Goanna peered through a lorgnette made from grass. "It could be made a little more attractive," she hissed with her head in the air.

"I hope the menu will tempt our jaded appetites."

"Do you think it is quite select enough for us?" Daisy Goanna asked, peeping this way and that.

"It all depends on who the other guests are," Mrs Goanna replied. "*We* at least will give tone to the place."

"Sh-h-h! There's the proprietress!" Mr Goanna hissed as Mrs Koala scrambled down the tree to greet them.

"How do you do?" Mrs Goanna wheezed. "Is our suite ready?"

"Come this way, please," Mrs Koala replied with a bow. "Everything's in readiness. One double bed and one single bed."

"We'll rest for a few minutes before tea," Mrs Goanna replied.

"Follow me," Mrs Koala said, leading the way until the suite was reached.

"Where's the double bed?" Mrs Goanna asked, raising her eyebrows.

"There it is!" Mrs Koala replied pointing to the pile of leaves.

"*That's* a single bed!" Mrs Goanna said haughtily.

"No, it isn't!" Mrs Koala replied indignantly. "Look at all the leaves I've piled up. I took the top lot from another bed—that makes it double."

"How pathetic!" Mrs Goanna sniffed, turning her head away. "One can see yours is *not* a select guest house."

"How pathetic!" Mrs Goanna sniffed, turning her head away.

"It *is* select!" Mrs Koala replied crossly. "And *I'm* the selector. I'll be pleased if you and your family will go elsewhere. I entertain only the *best* people."

"Oh! Did you hear that?" Daisy Goanna hissed in horror. "*We* the banded monitors, to be spoken to like that."

"Take your bands and your hissing away!" came a deep growl from Mr Tree-Kangaroo's direction. "I'm waiting for my dinner and you're holding it up."

"What's for dinner?" Mr Goanna suddenly asked, his eyes nearly popping out of his head. "Any rabbits?"

"Certainly not!" Mrs Koala replied tartly. "The rabbits are our guests, and not to be put on the menu."

"Guests!" All the Goanna family hissed loudly. "Rabbits for guests!"

"Do you know, we eat them by the dozen?" Mrs Goanna said with her head in the air.

"I wouldn't be surprised!" Mrs Koala replied. "In fact *nothing* you did would surprise me."

"Come! Bertram. This is no place for respectable people like us," Mrs Goanna said turning to her husband, and in less than a minute all three were shuffling down the tree again.

"Old coppers! That's what they are!" Mrs Koala said to Nutsy. "Hissing and spluttering around my place like a wash-day at the zoo."

"You should have poked them overboard," Nutsy said sympathetically. "I wish Blinky had been here. He'd have done it!"

"Is my tucker ready?" Mr Tree-Kangaroo sounded as though he was becoming impatient.

"Yes, yes," Mrs Koala called. "Come this way into the dining-room."

"Tie your apron and cap on," she whispered to Nutsy. "And when he comes up, hand him a few gum-nuts to chew while I prepare his tea."

Mr Tree-Kangaroo climbed with great alacrity to

Then Mr Tree-Kangaroo did a dreadful thing.

the dining-room, where Nutsy stood, holding some gum-nuts. She bowed ever so sweetly as the gentleman sat down on the branch, and offered him the dainties.

"What's this? What's this?" he said with a grunt, eyeing the nuts with suspicion.

"They're to chew. To keep you quiet till your tea is ready," Nutsy replied sweetly.

Then Mr Tree-Kangaroo did a dreadful thing. The rudest thing I have ever heard of. He raised his paw, gave a nasty smack with it, and sent the nuts sky-high. Poor Nutsy opened her mouth to cry; but Mrs Koala, who had seen everything (and very nervous she felt about it too), cried out:

"I'm coming! I'm coming! Don't get mad! Here's your tea!"

"What's for tea?" Mr Tree-Kangaroo asked Nutsy, looking at her sternly, while she shivered from head to toes.

"Chewing-gum or leaves," she replied stuttering.

"What's chewing-gum?" Mr Tree-Kangaroo asked, glaring at Nutsy. "Is it something new?"

"Not 'zactly," Nutsy replied, fumbling with her paws. "It's the same as gum-leaves, only you chew some leaves, and the others you just gobble."

"I see," Mr Tree-Kangaroo said in a slow deliberate manner, while his whiskers seemed to be quivering in all directions at once. "And *that's* what you expect guests to eat in a select house?"

"Here you are! Here you are!" Mrs Koala cried, fairly pushing the leaves under his nose. "They're the first of the season."

"*And* the last!" her guest roared as he pitched them in the same direction as the nuts.

"My goodness!" Mrs Koala said under her breath. "What a dreadful temper!"

"Give me my sixpence back!" Mr Tree-Kangaroo demanded loudly. "And my bank-book too!"

"Inquire for them at the office," Mrs Koala replied with her nose in the air. "Come, Nutsy, we will see if Blinky has returned with the cabbages."

"*Cabbages!*" Mr Tree-Kangaroo fairly shouted. "Have you any cabbages?"

"They're on order," Mrs Koala replied with dignity. "But they are only for gentlemen. Good day!" and so saying, she and Nutsy climbed higher in the tree.

"Pity I lost my temper," Mr Tree-Kangaroo murmured to himself as he slowly climbed down the tree. "It's years since I tasted a cabbage; but I suppose *their* cabbages would have slugs in them, so I've not missed much.

"My sixpence and bank-book, please!" he announced to the astonished Splodge.

"Aren't you satisfied?" Splodge asked in surprise.

"My sixpence and bank-book!" Mr Tree-Kangaroo thundered. "And look slick, my lad!"

"There'll be a penny charge for resting on the bed," Splodge replied coldly. He, too, was beginning to get cross.

"My *sixpence* and bank-book!" Mr Tree-Kangaroo roared.

"Oh, for the love of spiders, *take them!*" Splodge shouted as he hurled the rusty tin containing the treasures at the guest.

"Oh— for the love of spiders TAKE THEM!"

283

Blinky Bill and Nutsy

Mr Tree-Kangaroo tucked his sixpence and piece of newspaper carefully in his pouch, eyeing Splodge all the while. "I'll have a boxing-match with you some day, my young codger," he said shaking his paw at Splodge.

"Mind the step as you go out!" was Splodge's reply, then turning his back on the irate guest he spotted that gentleman's shoes.

"Hum-m-m!" he growled to himself. "He won't get those anyway!"

Mr Tree-Kangaroo had entirely forgotten his shoes, and it was not until his feet became sore, many, many miles farther on that he remembered them. "That's goodbye to *them*," he sighed sitting down to rest. Back at the office of "A Home Away From Home" the manager was slowly and carefully writing in a large book.

> Mr Tree-Kangaroo. Came and went.
> Profit—one pair of shoes.
> Loss—nothing.

"Not too bad for the first try," Splodge said to himself. "But I can see things want livening up a bit if we're to make this business pay. Moonlight picnics, dancing in the bush, fishing excursions, snake-hunts—that's the idea! I'll go now and tell Mrs Koala what must be done. By the way it's time that young shaver, Mr Blinky, was back. I wonder where's he's got to." Almost simultaneously with Splodge's thought Blinky came tumbling through the bush, a large cabbage tightly held between his front paws, and a very pleased look on his face.

"Where'd you get *that?*" Splodge shouted, staring coldly at the cabbage.

"Over at Farmer Scratchet's," Blinky said proudly.

"Did you come by it honestly?" Splodge demanded.

The Guest House

"Yes!" Blinky replied, hugging the cabbage more tightly. "I asked Farmer Scratchet if he'd lend me a few cabbages and carrots, and Mrs Scratchet's clothes-basket, and instead of saying 'Certainly, Blinky!' he roared at me and said he'd 'give me 'zactly one minute to get off his premises.' "

"And how did you come by that cabbage under those circumstances?" Splodge said sternly, pointing to the cabbage.

"I just walked out of the gate, round the back of Farmer Scratchet's house, popped under the fence and grabbed it before it had time to call out for help."

"That's stealing!" Splodge thundered, "and sure as eggs that very same cabbage will choke you if you attempt to eat it."

"O-o-o-h! I didn't know *that!*" Blinky said in surprise. "Will it choke all the guests too?"

"No, only the stealer of it," Splodge replied. "Here—hand it over while I taste it to see if it's perfectly fresh."

Blinky handed over the big crisp cabbage not without some misgivings. Splodge pulled a juicy leaf and quickly gobbled the dainty; the second and third leaves disappeared in the same way with startling rapidity.

"Here! You'll have the lot if you don't stop," Blinky shouted indignantly, making a grab at the cabbage.

"The outside leaves are no good for guests, and I'm only eating them," Splodge replied, holding the cabbage at a safe distance from Blinky. "You shin up the tree and tell your mother to come down and have a look at it. Besides, I want to talk business with her."

"Don't you eat another leaf, or I'll not be responsible for my actions when I come back," Blinky said as he started to climb the tree.

"Stuff and nonsense!" Splodge mumbled to himself as he crammed his mouth full of cabbage. "I'll just taste one more leaf, from the heart, and then I'll not touch another." Saying this, he

"Stuff and nonsense!"

pulled apart the creamy heart of the cabbage and instantly gobbled half of it. The remainder looked very silly indeed, so he decided to finish it, and be done with the whole affair. "A half cabbage will only cause ill-feeling and jealousy—so here goes!" Splodge added. And away went the last little particle of that beautiful green cabbage. "The very idea of *stealing* a cabbage!" he said to himself. "That'll be a lesson to young man Blinky. I can't bear the thought of him stealing."

In a few minutes Mrs Koala, Nutsy and Blinky stood in front of him.

"Where's the cabbage?" Blinky demanded, glaring at Splodge.

"I decided it was best to destroy it," Splodge explained. "Stolen goods only cause trouble."

"I hope you have the biggest and longest stomach-ache you've ever had in your life," Blinky shouted with rage.

"I think you might have waited until we could hold a consultation over the cabbage," Mrs Koala remarked, looking at Splodge. "After all, it was my son's cabbage and not yours."

"We'll say no more about it," Splodge replied, dismissing the subject with a wave of his paw. "More urgent business requires our attention."

"What's that?" Mrs Koala inquired.

"This place wants pepping up," Splodge said impressively. "Amusement for the guests—parties, dances, excursions, picnics, and a bit of whoopee here and there."

The Guest House

"I'd like to give you a bit of whoopee here and there," Blinky said still glowering at Splodge.

"That'll do!" Mrs Koala said sternly, giving her son a gentle push.

"I think we'll adjourn to my office, Mrs Koala, and discuss the matter in quietness and privacy," Splodge said, ignoring Blinky and Nutsy.

"Quite so, quite so," Mrs Koala replied. "Blinky—you and Nutsy play about for a little while, until I call you."

"Come on, Nuts, let's go for a walk," Blinky whispered. "That Splodge is the greediest gobbler I've ever seen."

"Can't we get another cabbage?" Nutsy asked. "I'm sure Mrs Koala would like one."

" 'Course we can! We can get dozens of 'em," Blinky said with a worldly air. "We can get carrots and potatoes too—and Mrs Scratchet's basket as well."

"What a surprise Mrs Koala will get," Nutsy said excitedly.

"Come on, let's hurry," Blinky replied, running ahead through the bush.

It was moonlight. As the two little bears approached Farmer Scratchet's house, they saw a light gleaming in the window.

"He's in bed," Blinky whispered. "We'll crawl round to the laundry first and get the basket."

Nutsy was trembling with excitement. "Has he a dog?" she asked.

"He's chained up, and besides, he's a friend of mine," Blinky answered.

Nearer and nearer they crept towards the laundry. The door was open and everything looked very simple and easy. A few more steps and they stood in front of the door. There was the clothes-basket, full of linen on top of the copper.

"We'll have to tip all that rubbish out," Blinky remarked. "I'll get up on top of the copper and throw the stuff down. You be ready to help me down with the basket."

Blinky Bill and Nutsy

"Well, hurry up," Nutsy said nervously. "Someone might catch us."

Almost immediately Farmer Scratchet's dog began to bark.

"He'll catch us! He'll kill us!" Nutsy whispered. "Hide in the copper."

"Come on then," Blinky said excitedly. "Hurry up or he'll be here."

The two little koalas scrambled into the copper, pulled the lid over them, and lay there with hearts thumping, while Farmer Scratchet's dog barked furiously.

"Lie down!" a voice roared from the house; but the dog still kept barking.

In a few moments heavy footsteps came padding down the path.

"What's all the noise about?" Farmer Scratchet demanded.

The dog barked and tugged at his chain.

"I've a good mind to let you off," Farmer Scratchet said.

"We'll have to tip all that rubbish out!"

288

The Guest House

"I wouldn't if I were you," Blinky said softly.

"Tell him not to," Nutsy whimpered.

"Be quiet," Blinky ordered. "We're as dead as turnips if he finds us."

Nearer came the footsteps, and then—horror of horrors, Farmer Scratchet came into the laundry.

"If there's any one about he's in here," Farmer Scratchet said under his breath as he turned over boxes, moved the gardening tools, looked behind the door, and actually in the clothes-basket.

"That dog's a fraud!" he exclaimed. "Yap, yap, yap, and no cause for any of it. For two pins I'd give him to the butcher."

Blinky gave Nutsy a nudge. They held their breaths, not daring to make the slightest sound.

"Kerchoo!" Farmer Scratchet sneezed, making the windows rattle, and nearly, very nearly killing the two little bears with fright.

"A plague on that dog," he said loudly and crossly. "Here am I catching my death of cold, all through his yapping. Bed's the best place for me!" Saying this he stamped out of the laundry and to Blinky's and Nutsy's delight, hauled his dog, chain and all,

KERCHOO!

round to the front of the house.

"Isn't he kind?" Blinky giggled as he and Nutsy wriggled out of the copper.

"I think I'm going to faint," Nutsy said weakly.

"I'll push you under the tap if you do," Blinky said sternly. "Just you try any of those silly tricks and you'll soon be sorry. Get down on the floor while I empty the basket."

Blinky Bill and Nutsy

Nutsy did so, without any further comment, while a shower of linen came hurtling through the air. Piles of it flew in all directions, and finally the basket arrived after a good kick from Blinky on top of the copper.

"Look out for your shins!" he called as the basket toppled at Nutsy's feet.

In another few seconds both little bears were tugging and pushing the cumbersome basket out of the door and over the lawn. Under the fence, and across the paddock to where the vegetables grew, they heaved and tugged, determined to accomplish their mission. Farmer Scratchet's best piece of rope, that he always used for hauling logs and iron about, was the cause of at least half an hour's tussle, as Blinky and Nutsy came upon it lying on the ground. They lifted and grunted, sighed and heaved, as they pushed it into the basket, then off once more to the cabbage patch.

"It's no use taking more than one cabbage, and one potato, and one carrot," Blinky said puffing. "We'll never get home if we do."

"I wish Splodge was here," Nutsy remarked. "We could harness him to the basket and drag home lots of cabbages then."

"It's a good idea," Blinky said looking at Nutsy. "But he's not to be trusted after what happened to the last cabbage—besides, he'll say its stealing, and we're only borrowing."

"But he'd be such a help," Nutsy persisted. "I could run home and get him while you fill the basket up, ready to pull off when he comes."

"If I get him he'll have to promise not to eat our things, and not to growl," Blinky answered, "and that means—we've got to get the rope out again."

Nutsy was already in the basket trying to heave the rope out. They pushed and poked, puffing and grunting until the rope lay on the ground.

The Guest House

"Go for your life," Blinky ordered, "and don't be long, 'cause Farmer Scratchet might come around again."

Nutsy flew along the track, while Blinky pulled up carrots and potatoes by the dozen. Into the basket they went, with six fine cabbages perched on top. By the time he'd completed his job, Splodge and Nutsy came in sight, Nutsy perched on top of her friend's back, while he made big bounds over to where Blinky stood.

"What game is this?" Splodge demanded looking as cross as he possibly could.

"Private business," Blinky replied loftily. "If you care to drag this basket home you'll be paid with *one* potato."

Splodge was speechless. Such impudence—and from so small an animal too.

"Hook your hind legs to the basket with this rope," Blinky began to command.

"Now look here, my young fellow. I'm not hooking any of my hind legs to any baskets for any one for only *one* potato," Splodge said definitely. "One potato, one carrot, and one cabbage is my price. Take it or leave it."

"It's overcharging," Blinky announced sternly, "but I'll have to hire you."

Not a word was mentioned in regard to stealing as Splodge licked his lips while helping Nutsy and Blinky to tie the rope to the basket handles, and then loop it over his shoulders.

"You and Nutsy had better get in the basket too," Splodge said as he eyed the load, which to him was a mere trifle.

"Hooray!" Blinky shouted. "Come on, Nuts, now for a joy ride."

Up the two of them scrambled, perching themselves between cabbages and clinging to the basket sides.

"All aboard?" Splodge called. "Off we go!"

With a tremendous jerk the basket bounded off the ground.

Blinky Bill and Nutsy

Bump, bump, bump, over the paddock it went, Splodge leaping ahead, while Blinky and Nutsy were bounced about among the cabbages and potatoes.

Round the corners they bounded, in and out of the trees, missing branches and rocks by a hairbreadth. Mrs Rabbit and her toddlers were out for an evening stroll. She looked with amazement at this new kind of danger that came tearing along the bush track, then with one startled scream called her babies to her side, and she and they dashed into the undergrowth away from the hideous monster.

"It's enough to turn all my children cross-eyed," Mrs Rabbit panted, as she lined her babies up under cover of a big gum-tree and examined each carefully.

Meanwhile Splodge and Co. went bounding along. "The quicker home, the quicker I'll get my cabbage," Splodge thought. Mrs Koala up in the tree could not believe her eyes as she saw Splodge and the contraption come tearing through the bush.

Wallop, wallop, wallop, they came, amid calls and shouts from Blinky and Nutsy.

Down the tree Mrs Koala scrambled, nearly slipping in her excitement.

Splodge came to a standstill, streams of puff coming from his nostrils.

"Look what we've got!" Blinky shouted.

"Potatoes and carrots and cabbages!" Nutsy shouted at the same time.

" 'Pon my soul!" Mrs Koala exclaimed. "And how am I going to pay for it all?"

"It's all borrowed!" Blinky replied, dancing up and down, "and the basket too—and the rope."

" 'Pon my soul!" Mrs Koala repeated. She was amazed.

"Of course we'll have to return the basket and rope," Splodge explained, "but I don't see how we can manage about the vegetables.

Bump, bump, bump—over the paddock it went.

Anyhow, there's acres of them over at Farmer Scratchet's going to waste—sheer waste—and just asking to be picked and eaten. It's a kindness to do it."

"Quite right," Mrs Koala agreed. "I never can understand humans allowing fields and fields of cabbages and carrots to remain there, week in and week out."

Chapter 6.
PUTTING "PEP" IN THINGS.

ALL through the night Splodge, Mrs Koala, Blinky and Nutsy worked at top speed. The whole place was transformed. From a stout limb of the gumtree dangled a rope, on the end of which Mrs Scratchet's basket swayed to and fro not far above the ground. At the foot of the tree, neatly arrayed in rows, lay the carrots, potatoes and cabbages, interspersed with watercress and gum-leaves. A large notice bravely planted in the heart of the largest cabbage bore the following words for all the bush folk to read:

Mrs Koala feeds her guests on these things. Take a good look. Have a good sniff (no tasting allowed). Then order your meals and beds from the manager.

P.S. Under no circs need snakes apply. Ants may apply for employment as garbage removers.

Signed, SPLODGE,

Manager of this concern.

Either the smell of the good things to eat, or that strange thing called bush telegraphy, had the effect of bringing animals of all descriptions from all corners of the

DOROTHY WALL

bush. They peered and sniffed with their noses against the vege-tables, dangerously close to their mouths. But Splodge had his weather eye open. When he found an animal a little too interested in the cabbages or carrots, he smartly rapped the offender on the back with the order:

"Sniff and move on, please."

Guests were booked in bunches. The climax came when Farmer Scratchet's old plough horse wandered upon the scene.

"How much for dinner?" he asked Splodge.

"Sorry, sir, we're full up," Splodge replied thinking very quickly. One dinner for Mr Plough Horse would mean no dinner for any one else.

"Fine cabbages you have there," Mr Plough Horse remarked nodding in the cabbages' direction. "They're mighty like Farmer Scratchet's, the ones I helped to plough in."

"They're first cousins," Splodge replied without twinking a whisker.

"Look here, my boy!" Mr Plough Horse said under his breath, thrusting his nose right into Splodge's face, "you give me a couple of carrots, or I'll let Farmer Scratchet know about this—cousins or no cousins."

"I don't usually bribe people," Splodge said haughtily, "but business is business and I hate the way you snoop around, so take a couple of carrots and go. Mind you—if I catch you holding private conversations with Farmer Scratchet it will be a bad day for you."

Mr Plough Horse gave a loud long neigh and grabbed the carrots between this teeth.

"I hope they get stuck in his wind-pipe," Splodge said to Mrs Koala who had been standing by, nervously watching the whole business.

"He's a pimp!" Blinky shouted. "We all should chase him off our premises."

296

"Fine cabbages you have there," Mr Plough Horse remarked.

Blinky Bill and Nutsy

Amid an uproar of growling, screeching and howling, Mr Plough Horse was sent about his business. After that everything proceeded quietly. From a branch of the gum-tree Nutsy, at a given signal from Mrs Koala, rang the dinner-bells, that is to say, she waved a pawful of Christmas bells backwards and forwards, making the sweetest tinkle imaginable.

"Hooray!" the guests shouted. "Hooray for a gobble!" All the eatables had been carefully hoisted up in the basket on to the biggest limb of the tree and there they were in full view of the guests below.

As the dinner bell sounded, a wild scramble up the tree commenced by those who were able to climb, while the birds flew like darts up on to the bough.

"What'll we do?" Mrs and Mr Wombat wailed.

"And me too?" Mr Wallaby echoed.

"You'll go up in the basket," Blinky exclaimed triumphantly, as he proceeded to grab the rope. "Get in—one at a time, and no pushing and shoving," he ordered.

"Ladies first," Mrs Wombat simpered shyly as she waddled towards the basket.

"Hurry up and get in," Blinky shouted.

Very clumsily Mrs Wombat fell into the basket with a shrill little scream.

"Let her go!" Splodge said beckoning to Blinky to haul at the rope.

He hauled and hauled, pulled and tugged; but the basket didn't budge an inch.

"You're the fattest wombat I've ever met," Blinky said crossly, the perspiration running down his nose.

"He's insulting me!" Mrs Wombat complained in a whining tone.

"I'll soon fix it!" Splodge remarked, bounding over to the basket.

With a rush Splodge sprang away in the opposite direction.

"Let me there, Blinky, and when I say 'Go!' pull with all your might."

"Get ready!" he shouted. "Now—*go!*"

With a rush Splodge sprang away in the opposite direction, the rope well around his shoulders. Up shot Mrs Wombat in the basket, while Blinky was tumbled over and over in the rush. Away the basket went, right up to the dining-room in the tree. Mrs Wombat gave a nervous shriek then, grabbing the limb of the tree with all her might, she pulled herself out of the basket and sprawled all over the cabbages.

"A most awkward landing," Mrs Koala remarked as she rushed forward to grab her guest, while the basket went whizzing to the ground again, ready for the next passenger.

All were hoisted up in time, not without great excitement and many howls of dismay as the basket swung perilously near to going over the limb on occasions; but no accident happened and every one was elated when the sign to start dinner was given.

It was a strange sight. Never before in the history of bushland had wombats, wallabies, kangaroos, rabbits and such-like ground animals, had the pleasure of dining up in a tree. The chatter and grunting was deafening. Shrill calls from the birds only accentuated the din. The whole bush rang with mirth.

Just when the fun was at its height—for Mrs Wombat had suddenly swayed backward, and finding no branch to support her, had nearly fallen head over heels out of the tree, had it not been for Mr Wallaby grabbing her around the leg and saving her from certain death—Mrs Grunty and her son Snubby came padding through the bush. Mrs Grunty had a scowl on her face. She

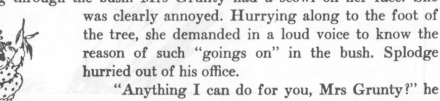

was clearly annoyed. Hurrying along to the foot of the tree, she demanded in a loud voice to know the reason of such "goings on" in the bush. Splodge hurried out of his office.

"Anything I can do for you, Mrs Grunty?" he politely asked.

Putting "Pep" In Things

"These larrikins—all this noise and cackle—what's the meaning of it?" Mrs Grunty asked, spluttering with indignation.

"That's our guest house," Splodge explained pointing to the multitude up in the tree.

"I wish I had a chopper—I'd give them all a bump if I had," Mrs Grunty snarled.

"How about going up and having some dinner?" Splodge said soothingly. "You don't know what you're missing."

"*Me*-go-up-there!" Mrs Grunty gasped. "Take my Snubby up there where that bold cub of a Blinky is. Shame on you all," she shouted.

"Go up and have some dinner," Splodge repeated. "We're all going to have a hop in the moonlight afterwards."

"Oh—oh! How *scandalous!*" Mrs Grunty could hardly speak with horror.

"You'll have the time of your life," Splodge said, laughing at the top of his voice, and gradually edging Mrs Grunty and Snubby over towards the basket, without her noticing what was happening.

Still arguing loudly and protesting strongly about everything, Splodge managed to get her right up to the edge of the basket, then without a beg pardon or gentle argument he gave her and Snubby a quick push and head over heels the pair of them lay flat in the basket.

"A-hoy!" Splodge yelled, as he rushed out with the rope. Up shot the basket, yells and screams coming from its occupants, while those in the tree all leaned out to see what the noise was about.

"She's stuck!" Blinky called at the top of his voice, and stuck she was.

In mid-air the basket was rocking violently, while Mrs Grunty walloped about inside, only making the basket swing more danger-ously, as she clawed at one side and then the other.

"Sit down!" Blinky shouted, amid cheers and yells from the onlookers. One kookaburra had the impudence to fly down and perch on the handle of the basket, laughing loudly as it almost tumbled upside down. Mrs Grunty made a wild lunge at the bird and out she fell—but not altogether; her wild grabbing at the side of the basket saved her from the final plunge to earth.

"Oh—how dreadful. How ghastly!" she moaned as she flopped back into safety, and then to every one's surprise fainted on top of Snubby.

Splodge in the meantime worked terrifically with the rope. In his lightning-like rush he had tangled the rope round a short tree and there it stuck, refusing to move until he backed and whipped it loose. That was the sign for further excitement, for, as the rope freed itself, the basket came with a rush down to earth again. "Bump!" it landed. Snubby gave a little squeal and popped his head over the side, while Mrs Grunty gave a deep sigh and opened her eyes. The bump had bumped her back into con-sciousness.

Splodge rushed over to the basket and fanned Mrs Grunty with a bunch of leaves, bringing the colour back to her face.

"You scoundrel!" she snarled. "Help me out of this trap at once."

Every animal that could climb down the tree came with amazing speed, and all rushed over to Mrs Grunty. Willing paws helped her to her feet, while Mrs Koala waved a few of her very best gum-tips under her friend's nose.

It had the desired effect. Mrs Grunty grabbed the leaves and ate them immediately.

"Poor soul!" Mrs Koala said sympathetically.

"Don't speak! Please don't address me," Mrs Grunty replied weakly.

Putting "Pep" In Things

"I'll take her home," Splodge said to Mrs Koala; but Mrs Grunty overheard him.

"You'll do no such thing," she snapped. "You're the cause of it all. And where's my Snubby?" She suddenly remembered her son.

Snubby was enjoying himself at the moment, being made a great fuss of by Nutsy, who offered him as many leaves as he could swallow.

"Let him stay for the hop," Nutsy pleaded, as Mrs Grunty ordered him home.

"Yes—do!" every one begged.

"It'll be the end of him," Mrs Grunty sighed. "The end of my discipline—the end of his childhood."

"Nonsense," Mrs Koala said softly. "Let him play with Nutsy, she's the sweetest little bear."

"Oh, very well, very well," Mrs Grunty sighed. "I wish I'd brought my knitting. It's a waste of time sitting around and doing nothing."

"But you're going to dance," Mrs Koala replied with a cheerful smile.

"Nonsense!" Mrs Grunty remarked shortly. "The very idea——"

Already the frog quartette were tuning up their drums and croakers, while Walter Wombat, who was generally considered the finest band conductor in the bush, was sitting in a corner all by himself, working up his deep gump, gump, gumps. Piping crickets sounded their notes, and then, without further notice, a butcher bird started to carol. That was the signal for all to commence. Walter Wombat sprang to his feet. "Gump—gump—gump," he grunted waving a stick in his front paws. Down it came with a crash on a rock, splitting it to smithereens.

Blinky Bill and Nutsy

"Pests and bothers!" he exclaimed, hastily grabbing another stick that lay at his feet.

"Whacko! Let her rip!" he shouted and once more raised his baton above his head.

"Look out for the splinters!" Blinky shouted; but Mr Walter Wombat was too much of a gentleman to even pretend he heard this rude remark. The band started. Every one jumped to his feet, grabbing the partner who happened to be nearest. Then as the music suddenly changed into "The Teddy Bears' Picnic", laughs and shouts started the greatest and happiest dance ever seen in the bush. Round and round the foot of the old gum-tree the animals danced, hopped and flew. Old Mr Wombat grabbed Mrs Grunty before she had time to protest, and Splodge rubbed his eyes to make sure he was seeing correctly when he spied these two fox-trotting, if you please. Mrs Koala waltzed with Mr Kangaroo, or tried to. His big feet *would* get in the way until he ended up by seizing her around the waist and whirling around with her in mid-air. Splodge danced with Mrs Wallaby and caused quite a sensation when both of them exhibited new steps to the audience. Splodge explained that the new dance was called "The Zoo Rush".

Nutsy danced with Snubby, until Blinky butted in and then all three decided to have a dance on their own. On the outskirts of the other dancers, these three little bears tumbled and hopped, laughed and pranced, until Mrs Koala and Mrs Grunty joined in. Alone the little bears danced, and if ever you've tried to imagine a teddy bears' picnic, just close your eyes for a moment at present, turn on the music of that famous melody and you just can't help seeing them as plain as daylight. The dear little cuddly bears.

This happy dance was the means of many bush friendships being made, and more important still it was the cause of Mrs

Putting "Pep" In Things

Grunty becoming quite gay and hospitable. Ever after, she and Snubby paid regular visits to Mrs Koala, while Blinky and Nutsy were overjoyed to have another playmate. The last peep I had of Blinky before I left the bush, was to see him instructing Snubby how to use a catapult, and Nutsy how to make frogs hop when they didn't want to.

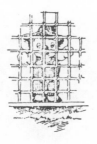

If any little girl or boy should be the proud owner of a koala, please remember the poor wee thing cannot eat sweets, fruit, nuts, or all the nice things you like so much. His digestive organs are very primitive and all he needs is his own food—gum-tips; but remember not every gum-leaf is good for him, only those from the York, Flooded, Manna, and White gum-trees are suitable.

These little animals need a great deal of petting and attention when in captivity, as petting is very necessary for them. They fret and grieve and finally die, if they are left alone, just as a baby would. The kindest action of all would be to leave the koala baby in his own bushland, among his own playmates, with the sun, the sky, the birds, and the gum-trees, where he will grow to manhood and live for many years—happy as he should be.

Dorothy Wall.

The End

The End